THE PUDDING LANE WITCH

A. W. JACKSON

Copyright © A.W. Jackson (2024)

The right of A.W. Jackson to be identified as author of this work has been asserted by them in accordance with section 77 and 78 of the Copyright, Designs and Patents Act 1988.

All rights reserved. No part of this publication may be reproduced, stored in a retrieval system, or transmitted in any form or by any means, electronic, mechanical, photocopying, recording, or otherwise, without the prior permission of the publishers.

Any person who commits any unauthorised act in relation to this publication may be liable to criminal prosecution and civil claims for damages.

This book is a work of fiction. Names, characters, places and incidents are either products of the author's imagination or are used fictitiously. Any resemblance to actual events or locales or persons, living or dead, is entirely coincidental.

First published by Cranthorpe Millner Publishers (2024)

ISBN 978-1-80378-233-1 (Paperback)

www.cranthorpemillner.com

Cranthorpe Millner Publishers

Printed and bound by CPI Group (UK) Ltd
Croydon, CR0 4YY

A Note from the Author

This story is a modern magical twist on the classic tale of the Great Fire of London. It exists within the same universe as *Madame Voodoo*, but is still very much a standalone story that can be enjoyed without having read *Madame Voodoo*.

If you are reader from *Madame Voodoo*, however, I must warn you that there is a darker tone to this story. While it tackles many of the same themes and issues as *Madame Voodoo*, it does so with some very real examples.

The content of this story is very dark, with parts which some individuals may find triggering. These include domestic violence, sexual abuse, and extensive racism.

If you are suffering from any of the issues raised in this story, then please do seek help. Do not suffer in silence!

Now, without further ado, please immerse yourself in the story of Gweneviere Baxter – *The Pudding Lane Witch*.

Sincerely,
A.W. Jackson

PROLOGUE
June 1665

Amongst the dark, dingy streets of London lay a wayward school for young orphaned and abandoned girls, or rather, witches. A school where the headmistress was referred to as Matriarch by all students and teachers. She created this safe space for them, and in return she demanded the respect she so rightfully deserved. She fed them, clothed them, protected them, but, most importantly, she taught them how to blend into a society that would rather see an innocent witch hang than a guilty man slapped on the wrist. The Matriarch was known to the outside world of mortals as the Crone. Anyone who dealt with her face-to-face knew exactly what she was, and those who found out through chance would surely not know for very long.

One particularly gruesome night there was a mighty thunderstorm overhead, and the girls had been instructed to return to their dormitories early, meaning they missed out on dessert. The streets outside, however, were still full of the drunken and 'fearless' men that traipsed them. The unfortunate reality of funding such a secretive school for witches meant that it was amongst a rather unsightly neighbourhood. Stuck between brothels and taverns, the school was often a front line for batting off the unwanted attention of sad, filthy old men.

It was midnight, otherwise known as the witching hour, and all about the school were abed. The Crone and senior teachers had placed a spell of protection upon the school in a bid to evade any lightning strikes that might start a fire. Afterwards, they decided to get some rest too, as there was no need for them to sit up worrying all night. Besides, graduation was soon approaching, and there was much to be done.

"Ahhh!" a young student screamed from the cafeteria like a banshee.

The Crone rose from her bed into an upright position with ease, as if the scream had sparked some youth back into her. Though her body reacted with haste, her mind was still hazy as she briefly remembered dreaming of a young girl with auburn hair. She couldn't remember anything else about the dream, just the girl, but as her mind slowly caught up with her body, she remembered what had awoken her in the first place and made her way to the cafeteria.

The Crone, being rather old and hunched over, hobbled through the cafeteria doors to find the girl quivering in shock. The poor child must've been about eight years old.

"What are you doing out of bed?" the Crone croaked.

"I was still hungry, so I came looking for something to eat... and then I saw a... monster, over there," the girl stuttered in fear, as she pointed to the pantry door.

"Well, it's a good job monsters don't scare me," the Crone replied, leaving the girl alone while she went in search of what had caused her such terror.

As the Crone approached the pantry door, she grabbed a candle to take with her. She could hear the rest of the faculty catching up behind her to see what the fuss was about. The Crone struck a match to light the candle before gently pushing the door open. All of the teachers' eyes immediately scanned the room at their natural height, only to see nothing, but as the Crone smelt a foul stench in the air, she lowered her candle to the ground to see something truly unsightly.

"Is that what I think it is?" a teacher muttered over the Crone's shoulder.

"No, it... it can't be," another whispered behind them.

"I'm afraid so, ladies. It is a rat king," the Crone said, confirming their suspicions, and fears.

A rat king occurs when a pack of rats become entangled in one another's tails. Unable to free themselves, they remain trapped, ghastly thrashing, until they all starve to death. To the people of 1665, this was a bad omen indeed.

"You, discard of it," the Crone instructed, pointing at one of the teachers. "And you, take the girl back to bed," she said, pointing at another. "Don't fear, ladies, though there are clearly trying times to come, I will see us through. Remember to stay vigilant, even more so than usual."

With that, the Crone headed back to her room. She laid in bed contemplating what this could mean for the future of the school, or the future of witch-kind, for that matter. Not before long, she drifted off, her ongoing inner rambles tired her mind once more. As she fell back into a deep slumber, her dreams of the girl from earlier in the night returned. Only now they were much clearer, and the Crone saw it to be less of a dream and more of a vision. A vision that showed the Crone who would be the witch to save all witches from further trials and tribulations.

A witch named Gweneviere.

CHAPTER 1
Trial by Fire

Nine months later, in a small village north of London.

Gweneviere laid in her bed as her thick, curly, auburn hair swallowed her tatty pillow. The rich colour was a beautiful blend of her mother's coppery locks and her father's deep brown coif. She had a pretty face, with a more olive skin tone than most Britons of the time, luscious rosy lips, a cute button nose, and bright, silvery blue eyes. The only thing she lacked was social skills, as her's were horrific. Watching Gweneviere attempt to make friends was like witnessing a bad improv, with nothing but an awkward silence filling the air. It also didn't help that when people spoke to Gweneviere, she often found herself getting lost in her own mind – in a self-induced trance from her own thoughts.

The eighteen-year-old beauty stared at the ceiling, contemplating the fairness of her life. Gweneviere was coming into her witch-hood in a time when women were being trialled, or more accurately, publicly murdered for being witches. There was a common misbelief that all witches were malevolent and Satan worshippers. The reality of the situation was that most witches were peaceful creatures who used their magics to provide remedies and services to the local women. This didn't mean satanic witches didn't exist. There were indeed some satanic witches who did the dark lord's work by kidnapping children and bringing about plagues. They were never the ones trialled, though, as they were far too crafty and nefarious to be caught. Instead, the majority of women that were trialled were simply that: mortal women. Women who were strong minded and unlucky enough to sport a birthmark that didn't sit well with their local pastor.

Platoons of misogynist, incompetent men would scour villages for witches where demonic witchcraft had been present – or areas where the women had become too vocal and independent. They would, under their pastor's guidance, look for any women who had a mole or birthmark of a certain look or size. Pastors would often try to verify their reasonings with 'visions' and 'messages' from God that, conveniently, only they could receive. The punishments included being hung or burned at the stake in the town square, and those who were *lucky* enough to live near a body of water would be drowned. The gruesome test was to drop a tied-up woman into a lake and see if they would sink or swim. Of course, any ordinary women would have passed the test by drowning, therefore too late to be saved. Any witches taking place in the test, however, had a decision to make – free themselves and face being hung or burned alive for proving their identity as a witch, or purposely drown in the hopes their captors might realise what a barbaric practice it was. The only winners of these trials were the sick pastors who profited on growing their following and demonising outspoken women. Also, of course, the satanist witches who could do the Devil's bidding whilst getting off scot-free.

Gweneviere's mother was a gorgeous young woman despite having lived for centuries. It was a rare trait amongst witches to have longevity such as hers. The majority of witches aged at the average human rate, though usually managed to expand their lifespan a few years by using certain remedies. Nevertheless, Gweneviere's mother was special indeed. Aging extremely slowly, and with the addition of her skin rejuvenating remedies, she didn't look a day over thirty. Gweneviere had inherited longevity, meaning her fresh, tight, eighteen-year-old face would stay that way for a good few decades.

Gweneviere's mother was a witch who practiced healing magics. She created medicines and remedies for women of the town. She was a modest woman and, in most cases, worked for free or whatever they could afford. She also dabbled in aiding suffering women with certain potions that would tame their abusive husbands. She felt sorry for the women who had such sleazy men for partners, knowing that her own husband would never lay a finger on her. All the women she helped were extremely grateful for her gifts and kept her abilities secret as thanks.

One woman, however, couldn't keep that secret any longer...

One evening, a man on the other side of the village caught his wife sneaking a potion into his evening supper. He tossed the bowl of food that his wife had slaved for hours making to the ground. He grabbed the poor woman by her hair and dragged her to the open fireplace, where he snatched the fire stoker from its resting position.

"Where the hell did you get that from?" he growled, his spit drenching her face.

"Please, I don't know what you're talking about," the poor woman cried, trying her best to play dumb.

"The potion!" He shook her by the hair, causing a lock to come out into his hand. "Where did you get it from?!" he screamed, now foaming at the mouth.

He pulled her face closer to his, so that she could smell the foul mead on his breath. He'd spent all afternoon in the pub after being fired earlier that morning; it was safe to say that she would be the outlet of his anger. He had been holding the iron fire stoker deep into the flames long enough that the tip had become red-hot. He turned her face to it. He didn't have to say much else, it was pretty clear what his next steps would be.

"No! Please, NO!" she howled, as he shuffled up her dress and pressed the burning metal into her thigh, searing her skin. It practically carved a chunk out of her leg – he had pressed down that hard. Steam and the smell of burning flesh filled the room.

"Now, tell me. Who gave you the potion?" he whispered into his whimpering wife's ear, as he retightened his grip on her hair.

She reluctantly answered him with a shaky voice and tears flowing down her cheeks. He threw her to the ground and headed out to gather a few of his burly pals to hunt down the witch.

Gweneviere's mother.

A solitary tear slid down the side of Gweneviere's face, dropping into her ear as she laid in her bed looking up. She turned onto her side and looked out of her bedroom window to see the night sky void of stars as dark grey clouds blanketed the town. Her father was surely on his way home from work by now, though he often worked late to make enough money to provide for his family. They lived on the edge of town in a farmhouse, with a couple of animals and crops for their own use. There was nothing plentiful enough to be able to sell at the market, therefore her father had to work the long days as a blacksmith. It was worth it to come home to his beautiful wife and daughter, even if he and Gweneviere didn't always see eye to eye. Alas, tonight, he would only be coming home to Gweneviere.

The reason Gweneviere was so torn up was because she had witnessed her mother's public execution just a few hours earlier.

Gweneviere and her mother had been browsing the market for some meat for the night's supper when a swarm of potbellied, balding, toothless men stormed through the market and swept

Gweneviere's mother off her feet. Gweneviere screamed and tried her best to free her, but it was no use as one of the beefy men smacked Gweneviere to the ground.

"MOTHER!" Gweneviere screamed.

The men carried her twenty metres down the road to the stake in the town square. It was surrounded by the town's most treasured buildings: the church, the town hall and the mayor's house, where the mayor stood awaiting the *show* on his balcony. The pastor rushed out from his parish and took charge of the 'trial'.

"Here, another one of Satan's foot soldiers. Tell us, honorary gentleman, what are the crimes of this particular wench?" the pastor asked, condemning her.

"She bewitched my wife to slip poison into my broth!" he shouted, slurring his words slightly.

"No, I promise, I didn't do that. I wasn't trying to poison anyone. I swear it!" she called out, trying to plead her case to a mob of uneducated men – and women, who were too scared to go against the status quo.

Gweneviere's mother noticed the woman who had ousted her at the back of the crowd in tears, with a black hood over her head to hide her newly mangled, patchy scalp. Gweneviere's mother didn't blame the poor woman as she knew this world wasn't ready for strong women, though she hoped that Gweneviere would live long enough to see a day where it was.

The mob of 'townies', as Gweneviere often referred to them, began to heckle and slander her as she was tied to the stake by the other two idiotic men who had aided in her capture. Gweneviere's cries became quieter but no less intense.

Her mother had spotted her in the crowd and pursed her lips together as if to hush her. Her mother knew they would turn on Gweneviere if she didn't silence her tears.

Gweneviere's innate magical talent was control over fire, making her a pyrokinetic witch. What played out next felt like a cruel form of poetry, as her mother was set alight at her feet. Gweneviere watched as her mother's hair became lost in the roaring flames that engulfed her slim frame. As the tears flowed, Gweneviere couldn't help but feel angered by her mother's injustice, but her anger slowly personified itself. The fire that had burned her mother to a crisp began to spread to the surrounding grounds. The townies screamed as they got a taste of their own medicine when a few of their cloaks caught on fire. Gweneviere turned and ran home before her anger got too out of hand and she burned the whole village to the ground.

As her tears continued to soak her pillow, Gweneviere heard the clunky sound of her father's boots hitting the doorstep. Her father, Harold, was a tall, husky man with a full head of dark brown hair and a fully sculpted jaw line that made all the women who saw him instantly lose their train of thought. He was the seventeenth century equivalent of a DILF, with his large, puffed out, hairy chest and beefy arms. Harold grew up extremely poor, as an only child, whose parents worked their whole life, until they died of a ripe old age of fifty or so. He had learnt his unrivalled blacksmithing skills from his father. Harold, however, wasn't respected by his employer, and spent most of his days in the very back of the shop whilst the owner's son worked the market front. The owner's son was in his twenties and, though his looks brought the ladies in, his blacksmithing ability was far less than average, and he took the glory of adding the easy finishing touches to all of Harold's pieces. Having spent all day taking shit from his boss and slaving away at the back of the shop for mere pennies, all Harold wanted to do was sit with his family and enjoy a meal expertly cooked by his wife.

Gweneviere heard a knock on her bedroom door, her stomach twisted in knots as she couldn't comprehend how to break the news to her father.

"Gwen? You in there?" his husky voice carried through the door.

"Yeah," Gweneviere breathed, as she tried drying her eyes.

He opened the door slowly and, as he entered, asked, "Gwen, where's your mother?"

Gweneviere sat up in her bed and turned to answer her father, but no words came from her lips, just splutters as she began to sob again. The crevasse of her ears had already been filled with tears from laying down, but now so did the dip in her collarbone as the salty water flowed without break.

"Gwen? What's wrong, Gwen?" he asked, as he took a seat beside her and tucked her head beneath his strong chin.

She pulled herself away and looked up at her father. "It's Mum. The townies, they..." She struggled to finish.

"They what, Gwen? What happened?" Harold demanded, fearing he already knew the words she was about to utter.

"They killed her! They tied her up and burned her," Gweneviere finally blurted out, her reddened eyes beginning to weep once more.

Her father didn't shed a tear, not because he didn't love his wife, but because he was angry. Angry at the miserable town that murdered her, and angry that she was so stubborn and hadn't listened to his warnings.

"Goddamn... I told her that we should've moved further from the town and just lived off the land. I could've hunted us food. But no, she wanted to help people, and look where it got her!" He stood up, punching the wall in his frustration.

"Dad, stop! It's not your fault, and it certainly wasn't Mum's either," Gweneviere pleaded, as she wiped her stinging eyes.

"Pft, it doesn't matter now, anyway, she's gone and she's never coming back. Make no mistake, Gwen, it won't be long until they figure out that you're her daughter, and you'll be next." He was too overwhelmed by his own anger to show any warmth and compassion to his grieving daughter.

"Dad, don't say things like that!"

"I'm sorry, Gwen, but it's true. As soon as *they* realise, it'll be you that's on that stake."

"Dad, I won't let that happen. I promise. I'll protect myself," Gweneviere tried to reason.

"No. *I* won't let that happen, because we're getting out of here, tonight!"

"Don't be ridiculous, Dad. We can't leave our home and everything behind!"

"There's nothing left for us here. If we stay only more pain and death will ensue," he answered, coldly.

"What about friends?" Gweneviere pleaded, knowing she was grasping at straws.

"What friends? Come on, Gwen, let's not kid ourselves here. We both know that *you* don't have any friends; you'd have to leave this godforsaken house to even have a chance at that. The only one out of the three of us that had any *friends* was your mother. I suppose the only upside to you being a loner is that no can ever get close enough to stab you in the back. Now, pack your things, we're leaving within the hour."

He left no pause for Gweneviere to answer back, swiftly leaving the room and slamming the door closed.

Gweneviere stopped fighting the inevitable; she knew that the only person who could ever convince her father to change his mind was now gone. She began to pack what little belongings she had when she heard a rattle in her top drawer, a drawer which she had already emptied. She assumed it was a mouse, as her mother usually let them be, not wanting to throw them out into the cold. Something felt different. It was as if something was telling Gweneviere to look. She slowly opened the draw to see a book with a leather cover – it was her mother's grimoire. She recorded all her healing remedies and potion recipes in it, as well as spells that she had come up with herself. There were hundreds of years' worth of arcane magical knowledge on those pages, and now they belonged to Gweneviere. She had seen her mother writing in it all the time, and realised that her mother must have used her last breathy words to cast a spell so that it would appear to her in that moment, so that she wouldn't forget it, or forget her.

Gweneviere didn't subscribe very much to healing magics as it certainly didn't come naturally to her like it did her mother but, of course, she was more than relieved to have it, to have something of her mother's to take with her wherever they'd end up. She stuffed it in her bag before her father called out.

"Are you ready?" Harold called from the base of the stairs.

"Yeah, coming," Gweneviere softly called back, as she took one last look at her childhood bedroom.

She joined her father in the living room, and they put out the fire for the last time before heading out into the woods behind their home.

Not long after they began their journey, a loud bang came from behind them.

"What was that?" Gweneviere jumped as they turned to see a roaring orange glow through the trees.

"*That* would be me being right. They've torched the house. See, I told you it wouldn't be long, and no doubt the cowards thought we'd be asleep by now," Harold snarled in anger.

"I'm sorry I didn't believe you, Dad," Gweneviere apologised, as her glossy eyes reflected the fiery glow of their burning home.

"It's okay, Gwen, but we need to go. We must make it to the next town over by sunrise, so that when they realise that we weren't home, we'll be long gone. Now then, set this lantern alight, will you? I forgot the matches in the house and it's getting too dark to see where I'm going."

"I can't," Gweneviere muttered, feeling deflated.

"What do you mean you can't? It's your power, is it not?" Harold questioned, bewildered by his daughter's answer.

"Well... yes, but after seeing mother burn and my power only making it worse, I don't think I have it in me to use it anymore. Nothing *good* comes of fire." Gweneviere tried explaining her feelings, but was met with a scoff.

"Gwen, don't be so stupid. It's not like you tied your mother up and burned her at the stake, for Christ's sake. Now, come on, light it. We need to see where we're going. Is that not a good thing to come of fire? Sight? Warmth, even? Because it'll be getting cold soon, too," he snarked.

"Fine." Gweneviere reluctantly lit the way into the ever-thickening forest.

"See, that wasn't so hard, was it?" he said, rolling his eyes at his weak daughter.

Gweneviere felt overcome with a sense of failure: she was powerless to save her mother, and now she struggled to even perform basic tasks for her father.

"Gwen, you need to stay alert, okay? This forest is a shortcut to the next town over, but there's good reason why a road hasn't been ploughed through it. Your mother warned me once of the kinds of mystical beasts that roam these woods at night," Harold cautioned, spooking Gweneviere a little.

"Like what?" she asked shakily.

"In all honesty, Gwen, too many to remember. But one that specifically comes to mind is werewolves. She said they're one of the most dangerous creatures out here. They usually travel in packs and are especially dangerous during a full moon.

They become extra territorial and aggressive."

Gweneviere didn't quite believe her father's attempt at scaring her. Townies, who hunted witches, were scary to her because they were a very real threat. Werewolves, on the other hand, still seemed outlandish to Gweneviere, despite the fact she, herself, could set fires with just a thought.

"Really, Dad? Werewolves? I'm not a little girl anymore."

"I'm not joking, kid. For once in your life, will you just listen to me and do as I say? I was right about the townies, wasn't I?"

"Yes, alright, sorry," Gweneviere conceded, wishing she had just bit her tongue instead of speaking. "So, how do we protect ourselves from the werewolves?" she asked, rolling her eyes behind her father's back.

"You will use your magic, and I will use *these*," he said, proudly patting his hands on the hammer and dagger, of his own beautiful craftmanship, that were slid into his belt on either side of his hips.

"Well, that sounds like a great way to get killed," she muttered under her breath.

"What?" he questioned, not quite catching her breathy backchat.

"Nothing," Gweneviere answered, snapping back in line, not realising quite how loud her whispering had been.

A few hours passed and they were deep into the forest. The ground was covered in mounds of moss that slowed them down. Crooked trees towered over them, covering the night sky and diminishing any additional light that they may have garnered from the moon, the *full* moon.

Both Gweneviere and her father grew tired of their perilous journey. She constantly asked how much longer it would take until they reached their destination.

"Shouldn't be far off now," he answered. Though, if he was being honest with himself, he couldn't really sense how much further they had to travel thanks to every square inch of the woods looking the exact same, even with the help of Gweneviere's lantern. Luckily, Harold had been marking trees with his dagger as they walked by to ensure that they didn't go round in circles.

"Where are we even going, anyway? And don't say 'the next town'," Gweneviere grumbled.

"We're going to one of your mother's old friends," he answered, vaguely.

"I thought you said her friends were backstabbers?"

"Yes, well, let's hope this one isn't, ay!"

Harold had met this friend once before, a long time ago, and if he was being honest with himself, he wasn't sure if they would even remember him, let alone care enough to help. Nevertheless, it was their only chance at salvation.

Harold was walking a bit further ahead than Gweneviere, so when she heard a rustle coming from the bushes beside her, it was just out of her father's earshot. Gweneviere scrutinised the bushes as she tried to pinpoint the sound. She reluctantly lit her hands, gently, with small flames to aid in her search for the source of the noise. The bushes rustled once again, but louder. So loud that this time, her father had heard and doubled back on himself.

He raced to be by Gweneviere's side. "Did you hear where it came from?" he asked, with a frantic look in his eye.

"Er... no," Gweneviere lied. She didn't feel scared of whatever it was that was stalking them. She couldn't explain why, but she almost felt safe and watched over, rather than stalked.

"Get back-to-back with me, Gwen," he demanded, with his hammer and dagger firm within his grasp and at the ready to swing.

Though she hadn't felt scared, her father's reaction coaxed a wearier side of her to come out, so she turned her small flames into fiery globes that hovered in each palm. Gweneviere did as he said and, as the noises began to dart about them, no longer focusing on one point, the two of them began to slowly turn around, staying back-to-back to get a good view of the surroundings.

"Gwen, don't hesitate to shoot, I can't lose you too," he pleaded.

"But Dad, what if it's not trying to hurt us. Maybe it wants help, or is just curious," she said over her shoulder.

"No! You do as I say, it's too much of a risk, it could be dangerous." Harold made sure to keep both eyes peeled as he instructed his daughter.

"Exactly, *could* be. You know, you're starting to sound like a townie," Gweneviere sniped.

"Gwen, let me be very clear that, if we weren't in grave danger right now, I would back hand you for your insolence," he said, with a growl similar to the very creature he was afraid of.

Gweneviere knew that he was only saying these things because he knew that she was right.

Suddenly, out of the bushes in front of Gweneviere, came a wolf, a werewolf. It had a slight low-toned grumble, but didn't seem to be aggressive. She almost felt like it was trying to communicate with her. Before she had chance to open her mind to it, though, her father spotted the foul beast in the corner of his eye and jumped around to Gweneviere's position. He placed himself between his daughter and the wild dog before clanging his hammer and dagger together aggressively. Gweneviere wasn't sure if this was to scare it off or challenge it. The wolf didn't take a step closer but did louden his growl in order to stand his ground. After all, the forest was his domain, Harold and Gweneviere were the trespassers. Harold launched at the wolf, taking a big swing for it and missing. The dodged attack confirmed in the hound's mind that this fight was do or die, so he sunk his teeth into Harold's arm. Harold cried out for Gweneviere to help, dropping his weapons in the commotion.

"Gwen, kill it. For God's sake, kill it!" he shouted, as he tried to wriggle his arm free, but the wolf's teeth were far too deep into his muscly flesh. If he pulled his arm out at that moment, it would have likely taken half his forearm off with it.

Gweneviere stood, frozen in fear. She had seen too much death today already and, though she didn't want her father to die, she couldn't reason killing the wolf. It was just defending itself. Harold continued his screams and cries for help, begging Gweneviere to burn the beast, but she remained in her frozen state as she watched the scene unfold. Harold, with his free arm, had tried punching the beast, but it was no use. Even with his impressive physique, his strength was no match for that of a werewolf. As the wolf thrashed Harold about by the arm, he edged closer and closer to his dagger, which finally became within reach of his fingertips. He nudged the blade closer with his fingers until he could fully grasp it in his hand. He thrusted it straight into the wolf's fast beating heart, causing the most gut-wrenching welp Gweneviere had ever heard. The wolf let go of Harold's arm and he released his dagger from its heart. The poor dog managed to stumble a few more steps before collapsing onto the woodland floor. Harold lifted himself up as Gweneviere ran to the dog's aid.

"Gwen, get away from that thing! It probably has all kinds of diseases."

"Just stop it, Dad. It's bad enough you slaughtered the poor thing, leave it to rest in peace."

Gweneviere looked into the pup's eyes as it took its last breaths. She stroked its head in a bid to calm the dying creature. As the wolf's eyes became lifeless, its body changed back into human form in front of Gweneviere's very eyes. It revealed a handsome, otherwise normal looking, young man who couldn't have been much older than Gweneviere herself.

"See! Do you see what you've done? He was a kid, a pup. You just did to him exactly what the townies were going to do to me. You killed him because you were scared of something that you didn't understand!"

Harold slowly walked over to Gweneviere, who was still kneeling besides the naked man silently. With his bitten arm cradled into his stomach, he swung his other arm back and launched it towards Gweneviere. The back of his hand smacked Gweneviere's face, rippling her cheek in slow motion. She fell to the ground next to the dead pup as her father towered over them both.

"I told you what I would do if you said that. Don't ever speak to me like that again, understood?" he demanded, returning his good arm to a supporting position for the other. There were deep teeth marks into the wounded one, and yet nowhere near as much blood as he'd expected. It appeared that the wolf's saliva caused the blood to clot.

Gweneviere simply nodded, having never seen her father act so cruelly before in all her life.

"Now, I promised your mother I would always look after you, and that's what I've done, but you better believe the second I find a decent man that will wife you, you'll belong to him."

"Did Mum *belong* to you?" Gweneviere just about managed to mutter, as she held her throbbing red cheek.

"No, because she wasn't an incessant freak. She was a strong woman who could survive on her own, make connections, and bonds with people. You can't even do that with your own father. Now, get up, we're only a couple of miles out." Harold ended his rant and carried on their journey.

Gweneviere sat up and began pulling the twigs and leaves out of her entangled hair. She turned to face the poor boy her father had just brutally murdered moments ago.

"I'm sorry," she whispered, as she closed the lids of his beautifully brown eyes for the last time.

With her father already departed, there was no time for a burial, so Gweneviere did her best to give him some dignity in death. She laid him flat on his back and gathered a few flowers together from the surrounding shrubs. She placed them in his hands, covering the gash on his chest, and grabbed some foliage to place atop his manhood to give him some modesty before finally placing her lips on his forehead.

"I'm sorry."

She picked up her bag and brushed herself off before slowly catching up to her father, who was barely still within view. There were no more words exchanged during the rest of their trip. Gweneviere just kept her distance, rather literally, always walking a few meters behind him.

A few hours later, as they finally left the enchanted woods behind and walked out into more open fields. Gweneviere assumed they must be close, and just in the nick of time, too, as the sun began to rise over the horizon. The light was almost blinding, but Gweneviere noticed that it did cast the silhouette of a farmhouse in the distance. They had run out of water sometime during the night, and Gweneviere's stomach was in cramps having missed an evening meal the night before, thus she hoped that they could at the very least stop for a drink.

"Is that the place?" Gweneviere asked, her voice barely audible, her mouth too parched for her to speak any louder.

"Just let me do the talking," he said, somewhat confirming their destination.

Gweneviere didn't bother answering back, not having the energy to engage in another fight. She just nodded instead.

Harold knocked on the farmer's door and awaited a response with heavy anticipation. *Will they help? Will they even recognise me?* he wondered.

A middle-aged woman – which in those times meant about thirty, if you were lucky – opened the door. She embraced Harold immediately as she explained that the news had already travelled of his wife's trial, or lack thereof. She also explained to him that, although, she of course, remembered them and wanted to help, she couldn't risk putting her own family in danger by harbouring them. It certainly wouldn't be long before the townies began to search their village as well. She did, however, offer up her barn, for the night, and a hot meal. She apologised for not being able to help any more than that, but did tell him of a witch in London who may be able to help. She briefly gave him directions on how to reach her. She scrawled them onto a piece of parchment, and reassured them that she would bring some food to the barn shortly.

They headed over to the barn which was laced with hay and animals: mainly pigs and chickens that seemingly roamed freely about the place. Gweneviere sat upon one of the hay bales and prepared for another lecture from her father.

"Stay put. I'm going to go get some things for our journey, okay?"

Gweneviere, once again, simply nodded, having taken an unofficial vow of silence. Harold saw the hurt in his daughter's expression and walked away feeling guilty. Gweneviere sat there pondering her father's actions in the last twenty-four hours.

He had never been an overly affectionate father, but he did always do his best by her and her mother. Maybe she needed to cut him some slack. After all, his wife had just been publicly murdered, and he feared the same fate for Gweneviere, too.

Harold returned with some bread and cheese, and his arm bandaged up. Gweneviere saw her injured father and knew she had to try to start again on a clean slate.

"Hey... Dad?"

"Yes, Gwen?" he replied warily, fearing another argument.

"Listen, I know we don't always see eye to eye, and last night got very out of hand, but I understand how you feel. I miss her too, and grief makes people do crazy things. So... please can we just forget about everything that's happened and start fresh?"

Her father stood in front of her with a slightly angry smoulder, though that was just his resting face – it was partly what made all the women swoon around him. "Gwen, that's probably the most sensible thing you've ever said. And for what it's worth... I'm sorry about last night. You're right, I was scared and angry, and maybe I could've dealt with the situation better, but please understand that everything I did, and everything that I continue to do, is to try and keep you safe," he confessed, genuinely.

"I know, Dad, it's okay. Besides, you're right, too, about me needing to be better at socialising. I always relied on Mum for that but now that she's gone, I know I have to start making connections for myself."

"That's great, Gwen. Now, here, have some cheese and bread. I'm sorry, it's all she had. So much for a hot meal, huh?" he joked, for the first time in who knows how long.

"Here," Gweneviere said, holding out her hand for the bread. She warmed it in her palms. The smell of freshly baked bread filled the barn, garnering the unwanted attention of the pigs.

One growl from Harold was all it took to scare them off.

"Thanks," he said, smiling.

They sat, eating their fresh bread and cheese before packing some more away in their bags for the next leg in their journey. They didn't bother taking up the offer of staying a night as Harold didn't want to risk the townies catching up to them.

"Where are we actually going?" Gweneviere asked.

"London."

"Ugh, London?" Gweneviere groaned.

In those times, the city certainly wasn't what it is now.

To reach their destination, they would once again have to trek through nightfall, though, luckily, there weren't any more enchanted woods along the way. By the next sunrise they would be close enough to hopefully hitch a ride on someone's horse and cart.

The next morning they strolled the roads leading to London, trying to flag down any passers-by for a ride, until finally one kind man was willing to take them free of charge. He must have been on his way to pick up cargo, as his cart was seemingly empty, which was fortunate in Gweneviere and Harold's case as it made for a less cramped journey. It was nice for Gweneviere to see that humanity wasn't completely lost, though, that naive dream was soon shattered as the driver's mouth began spouting misogynistic views on witches. Clearly witches were no better received in the capital than they were in the backwards rural towns. Gweneviere managed to bite her tongue long enough to reach the inner streets of London – the smog, disease ridden streets of London – where houses were piled atop each other, with rats and piss flowing down the streets like rivers. They stopped outside one of the rickety town houses, which was seemingly surrounded by brothels and cheap taverns.

Harold thanked the man as he and Gweneviere hopped off. Gweneviere was just glad to be away from that man and his views. She hadn't had to deal with people as regularly as her father did so didn't have as much practice gritting her teeth and bearing the ideocracy around witches. Her father heard it all day *everyday* working on the market – men and women believed anything their god-loving pastors preached. As Gweneviere got away from one grotesque man, she looked around to notice that she was seemingly amidst a street full of them.

"Please tell me this isn't the place," Gweneviere said, latching onto her father's unscathed muscular arm.

Dirty men with rotten teeth walked by, eyeing her up like a slab of meat. It may have been the middle of the day, but that certainly didn't stop the men surrounding them from being inebriated already.

"I'm afraid so," he confirmed, double checking the address that was scrawled onto a crumpled-up piece of parchment in his pocket.

He knocked on the door and out came a young, pretty

woman, who was seemingly used to being mistaken for the whore house next door.

"What do you want? If it's a good time you're looking for, it's next door," she said sharply, about to slam the door in his face before he even had a chance to answer.

Harold stopped the door with his foot and the woman peered her head through the remaining gap, as he announced, "I'm here to see the Crone."

CHAPTER 2
The Crone

"Right this way, sir." The young woman invited them in, opening the door just wide enough for them to squeeze through. "Now, wait here, and I will fetch the Crone," she added, having led them into a small entrance hall.

"Dad, what is this place?" Gweneviere asked, as her eyes darted about the hall.

"I'm not sure, but let's hear them out," he answered.

An old woman descended the staircase before them. She wore thick heavy robes that caused her to hunch over. Once at the bottom of the stairs and just a metre in front of them, she stuck out her frail bony fingers and pointed to Harold.

"What's your business here? Are you looking to wed one of my girls?"

"No, no, certainly not. I was told by an old friend that you could help my daughter. She's a witch," he explained.

"Hmm, I'll be the judge of that," she said, looking Gweneviere up and down, examining her. She sniffed the air with her protruding slender nose, and her nostrils turned from two grains of rice to almonds as they flared. "Pyrokinetic?"

"What?" Harold asked, his face looking even more bent out of shape than usual.

"Is she a pyrokinetic witch?" the Crone asked, growing tired of Harold's insolence.

"Yes, I am," Gweneviere interjected, speaking for herself.

"Very well," the Crone answered, waving them to follow on behind her.

As they walked in the slowly moving witch's shadow, they had plenty of time to take in their surroundings, noticing that the hallway was full of portraits depicting young, vibrant looking women, or rather, witches. Each of them looked as elegant and stately as the last; certainly not the kind of ladies you'd expect to see in the district.

"So, what is it that you do here?" Harold asked the Crone, to which she remained silent.

She lured them to her study and they sat down on opposite sides of the desk before she would once again speak.

"Now then, tell me why you are in need of my help? Then I might consider answering *your* questions."

"We're from a small town, north of the city, where Gwen's mother was trialled as a witch and burned at the stake, when—"

"Dim, was she?" the Crone cut him off.

"Excuse me?" Harold said, taken back by the interruption.

"Was she rather dense? After all, she was trialled for being a witch – how was she incompetent enough to be found out?" the Crone rudely asked.

Harold's teeth ground together like the stones he used to sharpen swords. Gweneviere could practically feel the vibrations from it. She could see he was searing with anger at the Crone's disrespectful words. He stood up, slamming his hands on the desk and raising his voice, just inches away from the Crone's face.

"Listen here, Crone, my wife was an incredible woman, much wiser than you. And if you must know, she was betrayed by one of the women she helped with her magics."

"SIT DOWN, NOW!" she bellowed, loud enough that it rippled through every room of the building, causing girls all about the house to be on their best behaviour.

It was seemingly unnatural how her voice had become so deep and voluminous compared to her scratchy, throaty tone a few seconds earlier. Though it would've fazed even most grown men, Harold wasn't easily spooked. Luckily, Gweneviere placed her hand on his to calm him and asked him to sit down.

"Clearly your daughter knows what's good for you. Now then, this is a school for young witches, where we train them to become perfect wives. We teach them about how their powers can be used in a God, and man, honouring way. Then, once our girls have matured into fine young women at the age of eighteen graduation occurs. I spend months each year seeking out the wealthy men of London who are sympathisers to our kind and are willing to wed a witch. At graduation, the men take their pick, and my girls live out happy lives as respected wives, never having to suffer a public, humiliating death, unlike *some*." She looked meaningfully in Harold's direction. "Now, allow me to show you some of our girls at work."

Standing, she led them to one of the classes in session.

As they once again followed in the Crone's footsteps,

Gweneviere looked up at her father for reassurance that he wouldn't leave her in a place like this. "Dad, please tell me you're not considering this," she whispered.

"Let's just hear the old hag out," he replied quietly.

They reached a classroom where they watched young girls learn how to place an enchantment on a charcoal iron so that it would operate itself. Of course, telekinetic witches didn't need such spells – they merely waved their hands about from the comfort of a chair in order to complete the task.

"As you can see, a witch makes for a much more efficient wife," the Crone boasted.

"Ah yes, just what every girl wants to be, an 'efficient wife'," Gweneviere said under her breath.

It was just loud enough for her father to catch her sarcastic comment, and he cracked a smile behind the Crone's back.

"After all, every great man has a great woman standing behind them," the Crone continued.

"Yes, well, I thought that witches were supposed to be strong, outspoken women. To me, you all look like slaves to men-kind," Gweneviere scoffed.

The Crone turned around with a surprising amount of ferocity as she pulled her thick robes away from her neck revealing a red patch of scaly skin that was carved deeply around her throat. "*This* is what happens when we act as you describe. So, yes, we may adapt to survive, but that's all some of us can afford to do!"

"I'm sorry for what happened to you, I truly am. But I can't let myself believe that I was put on this earth with these abilities just to conform to a man's twisted ideology of what I should be. Come on, Dad, we're going," Gweneviere demanded, as she turned and stormed to the exit.

Her father followed and, though he certainly wasn't fond of the Crone, he didn't appreciate Gweneviere's lack of respect either.

"Gwen, that was really rude," he said, catching up to her on the filthy street.

"I'm sorry, but you can't seriously expect me to do that."

"Of course I don't. Listen, we'll find a place and I'll get a job blacksmithing here, it shouldn't be too hard. Besides, no one knows who we are here, this can still be our fresh start."

"I'd like that too, and I'll find a job, Dad. I promise."

Harold had quickly managed to bag himself a job, once again, as a blacksmith and thankfully his arm had healed quicker than either of them had expected, meaning it didn't hinder him in his work. One perk that came from living in the city was that he got a slightly higher rate of pay, though, without being able to produce any food for themselves anymore, he still had to work long shifts, like a dog, to make up the extra cash. He had also secured the two of them a small one-bedroom flat above a shop. It wasn't much, but it was all they could afford on such a low income. Gweneviere had been trying her luck to get a job, but the only establishments that would entertain hiring a woman were sketchy taverns and whore houses. Neither her, nor her father were in support of those jobs and so they made do. But with their greedy landlord increasing the rent almost as often as he collected it, they soon realised that Harold's wage alone wasn't cutting it. They needed extra cash if they wanted to have a decent meal each night.

Gweneviere reluctantly took the job as a bar wench in one of the taverns in the same neighbourhood as the Crone's school. She often saw some of the older witches running errands and wondered if maybe she'd have been better off there. After all, her occupation didn't exactly scream female empowerment, as drunken men gawped at her daily, and the 'uniform' only encouraged the men's catcalling. They wore tightly corseted dresses that pushed up and smashed together Gweneviere's already rather large breasts. She loathed wearing it and was always achy afterwards. Her father also didn't approve very much of the job but, with her wage, they were finally managing to eat a healthy amount and maybe things would finally be on the up and up.

"Morning, Gwen," her father said gently, as he opened the bedroom door to wake her.

"Uh, yeah, morning Dad," she muttered, slowly coming around.

"Long night again, huh?"

"Yep," Gweneviere replied.

She was almost always on the late shifts, often arriving home so late that her father had already passed out for the night in the living room. Due to the size of their home, Harold had been making a bed for himself by the fire in the living area. It wasn't a great night's sleep, but he knew he'd be able to stomach it better than Gweneviere.

"Gwen, if you can't handle the late nights, it's fine, we can live off my wage for a while," Harold offered kindly, though, he knew he was just kidding himself.

"Don't worry, Dad, I'll be alright. I'm actually finishing just a little after you today. If you want, you can come walk me home?" she suggested, still stretching in bed.

"Okay, sure. I'll see you later."

With that, Harold set off for work, having already necked half a bowl of porridge while Gweneviere was asleep.

Gweneviere slowly dragged herself out of bed. She made herself some porridge with a teaspoon of honey – the only thing that made it edible to her. She scraped the last spoonful into her mouth, making sure not to waste any. They weren't in a position to waste any inch of food that might give them a bit of extra energy for the day. They were never sure when, or how plentiful, their next meal would be. Occasionally, the pub's landlady would offer Gweneviere something to eat on her long shifts. Though she wasn't exactly rolling in money herself and had to watch her profits, what with rats often getting into the supply room and nibbling away at her profit margins. Gweneviere quite admired her landlady's business-savvy mind, but then instantly lost respect for her every time that she allowed a man to treat one of the girls like a piece of meat.

Gweneviere headed out on her walk to work, they didn't live too far away from the sketchy street, as they couldn't exactly afford the Ritz themselves. They did, however, live far enough away that the drunken fights and screams couldn't be heard from their home, which was a relief to Gweneviere. She often had to watch women be dragged away by three or four men at a time during her shifts and didn't need the sound of that *scenario* in her mind whilst she tried to sleep. Even the whorehouse women who 'chose' that life didn't deserve be treated that way.

She reached the grubby tavern and started her shift. It appeared to be a rather quiet one at first, which was a welcome change as Gweneviere hated dealing with the rowdy crowds of men. When the bar staff outnumbered the customers, it made it much easier to push off any dirty chancers. Typically, though, business picked up, making the landlady smile as she saw every man as a walking opportunity to make more money. In her mind, if she had to flirt a little and take the odd groping in exchange for their money, it was worth it. Gweneviere definitely did not have this attitude to the unwarranted touching. It made her feel dirty when a man would slap her arse as she walked past their table. It was if every man in the joint thought they had some claim to her, simply because she was serving their drinks.

Gweneviere's shift was coming to an end and, for the most part, it hadn't been too bad a day, though she had noticed a regular come in who'd been eyeing her up for some time. He was a short, stumpy man with a long beard and balding head. When he smiled it looked more like a dilapidated graveyard, with each tooth a different shape, shade, and direction. He waved her over and, of course, being the good little bar wench that she was, she arrived to tend to his needs.

"Yes, Robert?" she asked with a blank expression, hoping to survive the last ten minutes of her shift without any altercations.

"Hmm, what's with this Robert malarky. I told you to call me Robbie, didn't I?" he slurred, grabbing Gweneviere's waist and sitting her on his crotch.

"Okay, *Robbie*." She smiled tightly, trying to go along with his disgusting advances in the hopes he wouldn't become aggressive.

"Now then, I've paid for a room across the road in the whorehouse, but I don't want any of them dirty skanks, I want pure, fresh, young meat."

He grinned towards his table of fellow foul-smelling, drunken idiots as he tightened his grip, sliding his hand further down Gweneviere's waist towards her bum while swigging mead in his other hand. Gweneviere jumped up, not being able to take anymore, causing him to spill his drink everywhere, soaking his crumb filled beard and shirt. As his entourage laughed, Robbie became embarrassed and ultimately, angry. His cheeks flooded red, and his eyes turned to Gweneviere.

"Right, that's it, wench, you've just sealed your fate, get here now!" he roared, his voice filling the whole tavern. "I'm going to take you, and some of my pals here, to teach you a lesson on being a man-honouring woman."

"Fuck off, Robert. I'm not going anywhere with you, especially not over *there*," she shouted back.

Robbie stormed over to her and grabbed the back of her hair with one hand and her waist with the other. He sniffed her sweet scent as he inched closer to her face. He pressed his hard member into her stomach through layers of cloth, but it was still enough to make Gweneviere feel sick inside. She closed her eyes as she wriggled and squirmed in his clutch, too scared to watch what he would do to her next. To her surprise, she felt his small prick pull away from her stomach, and her hair slip through his fingers before he unclamped her waist and she was finally free. She opened her eyes to see her father towering over Robert. He had tapped him on his shoulder, provoking him to turn around.

"Who are you?" Robert slurred. "Me and my missus are about to go and have a good time, aren't we, lads?" he announced to the whole tavern, causing a few of the men to cheer.

Harold's jaw clenched so tight it looked like his skin might tear. "You're not going anywhere with *her*," he growled, squaring up to Robert, or rather down, considering Harold was a good foot taller than him.

"What's it to you, big man?" Robert laughed, looking to his mates cockily.

"*She* is my daughter." Harold grinned menacingly, knowing he was about to enjoy kicking the guy's arse.

Robert swallowed a gulp of saliva, before sobering up slightly in fear.

"Go on, Robbie, you can take him," his mates shouted.

Robert turned around for a split second to Gweneviere, taking a good look at her breasts, disgustingly thinking that was what he was fighting for, before turning back and sucker-punching Harold in the jaw. Harold's face flinched slightly by the weak jab. Harold turned back to Robert and spat the blood that filled his mouth in Robert's face, partially blinding him. Harold then headbutted the man on the nose. He grabbed a disorientated Robert by the wispy bottom of his wet beard and dragged his face to the table, smacking the wood with great force before grabbing the very glass tankard he'd been drinking from and smashing it over his head, rendering the man unconscious. Harold didn't want to waste punches on such a pathetic man, it wasn't worth the risk of damaging his skilled blacksmithing hands.

Harold turned to Robert's mates with a growl, asking, "Well? Anyone else want some?"

As they took one look at Robert's unconscious, blood-coated, disfigured face flat on the table, they all quietly shook their heads, realising that Robbie was supposed to be the strongest among them.

"Oi, you, out!" the landlady shouted across the tavern at Harold.

"With pleasure. Oh, and consider this my daughter's resignation," he shouted back, before grabbing Gweneviere under his muscular arm and walking out.

"Dad, what are you doing? We need that job!" Gweneviere argued, once they were out of sight of the tavern.

"Gwen, I know life isn't great at the moment—"

"Well, that's an understatement," Gweneviere muttered.

"But," he continued, "I didn't bring you all the way here, away from those kind of townie men, to be treated like that. I'll do some extra shifts at work until we can find you a job where you don't have to be ogled at by filthy men all day."

"Thanks... Dad." She smiled, wrapping her arms around

his waist, as she squashed her teary-eyed face into his chest.

"You don't need to thank me. I know I've not always been the best dad, but I promise, as long as I'm around, you won't have to deal with men like that."

He pressed his lips gently to the top of his daughter's head as he held her, breathing in the smell of her hair, as if she was still his little baby girl. With their arms around one another, the pair of them walked home to their tiny apartment to figure out how they would find Gweneviere a decent, more wholesome job.

As the weeks went by, Gweneviere was having no luck finding another job. Any other bar work was off the table as word spread about her father's outburst, and any job that required a slither of intellect was reserved for men, most of whom didn't even possess the required brain power. Even with her father working any extra shift he could get, they still weren't making enough to healthily sustain their life in London. Harold was beginning to look gaunt, a look Gweneviere had never seen him sport before, he was always so brawny and strong. Now, though, he was a mere shadow of his former self.

They were starting to get a few weeks behind on paying the rent, and to make matters worse, the plague had hit London. With each passing day, more and more fell ill to the gruesome disease and died. It was spreading like wildfire, thanks to the awful personal hygiene and rampant rat population. With Gweneviere still needing a job, she took it upon herself to try and learn her mother's remedies. She scanned through her mother's grimoire so that she might be able to brew and sell some potion as a pain reliever to the plague sufferers. Harold was very set against the idea, fearing that she would meet the same fate as her mother. It was bad enough that the locals were blaming witches for the plague, they didn't need any more ammo to start another witch hunt. To Gweneviere's disappointment, she was unable to replicate her mother's gifts. She felt useless, and struggled to think of what else she could do to help. She felt especially guilty when she heard through the grapevine that witches were immune to the disease. Apparently, the plague was indeed started by a witch, a satanic one though. Some sick devil worshipper that viewed humans as worse than the vermin that ran through the streets. Although Gweneviere wasn't exactly sympathetic of the mortals, who were so small minded that the slightest odd-looking mole was enough to kill for, she certainly didn't agree with the way this satanic witch went about solving the problem. It only fed and supported the mortal's fearmongering.

As more weeks passed, men, women, and children were dropping like flies in the streets. There were many buildings boarded up and branded as plagued houses. The quarantine only did half the job, though, as people at the time hadn't realised that the witch had spread the plague through fleas that lived on the millions of rats in the city.

Gruesomely, Gweneviere's father had gotten a promotion due to his predecessor falling victim to the plague. The extra pay also came with extra work and Harold became weaker and more tired each day that went by. Gweneviere had to help clean and clothe him most days, which was the least she could do under the circumstances.

One day, on his way home from work, Harold spotted a job advertisement in a window for a bookkeeper. He couldn't wait to return home to tell Gweneviere about it. Upon opening the door, he called out for Gweneviere to tell her the exciting news. He knew his bright daughter would be more than smart enough for the job.

"Gwen?" he shouted, as soon as he opened the door.

"Yes, Dad?" she called from the bedroom.

Harold closed the door behind him and, before he could take another step, he dropped like a sack of potatoes. The loud thud that ensued grabbed Gweneviere's attention and she ran into the living space. She entered to see her father lying face down on the floor. She used all of her might to flip him over onto his back, and as she did, his shirt ripped slightly, revealing part of his chest.

"Dad! Dad, can you hear me?" she shouted, before noticing that his flesh was covered in boils and scabs. He had asked her the past few days to allow him to wash and dress himself, she did think that it was weird at the time, but now it made sense. He was trying to hide that he had the plague. "Dad, what have you done?" she cried into his chest.

Without hesitation she conjured up a fire ball and slung it into the dainty fireplace, causing it to roar to life. She swiftly filled a large pot with water and placed it on the fire. She dragged him as close to the fire as she could before stripping him of his shirt. She soaked a cloth in the now warm water before gently brushing it along his sores, trying her best to clean them and soothe the pain. Once she had finished cleaning him, she placed a pillow beneath his head and laid beside him in the hopes he would soon awaken.

An hour or two later, he finally woke.

"Dad, are you okay?"

"Yeah, I think so," he replied, dazed, and having forgotten about the job that he was so excited to tell her about.

"Why didn't you tell me you had the plague?" she asked.

"Because I knew you'd want me to stay home so you could look after me, but if I don't go to work, we'll be out on the streets in no time," he confessed, wheezing.

"Yes, but, if you carry on like this... well, you're going to die. You need to stay home at least for a few days to try and allow your body to fight through it and heal. I will scour Mum's spell book again until I find something to help, okay?"

"Fine, you've got two days, then I'm going back to work," he agreed stubbornly.

"Now, here, I made you something to eat," she said, holding out a bowl of broth.

"I'm not hungry."

"Dad, you need to eat something," she demanded, acting as if their parent-child relationship had been reversed.

"Ugh fine, it's just that... you didn't exactly inherit your mother's cooking skills, either." He sat up, chuckling, before the pain crippled him back to reality, and the floor.

"If you weren't on your deathbed right now, I'd slap you,"

she lovingly joked. "Now, eat your slop and get some rest."

Gweneviere spent the rest of the night examining every inch of her mother's texts in search for a cure, or even just something to boost his energy to help him fight off the violent disease. Late into the night, Gweneviere pried her eyes open in order to keep researching. Finally, she stumbled on something that she believed would help. Gweneviere leapt from her bed to tell her father the good news.

Still asleep, bless him, she thought to herself as she entered the room and saw him cosied up to the fire. She leant down beside him and began to gently shake him awake. "Dad, wake up, I think I can help."

After there was no response, Gweneviere tried again and again, but as her father remained silent, she became more vigorous with her shaking before she placed her ear to his chest.

"No, Dad, please don't leave me," she sobbed into his chest, but the only response was a faint echo of her own voice in the otherwise silent room. "Dad, please, I need you. I'm not ready to be alone, I can't do this."

But she was too late. Her father had passed.

Gweneviere sat there with her head on his chest as the tears dripped onto his stomach. What would she do? She had no one.

Gweneviere wanted nothing more than to give her father the dignity that he deserved in death, but she knew she wouldn't be able to do so. There would be no funeral, no eulogy, not even his own grave. She didn't even truly have time to mourn. She knew she couldn't get any help with disposing of his body: if she told one of the watchmen or searchers, they might suspect her to be a witch for lack of the disease being prevalent in her. Even if they didn't suspect her of being a witch, she would have gotten into trouble for not notifying them in the first place as any house with a plagued person would've been sealed, with her in it.

Her mother burned and father soon to be tossed into a pit of rotten corpses. How had her life come to this? A year ago she would have been frolicking in the spring meadows near their home, and now she was devising a plan to dispose of her father's remains.

Gweneviere, instead, had to do the unthinkable, and in the cover of night no less. She had to dispose of her father's body. She reluctantly sneaked him onto one of the plague carts which, come sunrise, would ship all of the bodies on board out to the nearest mass plague pit. She'd found a spell in her mother's book to aid her in transporting his hefty body. Even though he had become much scrawnier in the past few weeks, his height alone made him too heavy and awkward for Gweneviere to manoeuvre. It broke her heart to leave her father alone in death – no one deserved that, especially him.

Upon returning to her home, she sat in the spot where he had passed and lit a candle with her finger. She sat silently in a lonely vigil, promising her parents that their deaths wouldn't be in vain, that she would make something of herself and make them proud.

Two weeks after Harold's passing, Gweneviere was evicted by the landlord, as the last of her father's earnings had dried up and he had never managed to tell her about that job that he was so excited by. Gweneviere was all alone in London and had nowhere to go.

Well, that wasn't completely true, she had one place she could go. The Crone's school.

CHAPTER 3
Back to School

Though Gweneviere despised the place and its ideologies, the Crone's school was her only option. Her father had worked so hard for her to have a second chance at life, and in honour of his memory, she couldn't waste it. So she put her grievances aside and went back to the school in the hopes they'd at the very least provide a roof over her head.

She once again walked through the dreaded street, knocked on the door, and waited for one of the witches to appear.

Sensing who was at the door, the Crone answered herself. She opened it while donning her hooded robe and hid half her body behind the door. "Back already, are we?" she croaked, sarcastically.

"Yes," Gweneviere sighed. "My father has passed from the plague, and now... now I have nowhere else to go." She broke down, inconsolable – not that it would do her any good to cry. The Crone wasn't the caring type.

"I'll allow you to stay, if you take our classes and keep an open mind to what we do here," the Crone proposed.

"Yes, I can do that." Gweneviere thanked her appreciatively

as she sniffed and tried to wipe her eyes. In all honesty, she was just glad to have a bed to sleep in.

"Right, very well. I'm not one to hold a grudge. Follow me, then, and I'll show you to your room."

Gweneviere followed in the Crone's footsteps, to a bedroom with four single beds inside, three of which had been made up and one laid bare, with just a mattress seemingly made of straw.

"First things first. All of the girls here make their own beds and are expected to clean their linens every Friday. Understood?"

"Er yes, Ms Crone," Gweneviere answered shakily, uncertain what she should call her.

"Ahh yes, we shall nip that in the bud now. To the outside world I am known as the Crone, not a name that I appointed myself or am particularly fond of. Nevertheless, it was the name that was given to me by the *lovely* citizens of London. To the girls who reside within these walls, however, I am known as Matriarch. You are now forever a part of my flock, and may confide in me, but you will always refer to me as Matriarch, and you will not question my final say on any matter."

"Yes, Matriarch." Gweneviere paused, then asked warily, "May I ask how they have not discovered your magic after all the years of residing here?"

"Well, you see, Gweneviere, I can control minds. That was my natural born talent, as yours is pyrokinesis. Unfortunately, I can only control that of mortals, as a witch's mind is too strong. Strangely, though, I did attempt to do so with your father on that first day, but it didn't work. Hence why I raised my voice, I believe your mother must have reinforced his mind years ago to protect him from anyone with gifts such as mine. Perhaps she was a better witch than I originally gave her credit for. Anyway, to answer your question, if someone ever cottoned on to me or one of my girls, a quick chat with me and I could make them forget all about it."

"I see, and does anyone know your real name?" Gweneviere asked, out of interest.

"No one that's not already dead," the Crone replied, ominously.

It was quite obvious that the Crone's life hadn't been an easy one and she had clearly lost loved ones just like Gweneviere, though the Crone hoped that Gweneviere would one day become more powerful than herself, *much* more.

"Right, now then, make yourself comfortable. Supper will be at seven in the food hall, and if you get lost just ask one of your dormmates. I'm sure you'll get on like a house on *fire*." She croaked a laugh at the unintended pun. "I'll have one of them bring your designated bed linens shortly. You may wear your own garments during the day, however, at evening meals and other occasions you are to wear a dress made of your own volition. Girls are expected to make these in their down time and, once completed, must be vetted by myself or one of the other senior tutors. If it does not meet the high standard in which we set, then you will have to revisit the garb until it is satisfactory. In the meantime, I'll also have the girls provide you with a dress that the juniors wear while they make their dresses."

"Oh, I see, okay. Thank you," Gweneviere said, becoming less enthusiastic as the Crone explained the certain conditions of her stay.

"I shall see you at dinner," the Crone concluded, leaving Gweneviere to become acquainted with her corner of the room.

Gweneviere sat on her bed trying her best to hold back the tears, as all she could think about was her parents. She missed them so much, and now she was going to have to rely on her lacking social skills to make friends – or at least some semblance – to get her through to graduation. She was hoping to graduate with the other eighteen-year-olds in a couple months as she winced at the thought of having to stay there any longer.

Shortly after the Crone left, Gweneviere's new roommates strode into the room laughing and giggling. One of them carrying a pile of freshly ironed and folded linens with a dress atop it.

"Hello, I'm Poppy," said the chipper young witch.

She was a beautiful girl with soft features and a smooth pale complexion, though most people were pale in those days. Her long blonde hair was tied up in a pink and white checked cloth. The two witches either side of her were twins, with almost identical faces apart from the giant mole that one of them had on their chin. Not that it seemed to affect her confidence, as she and her sister were quite poised upon their first-time meeting Gweneviere, giving her a disapproving look up and down.

"And this is Gertrude and Glenda," Poppy added, introducing the girls whose faces looked as though they were constantly sucking a lemon.

"I'm Gweneviere, nice to meet you." She awkwardly smiled, attempting make a good first impression.

"Nice to meet you too, Gwen. Is it alright if I call you Gwen? It's much easier, less syllables to get my mouth around," Poppy asked, giggling.

"Er, yeah, sure." It was a nickname that only her parents had ever used until now, but it did feel nice to hear someone say it again, especially knowing that *they* couldn't anymore.

"Great, well, *Gwen*. I believe these are yours." Poppy presented Gweneviere with her bed linens and dinner dress.

"Thanks, I suppose I better make my bed and change for dinner, then," Gweneviere replied, as she took the pile of cloth from Poppy's arms.

"Yes, won't be long now. Let me know if you need any help or anything, okay?" Poppy offered, clearly the kinder of her three new roommates.

In fact, Gertrude and Glenda hadn't said a word to Gweneviere; they just watched her from afar.

An hour or so later, dinner was about to be served. Each girl had a named seat, usually among their roommates. Gweneviere's name placement was next to Poppy who, so far, had seemed rather nice, and was sat across from the twins who still hadn't spoken a word to Gweneviere. There was a buzzing sound from all the girls nattering amongst themselves. Poppy seemed rather popular at the dining table, but made sure to not leave Gweneviere to fend for herself.

"How are you settling in then, Gwen? Not too anxious, I hope?" Poppy asked.

"It's okay. Though, I get a feeling that the twins don't like me," Gweneviere answered. Every time her eyes glanced over at the two other witches, they were simply glaring back.

"Oh, don't worry about those two, it's a twin thing; they just don't mingle with the rest of us all that much. To be perfectly honest, I wouldn't be surprised if they opted to share a husband at graduation."

"Ah yes, *graduation*." Gweneviere slumped in her seat. "I think I'm more worried about that than the actual school, come to think of it. I mean, do you really adhere to the idea that all we can become in life is a tool to better a man?"

"Of course not, but listen, there are many reasons people choose this life. Some have no choice, others want a rich man and don't mind being a lacky, but *I* want to do something with my life. This is a much more sure-fire way to get some status by marrying a Lord. This world isn't made for us, you're right, so we must exploit it in every way we can. The sooner you realise that, Gwen, the sooner you'll be in control of your own destiny. Besides, when I watched graduation last year, the men were actually rather fetching, so here's hoping for a good one."

"Yeah, here's hoping," Gweneviere replied, as she mulled over Poppy's speech.

"Oh, shh. Matriarch is here," Poppy announced to the table.

When the Crone entered the dinner hall it was always common courtesy for all the girls to stand until she was seated at the head of the table, the table that sprawled the entire length of the food hall, and amazingly seated all forty girls, four teachers, and the Crone. Lanterns hung from chains above at different heights to keep in touch with the mystical, medieval vibe that the school had. The walls were decorated with even more portraits of past alumni. Gweneviere looked around wondering if she might be among them one day.

Once the Crone had made it to her seat, she waved her hand, signalling that everyone else may take their seats again. She raised a glass and tapped the side with a salad fork.

"Girls, as you may have noticed, we have a new recruit among our ranks – Gweneviere. I expect you all to make her feel welcome, as she has promised the same pledge to this fine institution as the rest of you. Now then, Gweneviere, stand for a moment, will you, and tell all the girls your natural talent," the Crone pronounced, raising her glass.

"Er... hello, everyone," Gweneviere nervously muttered. "I'm a pyrokinetic."

All of the girls oohed and aahed in response, before Gweneviere once again took her seat, unsure to whether they were being sarcastic or not.

"Oh, come on, Gweneviere, do a little more than that. Show the girls your powers," the Crone encouraged.

"Oh, okay."

Gweneviere stood back up, awkwardly smiling at the table of witches. She pondered what to do when Gertrude and Glenda simultaneously asked her to make the lanterns brighter. It was as if they knew what Gweneviere was thinking. She took them up on their suggestion as Poppy gave her a nod of encouragement. She looked up at the sea of lanterns above her and held her hands out to them, causing the room to become blindingly bright. The Crone applauded at the sight.

Gweneviere got carried away, however, making the entrapped flames grow larger to the point where it eventually became too much and shattered the glass lantern cages. Shards began to rain down, but Poppy stood up and braced herself with her hands out. She froze every single shard in the air before any could come close enough to harm someone. She redirected the dazzling fractured pieces of glass and gathered them into a pile in the corner of the room using her telekinetic abilities.

"I'm so sorry," Gweneviere grovelled, fearing expulsion on her first day.

"Nonsense, my dear. *That* was an excellent display of magics, from both of you girls, I'm very impressed. Though, we will need you to relight the room for the evening whilst we acquire some more lanterns."

"Oh, sure. No problem." Gweneviere summoned two globes of fire in her hands before enlarging them and floating them above the end of each table.

"Ahh, wonderful, Gweneviere. Right, girls, dinner is served," the Crone concluded.

"Gwen, why didn't you say you were a pyrokinetic witch? That's amazing," Poppy exclaimed giddily, as their food was being served.

"It is?" Gweneviere questioned, not really knowing much about witches other than her and her mother's abilities.

"Yeah, duh. Most of these girls would kill to have a power like ours."

"Ours?"

"Oh, sorry, how rude of me, I am a telekinetic," Poppy said proudly.

"Oh, that's how you managed to save us from the glass?"

"Yes, and girls with any kinetic powers like ourselves are usually the popular kids."

"Popular? Oh, I'm not sure if that'll be me. To be honest, I've never been much of a social butterfly," Gweneviere revealed, feeling rather sorry for herself.

"Nonsense, we'll have you a group of friends in no time." Poppy smiled.

"Can I ask what the twin's powers are?" Gweneviere whispered.

"We're telepaths," the twins responded almost instantly, not needing to hear Gweneviere. They had already read her mind.

"Is that why you told me to light the lanterns before? Because you could hear my thoughts?" Gweneviere asked.

"No, we just knew you'd cause a scene like that," they said, laughing in unison.

"Oh... I see, but you did read my mind just then, when I was asking about your powers?"

"Yes, bloody hell, anything else? Lighten up, question master," they said at the same time, before turning to their bowls of broth.

Gweneviere was taken back by their oddness and repositioned herself to convene with Poppy instead.

"What kind of broth is this, anyway?" Gweneviere asked, not being too keen on the presentation, as she scooped it up and poured it back into her bowl.

"I don't know, I just eat whatever is in front of me. It usually tastes good," Poppy answered, as she delicately slurped up the mysterious liquid.

Gweneviere began to swirl her spoon around her broth and looked around to see everyone else tucking in, before she caught the Crone's milky eye watching her, making her jump. She turned back to the bowl and took a sip of the broth with her eyes closed, hoping that somehow it would allow her to not taste the food, but to her surprise, it was amazing. It was far better than anything Gweneviere could ever cook up herself. She swiftly cleaned the rest of the bowl in no time, only to be surprised once more as dessert was placed in front of her. It was some sort of malted fruit loaf with a drizzle of custard. Gweneviere was practically drooling, as she couldn't remember the last time she had enjoyed a dessert. She and her father hadn't been able to afford such luxuries since they left home, so she lapped up every last sugary spoonful. It was like fireworks on her tongue; so much flavour that she had been denied for so long. Maybe this whole 'school' thing wouldn't be so bad after all.

Gweneviere spent the following months learning how to be the perfect house witch. She still loathed the lessons, which involved learning how to prepare meals, sew, and clean in the most efficient ways, as well as etiquette classes. Gweneviere had all the grace of a reversing dump truck. Although she didn't act the part, when she had been tied and squashed into her unbearably uncomfortable corseted dresses, she certainly looked it. Her slumping grades were much to her teacher's disappointment as they could see the potential that Gweneviere possessed.

Graduation was fast approaching, and Gweneviere was unsure whether she wanted to graduate or not. She had, surprisingly, come to enjoy living among peers, and the thought of having to trade that in for married life was scary to say the least. Gweneviere, on occasion, would sabotage herself in assessments that would count towards her final grade. It was all in the hopes that she might get one more year of being free, or at least as free as a witch could be. Although Gweneviere may have been cleverly fooling her teachers, the Crone was not so easily deceived.

"Gwen, Matriarch would like to see you in her study," Poppy told her, popping out of nowhere.

"Oh, do you know why?" Gweneviere pondered aloud.

"No, she just told me to fetch you, but don't worry. I'm sure it'll be nothing."

"Okay, wish me luck, I guess," Gweneviere said, walking away from Poppy and the twins.

Once she reached the Crone's office, she poked her head through the half-open door,

"You wanted to see me?"

"Yes, close the door and take a seat, dear," the Crone instructed, waiting for Gweneviere to be seated before she continued. "Now then, your teachers have been informing me that you haven't been performing up to scratch lately."

She said no more, looking to Gweneviere for an explanation.

"Er, yeah. I guess, I'm just finding certain aspects of the curriculum hard to achieve," Gweneviere stuttered.

"Is that right?" The Crone paused briefly, before continuing to speak. "Gweneviere, I'm not stupid, and I would implore you not to treat me as such. Now, please, tell me the real reason you are purposely failing your tests."

The Crone's voice was eerily calm, and Gwenivere could feel a cold sweat forming on the back of her neck.

"I would never purposely fail, I promise," she lied.

"Gweneviere! I just said do not treat me as a fool. The condition of me taking you in was that you swore to take this place seriously and learn all you can while having an open mind to our end goal. Or don't you remember?" the Crone barked, having had quite enough of Gweneviere's act.

"Okay, okay. I'm sorry. I have been failing on purpose," Gweneviere admitted, sighing in defeat.

"Might I ask why?"

"I'm scared to be wed. What if I end up with a horrible husband and end up hating my life forever?" Gweneviere asked, getting teary eyed.

"Gweneviere," the Crone said softly, "I would never intentionally provide any of my girls with a *horrific* man for a husband. I do my best to seek out the most exemplary and noble gentlemen about London to *persuade* them to take one of my girls in marriage. Now, I know you have never wanted this life and, believe it or not, I understand, but that doesn't change the fact that we're living in a world that is designed to cut away at our legs with every step we climb. You, Gweneviere, are the one who will live to see that change. I sense it in you; I've always sensed it, since that first day we met. I knew you had longevity in your blood. If you pick your battles wisely, you will live for hundreds of years and see in a new era, a new millennium, even, where witches aren't in need of marriage to do as they see fit. In the meantime, however, you need to make every ally you can and take advantage of every opportunity that you are presented with. Otherwise, you will never live to see that day. Now then, graduation is next week, you will re-sit your failed tests in a lone classroom with me as the invigilator and you *will* graduate, understood?"

"Yes, Matriarch," Gweneviere happily conceded.

She knew the Crone was right, if she was going to make something of herself, she would have to use any leg up she could get, starting with marrying a man of greatness.

It was the night of graduation, which consisted of the graduating witches dressing in their best garb before lining up in the dinner hall. The dinner hall had been turned into a ballroom for the night, where the girls would wait for their future husbands to take their pick and be married off. Only the girls from the year below were allowed to watch the ceremony, so that they could get a taste for what lay ahead for them at their graduation.

Gweneviere, Poppy, and the twins were all getting ready in their room. They had each designed and fashioned their own wedding-cum-graduation dresses as a part of one of their final assessments, though Gweneviere had a helping hand from Poppy, seeing as she had only just recently agreed to even graduate. The twins, of course, had identical black dresses matching the peculiarly dark outlook they had on life. May God protect the man that had to wed a telepath; they'd know about every little mischievous thought. Today, more than any other day, they couldn't be told apart – even the tell-tale chin mole had been hidden by the ruffled and ruched turtleneck on their gothic dresses.

Poppy had a large, billowingly beautiful, baby pink dress that accentuated her womanly features perfectly. It was clear that, out of them all, she was the most suited to become a man's beautiful arm candy. Gweneviere, on the other hand, having chosen the design herself, went for a forest green dress that was rather slim lined and silky looking. Poppy tried her best to add some glamour and sparkle where she could, but at the end of the day it was still Gweneviere's dress, so she had the last say.

"You know, I'm surprised you came around to the whole wedding idea," Poppy commented as she helped Gweneviere tighten the corsetry of her dress.

"Me too, Poppy, *me too*," Gweneviere agreed.

Unfortunately for Gweneviere, the uncomfortable undergarment was deemed a necessary element to pass the test, so she couldn't bypass it, much that she wished she could.

"For what it's worth, Gwen, I think you'll make a wonderful wife and mother one day."

"Thanks, Poppy, though I don't have a maternal bone in my body, so maybe they can come live with their fun Aunt Poppy instead," Gweneviere joked, knowing she had no intention of having children anytime soon, if at all.

"Oh, Gwen, you are a real laugh. I'm going to miss having

you around," Poppy confessed, tearing up.

"Oh, stop it." Gweneviere tried playing cool, but as Poppy leant in for a hug, she couldn't help but accept the fact that she had finally made a real friend as she let a single tear drop onto Poppy's hoop skirt.

"Right, come on, girls. Let's show these boys what a sexy witch looks like," Poppy announced, wiping her eyes and leading the girls through the school and into the ballroom. "Oh, Gwen. Don't forget to brag about how quickly you can heat up an iron, or pot of water."

Poppy's comment was sincere, but it just made Gweneviere giggle at her friend's innocent advice.

The graduating girls lined up in the centre of the room looking poised and ready to bag themselves a prospective husband. One by one, the eligible bachelors entered the room and walked past the line of girls. They made sure to allow each woman to introduce themselves, before deciding on which they would marry, because apparently that was all a man needed to know to decide what maiden he would want to spend the rest of his life with – if he was faithful, that is.

The Crone had mentioned that the order which the men were picked to enter in was random, though it soon became apparent that, clearly, the worst had been saved until last. The first couple of men actually seemed to be a catch – they were handsome, charming and even seemed to respect the girls. None of them, however, picked Gweneviere and, of course,

Poppy was the first to be picked. In fairness, she deserved it. She'd spent every waking moment in that school preparing herself to be the perfect wife and witch.

The twins were picked third and forth by no less than another pair of twins – brothers who had started a company together. They even seemed to enjoy the twins dark outlook on the world. As each girl was chosen and matched, they formed a parallel line against the wall facing the remaining single girls. Gweneviere's face slowly became dullened and miserable as she wasn't chosen again and again, which didn't help her chances of attracting any of the potential husbands. She just couldn't help it, of course, she wasn't expecting to be the first, second or even third, but being one of only three girls left, Gweneviere was losing all hope.

Stay calm and smile! Poppy mouthed as she grabbed Gweneviere's attention, raising her eyebrows in frustration. Gweneviere just sarcastically smiled in an over-the-top fashion in response. Poppy rolled her eyes just as the next man came in who, once again, didn't pick Gweneviere.

As the eligible women dwindled, so did the bachelors, as Gweneviere noticed that the men became progressively less attractive and more dismissive of the girls. Gweneviere and one more girl were left standing side by side as the second to last man stood before them, weighing up his options. Gweneviere tried her best to look more appealing than the witch beside her, who had two lazy eyes, but ultimately failed. She hadn't been desperate because the man was particularly good looking, but rather the fact that no matter how bad he was, judging by the ongoing pattern, the final man could only be worse. They joined the other couples, and Gweneviere was now alone. A line of eight women had dwindled to just one witch standing in the centre of a vast, empty space. The coupled-up girls watched in anticipation as they awaited the final man to stride though the room knowing it would inevitably be Gweneviere's fiancé.

Maybe it was a trick, maybe the last man would in fact be the most dapper and kind of them all...

Out came a short, chubby man with yellowed teeth that made is pale skin look even more translucent. He flipped his long, unruly curly hair as if it was something to be proud of, whereas in reality, it looked heavy and greasy; not something Gweneviere particularly wanted anywhere near her. He shuffled over with his stumpy legs and looked about the room seemingly surprised to only see Gweneviere there, before realising the rest of the girls had already been picked. It was at this moment that Gweneviere wasn't sure whether he knew he would be getting the other men's leftovers. She remained silent as she waited for him to acknowledge her.

"Hello, my name is Thomas, Thomas Farriner, and you are?" he asked politely, getting uncomfortably close to Gweneviere's face.

"Gweneviere Baxter," she answered, trying not to breathe as she felt his toxic breath hit her cheeks.

"Well not for much longer, aye? Ah, yes, Gweneviere Farriner has a much nicer ring to it. Don't you think?" He gave her a sickening grin.

This was what Gweneviere had been fearing the whole time. She knew she would end up with a grotesque man. He somehow managed to have shoulder length hair and a receding bald patch at the same time. She contemplated running there and then, but she would only end up back at square one: homeless and jobless. She couldn't let the months of training go to waste, so despite every primal urge of repulse that made her want to flee, she stayed. She just needed to remember the plan she had been working on in her mind since her talk with the Crone. All she needed to do was survive a good couple years with him, allowing her to make contacts and exploit every aspect of him that she could, before leaving to start her own entrepreneurial journey.

Thomas offered out his hand to Gweneviere as the unofficial proposal to marriage, which she reluctantly accepted, as she swallowed the lump in her throat. The room broke out into applause as the final couple was forged. All of the couples flooded back into the centre of the room.

It was then time for the communal wedding to begin. The Crone happened to *chance* upon a minister, who she had made backstreet deals with to keep their secret. One by one – as some of the younger students played classical music in the corner – each couple took their turn in becoming wed. Some of the girls, mainly Poppy, looked overjoyed as they pronounced their newfound loyalty to their husbands. When it came to Gweneviere's turn, however, she just considered it to be an achievement if she managed to get all the vows out without visibly gagging, seeing as Thomas' rancid breath leapt into her mouth each time she spoke. Of course, that was nothing compared to the rotten taste that filled her mouth when he forced his tongue into it as a part of their post wedding consummations. He whisked it around like he was cleaning her teeth. Gweneviere pulled away before any sick rose up into her throat.

Too late, she thought to herself as she swallowed back down the chunk of vomit in her mouth, though, even that was still more pleasant that kissing him. To think that her first kiss had been a disaster; nothing like the fairytales that her mother had told her about her own first kiss.

"Aw, are we a bit shy about kissing in public?" Thomas teased. "Don't worry, soon you'll be well versed with my ways." He winked, menacingly.

They were the last couple in line to be wed thus, once their vows had been exchanged, the afterparty could begin. There were glasses of wine poured and a feast prepared in honour of the gracious men willing to marry a bunch of wayward witches. All the women sat across from their husbands and began to tuck into the mountain of food in front of them. Gweneviere had managed to wangle a seat next to Poppy and her much easier on the eye husband.

"Hey Poppy, you want to swap?" Gweneviere joked under her breath, making Poppy giggle.

"Hey, give him a chance, he might surprise you and be a really sweet guy," she whispered back.

"That's easy for you to say when your husband looks like *that*," Gweneviere pointed out, looking at Poppy's man with her eyes almost popping out of her head. His cleanly shaven face was so handsome it almost hypnotised her.

"Yeah, he is pretty dishy, isn't he," Poppy agreed, losing herself in his, well... everything.

"You know, I hope he turns out to be a bed wetter," Gweneviere joked.

Poppy almost burst out with laughter, garnering their husbands' attentions and thus ending their chinwag.

"So, Gwen, what kind of powers do you possess?" Thomas asked as he shovelled food into his mouth with his fingers, seemingly forgetting that there was a perfectly good set of cutlery beside him.

Gweneviere also couldn't help but notice that he had already taken it upon himself to shorten her name without asking, as any other polite person would've.

"I'm pyrokinetic," Gweneviere answered, leaving out the part where she also had longevity and would likely outlive the slob ten times over.

"Ahh, a fire witch. Tell me, do you require fuel to create a flame, or can you create one of thin air?" he probed, intrigued by his new wife's gifts.

"Thin air," she confirmed unenthusiastically, already wishing that the conversation was over.

"Brilliant! You'll save me lots of money on fuel for the bakery," he grinned, rubbing his grubby mitts together.

"Bakery?"

"Yes, I have a well-established bakery at the heart of London, on Pudding Lane," he boasted.

Hmm, a man with a business in the centre of London, this could be useful indeed, Gweneviere contemplated.

The following hours contained dancing and making any last fond memories they could with each other before each witch went off to start their new lives. Some would surely become neighbours and see much of each other, however some may never see each other again. These unlucky few would include Poppy and Gweneviere, or so Poppy thought.

"Gwen." Poppy rushed over. "I'm so sorry, Gwen."

"What is it, Poppy? What's wrong?" Gweneviere asked.

"I just found out that my husband doesn't actually live in London, he lives in Cambridge. What if we never see each other again?"

"Calm down, Poppy, I'm only a letter away. I'll write to you all the time, okay? I'm sure we will find time to visit each other on the occasional weekend. Besides, it's Cambridge, not Scotland," Gweneviere reassured her, trying to calm Poppy's nerves.

"I don't know, maybe you were right. Maybe this marriage thing isn't for me either, and we should just run away right now," Poppy frantically suggested, clearly feeling slightly influenced by the amount of alcohol coursing through her veins.

"Poppy, relax," Gweneviere said calmly, planting her hands firmly on Poppy's shoulders. "You're just having cold feet, it's completely normal. Though, it does usually happen before the wedding. Now, listen to me, you've wanted this *forever* and now you have it. You need to go start your new life with your hunk of a husband and, most importantly of all, bloody enjoy it!"

"Yeah, I guess so."

"Come on, I'll walk you and your prince charming over to your chariot."

"Thanks, Gwen, you're a great friend."

Gweneviere realised, in that moment, she was one step closer to a better life and to making her parents proud because, for the first time ever, Gweneviere had a friend.

CHAPTER 4
Life as the Baker's Wife

After the wedding celebrations, Gweneviere packed her things and readied herself to move in with Thomas to start her new life as the baker's wife. The Crone waved them off and, Gweneviere, along with her newfound husband, exited the school where a carriage awaited them.

This is fancy, Gweneviere thought to herself. She had mostly only seen stagecoaches before: full of men, usually off to the same workplace, being pulled by several horses. This, however, was a rather nice carriage, still not royalty level, but far nicer than Gweneviere could've imagined. Thomas must've rented it for the special occasion. Though, as Gweneviere became lost in the fairytale moment, she was soon brought swiftly back to reality as she had to lug all her luggage to the carriage, with no help from Thomas. Luckily, the kind driver aided her in loading them onto the carriage when he had noticed her struggling.

Thomas was too distracted as he ogled through the steamy windows of the brothels on either side of the school. Gweneviere cleared her throat to grab his attention as she was about to enter the carriage.

"Ah, yes. I'm coming, dear," he responded, sounding as though they had already been married for a lifetime.

Thomas shuffled his stumpy body up the two steps and, as he climbed into the carriage, there was a noticeable dip in the height of it. It was much smaller on the inside than one would think looking outward in, and unfortunately, this meant that Gweneviere had no choice but to be touching distance from Thomas. He walked his fingers across his leg and playfully hopped them over to Gweneviere's thigh, before gripping her tightly and not letting go for the rest of the journey, which, luckily for Gweneviere, wasn't too long. The look on Gweneviere's face was disapproving to say the least; she knew what that hand signified, and she wasn't prepared to do it. Still being a virgin, Gweneviere had always hoped that she would lose her innocence to a kind, loving, but strong, man who wasn't afraid of an equally as strong woman. She therefore was not intent on giving that part of herself to Thomas. The look in Thomas' hungry eyes, however, made it seem as though she wouldn't have a choice in the matter.

They soon reached their destination and the horses halted afront the bakery. It was a nice enough looking building, with a large shop front window that would usually display all kinds of breads and cakes. Thomas wasted no time in showing Gweneviere where she would start her day each morning: in the back of the bakery, conjuring her magical everlasting fire in the furnace. He then went on to show her around the rest of the bakery, proud of what he had accomplished.

"It's really lovely," Gweneviere said, in a bid to appease him.

"Yes. Brilliant, isn't it?" he replied, still looking around at his pride and joy. "It's almost as beautiful as you," he added, rather charmingly, much to Gweneviere's surprise.

"Thank you." Gweneviere smiled shyly.

"Right, to the living quarters, then."

Thomas proceeded to show Gweneviere around his home above the bakery. It was much larger than the flat Gweneviere and her father had been sharing a few months ago. There were two large bedrooms, a living room with a beautiful open fireplace, and a kitchen with a small dining area off to the side of it. They still had to use communal toilets, though they did have a pot besides the bed for emergencies that would now be emptied by Gweneviere as one of her *many* chores.

"This will be our room," he said, finishing the tour as he winked at Gweneviere.

There was a massive bed with wooden posts in each corner, and tied up drapes that adorned them to add a little ambience for when it came to such *activities*. It did actually look rather tempting to Gweneviere. It appeared to be much comfier than any bed she had slept in before. That cosy feeling was tarnished, however, as soon as she remembered who it was that would be beside her as she slept.

"Now, then, I shall leave you to unpack while I go and make us a nightcap. Whiskey, okay? Great," he answered for her before she had time to reject the offer.

Gweneviere unpacked what few belongings she had into the bedside drawer, that would be hers, as Thomas waltzed back into the room.

"Ah, good to see you've made yourself at home." He smiled.

"Now, let's gets those clothes off you. It's far too warm tonight to be beneath so many layers. Look at your cheeks, they're practically tomatoes, you're so warm."

"Oh, erm... I'm actually feeling a little chilly still, I'll keep them on for now, I think," Gweneviere replied, rubbing her arms and acting as though she was covered in goose bumps.

"Nonsense, get them off. I'll keep you nice and warm under the covers."

He grinned sleazily, sending sickening shivers down Gweneviere's spine and giving her very real goose bumps. She felt sick to her stomach.

He denounced his clothes from his body and climbed into the bed with the covers off, leaving his full naked flesh exposed to Gweneviere. He scratched his large, hairy stomach with one hand and casually fondled himself with the other as he laid there watching Gweneviere take off her wedding dress to reveal her undergarments.

"I must say, they clearly saved the best till last with you, didn't they, my dear? Come on, keep going, don't be shy, I won't bite."

A slither of drool slipped out of his crusty lips as he encouraged her to remove the final layer of fabric that protected her bare body from his prying eyes.

"No, I think that's far enough," Gweneviere said, as she re-found her voice and stood her ground.

"Well, it's very sweet of you to think that, but I don't need a wife who thinks, I need a wife who obeys. Afterall, I could always chuck you out onto the streets and try again at next year's graduation," he threatened, with a cruel smile across his face.

"Okay, okay... fine." Gweneviere sighed, slowly slipping off her final layer, revealing her plump, perky breasts to his leering gaze.

"Now we're in business. They look fresh as a daisy. Let me guess, still pure, are we?" he asked, salivating as his penis began to elongate and thicken.

Clearly he was taking pleasure in Gweneviere's discomfort. Gweneviere silently nodded in response as she tried her best not to cry before him, for fear of him enjoying it.

"Come closer, I want to see those plums up close," he said, now fully erect. "Don't worry, I'll take good care of you."

As if that was supposed to give Gweneviere any reassurance.

Gweneviere reluctantly and slowly sat on the very edge of her side of the bed, but an impatient Thomas grabbed her by the breasts and dragged her to him. He planted his rough, greasy, bearded face between them and smelt Gweneviere's succulently sweet, scented skin. He was manhandling them to the point of pain.

Gweneviere screamed, but her pain only seemed to bring more pleasure to him. He flipped her over onto her front and began to mount her as he revelled in her squirms. The weight of his body atop hers was almost crushing. She was nearly suffocated as her face got flattened into his pillow that had already been stained by the stench of his breath. The same warm, dirty breath that she could now feel on the back of her neck. Gweneviere began to sob into the pillow as Thomas took no hesitation in ploughing himself into her small frame.

Her screams and cries loudened as he continued to pummel his filthy phallus inside her. The only silver lining Gweneviere could cling to was that he luckily didn't last very long, meaning that soon the ordeal came to an end. He released himself from within her and Gweneviere quietly shuffled back to her side of the bed, leaving a tear-soaked pillow behind. Not that Thomas minded, though, as he turned it over and swiftly fell asleep like a baby.

Though Gweneviere was finally free of his touch, she would forever feel soiled by him. His viscous liquid was inside her and the leftovers were wiped across her bum. She felt used and disgusting. She laid there cradling herself best she could, but no amount of false self-reassurance could make up for how she felt. She gazed up at the ceiling as the silent tears flowed down the sides of her face, soaking her pillow. She turned for a quick glance at the oaf snoring away as if nothing had happened, before returning her gaze to the ceiling, where it would be transfixed until sunrise. Gweneviere would not be sleeping that night.

The next morning, Gweneviere was still awake as the sun rose. She hadn't slept a wink during the night thanks to Thomas. She noticed him stirring awake beside her and so pretended to be asleep in the hopes that he would leave her be. Although, judging by the kind of man he was, that wasn't likely.

He woke Gweneviere by pushing her shoulder until she faked her awakening, to remind her that, as a part of their union, she was to fire up the bakery ovens each day, even if it was around five in the morning. Gweneviere walked over to the vanity table on her side of the room and sat naked in front of the mirror. It was only now, for the first time in early daylight, that she could see the aftermath of Thomas' doing. Her chest and stomach were covered in patches of red and purple. Some were bruises and others sores from being so violently rubbed into the bed. She exhaled deeply before trying to compose herself and getting on with the day at hand. She supposed that if this were to be her life, she had better deal with it, as sad as it may be. There was a bowl of clean water to her left and a cloth on the right. She held her hand above the bowl of water and warmed it through to make it less harsh on her tender skin. Dipping the cloth into the warm water, she, as gently as she could, cleansed herself, but even being as careful as she was, she still caught her face twitching in pain in the mirror. As much as her eyes wanted to carry on crying, there were no tears left, and besides, she wouldn't allow herself to waste any more on him. He didn't deserve the satisfaction of making her cry. Today would be the first day of her plan to absorb as much as she could from this fraudulent marriage and get out. She just needed to survive long enough to set up a life for herself, alone, or at the very least with a man who wasn't such a soul sucking pig.

Once Gweneviere had dressed herself, she made her way down to the bakery and, as she passed the living room, she could see Thomas sat in his chair, shovelling porridge into his mouth, most of which was just being stickily gathered by his beard. She was surprised to see that he had managed to do something for himself, as she half expected to be asked to make it for him. Nevertheless, she carried on down to the bakery, and luckily, after the banquet last night, she was still full and didn't need any breakfast before getting to work firing up the ovens.

She opened the door that led to the back room of the bakery. It was in total darkness, blocked off from the shop front's vast window and the morning sunshine that poured through it. Instead, Gweneviere lit a few lanterns, that she could just about make out, on the walls. Sensing the oil within them, she sparked them to life, causing the scene around her to become a much warmer one. Now that she could see what she was doing, she headed over to the furnace that looked as if it was large enough to house almost a hundred loaves of bread at a time. Gweneviere conjured up a fireball within her hands and slung it into the back of the furnace where it roared to life. She still needed to speak an incantation, as although she could create flames from nothing, she hadn't ever needed one to last longer than an hour without fuel. She created a spell to ensure the fire wouldn't snuff out.

"I forge this fire from the eternal flame. Let it continue to blaze until I say thy name. Gweneviere *Baxter*."

With that, the fire would remain burning brightly for Thomas' use until she returned, at the end of his working day, to put it out by merely whispering her name, her true name.

Gweneviere returned to the living room and informed 'his royal highness' that the bakery was ready for him to begin work.

"Ah yes, well done, Gweneviere. I knew you'd be a useful little witch. Here," Thomas said, handing her an extremely long, comprehensive list of chores that he expected to be done daily, with an added section at the bottom of those he would allow to be done weekly.

"Oh, thanks." Gweneviere only just managed to avoid rolling her eyes.

"Great, I expect I'll see you later, when you bring me my lunch at noonish."

"Lunch?"

"Yes, Gweneviere, it is a meal that well-off people have during the middle off the day. Did they not feed you lunch at the school?" he said condescendingly.

"Ah, yes, lunch. Of course they did, what would you like for lunch?" she asked through gritted teeth.

"I don't rather know what I fancy," he said, scratching his privates and clearing his throat. "There's some food in the pantry, so surprise me."

He smacked her arse in farewell and headed over to bakery, grabbing his apron on his way, before Gweneviere could further dispute his words.

"I guess I better get on with this list, then," Gweneviere voiced aloud, to the otherwise empty living room.

It was a very meticulous piece of paper instructing exactly what Gweneviere was to do, and in the ways that Thomas liked them to be done. It was seemingly designed to leave Gweneviere without a spare second in the day; even after enacting various spells and enchantments the school taught her to make life easier, she would still have no time to rest. Despite time being against her, Gweneviere went about her day the best she could and tried to get all her morning chores done before she had to make lunch for Thomas.

It was just past noon and Gweneviere headed down to present her 'master' with his lunch. He was seemingly underwhelmed and unimpressed by what she had presented.

"What on earth is this?" Thomas questioned, looking down on the plate of toasted bread with melted cheese atop.

"It's very tasty, I promise," Gweneviere attempted to convince him.

"Where's the meat?"

"Well, there wasn't any meat in the house."

"Then you go to the market and get some, for Christ's sake!" he raged. "You're also late. I'm starving here and now all I've got is this cheesy bread to last me my working day. Here, take this, and get some *meat* for dinner," he demanded, stuffing some money into her hands.

"Okay, I will try to do better tonight," she apologised, not wanting to piss him off anymore. At least going to the market for supper ingredients was already an item on the afternoon agenda, so it wasn't actually adding to her workload.

After scouring the markets for the makings of a delicious dinner, Gweneviere noticed that, to her surprise, Thomas had provided her with a hefty budget. She even had a little left over, and so when she walked past a stall selling fudge, she couldn't help herself; she purchased what she could with her remaining pennies and scoffed it on the way home, out of sight of the wicked man. After all, she had to make the most out of the small things in her day.

Once home, Gweneviere began preparing dinner in the hopes that she could produce something that Thomas would deem, at the very least, edible. It was frustrating seeing his arrogance during lunch as she had actually tried to pay attention in her cooking classes, after remembering her father's joke about her food not being nearly as good as her mothers.

Thomas returned from work and went straight over to the dining table to await his dinner. Gweneviere, trying to be a tentative wife – or at least appear that way – poured him a glass of wine. For which, she barely received as much as a thank you. She added the finishing touches to dinner and served it at the six-seater dining table, which was a ridiculous size considering that there were never more than two of them, it would seem. Gweneviere sat herself at the opposite end of the dining table to put as much distance between them as possible. She sat and watched with anticipation as Thomas eyed up his plate, inspecting the food before he tried it.

"Is it okay?" Gweneviere asked, as he sat in silence.

"My God, Gweneviere, that's a much better job than lunch. I especially like the meat," he complimented, guzzling down another mouthful.

Gweneviere was just happy that he wouldn't be in a foul mood for the rest of the evening. "I'm glad you like it."

"Yes, it really is delicious. Tell me, did I give you enough money for everything at the market?" Thomas asked, as his open mouth churned the food in front of Gweneviere.

"Er…"

Gweneviere's brain had an epiphany almost instantaneously after Thomas finished talking. The left-over money that she'd used to buy the fudge could be saved up for herself, and he would never know because he doesn't go out on the market to buy food. Even better, as now was her time to milk the opportunity for all it was worth by fabricating ever so slightly.

"Actually, it was a bit tight. A couple extra pennies ought to secure us the best food the market has to offer," she told him, hoping to expand her savings with immediate effect.

"Hmm," he pondered aloud, making Gweneviere nervous that he didn't believe her. "Very well, I can stretch to a couple more pennies, but that's it."

"Thank you. Anyway, how has your day been?" Gweneviere asked, swiftly changing the subject before he could rethink his kind decision. Though, she didn't listen to much of his answer, as now all she could think about was where she was going to hide the money from him.

"Oh, you know how it is when you get to a certain age – it's just the same shit every day. You get up, you go to work, and you come home to a nice meal prepared by your beautiful wife."

All Gweneviere heard was, 'Yada, yada, yada, beautiful wife.' She choked on her wine as the compliment took her out of her thoughts, smiling coyly to flatter him as she pretended she knew what else he had said.

"Cheers to you, Gweneviere," he said, holding up his wine glass before devouring the rest of his food like a ravenous dog.

Gweneviere held her glass up too, tilted slightly towards him, with another false smile. She internally revelled in the fact that she had already made a start in escaping from under his thumb.

After dinner, Thomas returned to his chair in front of the fire and put his feet up on a stool as he enjoyed another glass of wine with a book, all while Gweneviere was washing dishes, using up the rest of the day's clean water. Thomas was wealthy enough to afford to pay the local cob to fetch them a few gallons of fresh water each day, but not quite wealthy enough to be hooked up with the latest home advancements – a running water supply – like the truly rich did.

"Gwen," he called out from his chair.

"Yes?"

"When you're done with those dishes, my feet could do with a good massage, I've been on them all day and they hurt like hell."

"Okay," she called back, begrudgingly. "Like I've not been on my feet all day running around doing errands like an idiot," she muttered to herself while aggressively drying the last dish.

She walked over to his crusty feet, but kept in the back of her mind her new plan to get out of that house. She knelt between Thomas' feet and the fire, the heat of which only amplifying the stench. To put it bluntly, his feet were vile; they could have easily been mistaken for the hooves of the devil himself. His toenails were curled and ingrown, with a heavy dose of fungus. He had bunions the size of golf balls and the soles of his feet were like rock; she thought about whether or not to get the cheese grater out but swiftly changed her mind when she remembered it would be her who would have to sweep up the chunks of crusty foot. He wiggled his toes at

Gweneviere as if it was supposed to entice her. Instead, the sound of scraping wracked around her brain from his crunchy toes grinding against each other as he wriggled them. There was nothing enticing about the man in general, let alone his gruesome, stilton-like feet. Gweneviere rubbed some oil into his feet in the hopes that they might soften a little to make them more pliable.

"Come on, Gwen, put your back into it. These are working feet," he moaned, clicking at her face while taking another glug of the deep red alcohol that swirled his glass.

"I'm trying."

"Well, you're going to have to try harder, then, aren't you?"

Gweneviere decided to remain silent, saving her strength to try and pierce through to the part of his foot where he may still have living nerves.

"Oh, before I forget, at the weeks-end we're going to a party hosted by a friend of mine. So I'm going to give you some extra money this week to find a dress. I want you to look as good as magically possible, understood?" He grinned, winking at her. "There's no point in having a trophy wife if she's dressed like a common peasant."

"Oh, a party? That might actually be fun."

"Well, of course it'll be fun, it's a party. Oh, and don't worry, my friend's wife will be there, so you two can talk about how we are in bed, or whatever it is you women folk gas about. Now, get back to rubbing," he added with a wave of his hand.

"Oh, goody." Gweneviere faked an appreciative smile. Of course that's what Thomas thought women talked about. If it was up to Gweneviere, she'd quite happily never speak of what

Thomas had already done to her ever again. She felt physically sick every time it crossed her mind, if she was honest.

Gweneviere continued to rub his feet as she tried to concentrate on the benefits of going to the party. She could imagine meeting rich and powerful men and women there; it could be a great chance for her to make some powerful friends who might help her get a leg up in the world. She wondered if she might be able to remember her socialising classes on proper party etiquette; she'd have to rehearse with herself during the week.

As she daydreamed about the kinds of people she may get to meet, the sound of Thomas' snoring brought her out of her trance. He was out like a light and, thankfully for Gweneviere, this meant she had time to find a hiding spot for her new income. It also meant that she wouldn't be defiled that night, which was something to celebrate in of itself.

When Gweneviere and Thomas arrived at the party, it soon became apparent that Thomas' friend was much wealthier than himself. Their carriage pulled up to a humongous brick manor with iron gates where guards were stationed, asking for invitations. Gweneviere had never felt so fancy in all her life. She had spent her gown money on a rather classical dress compared to the one she concocted herself for graduation. It seemed she was trying to fit in. She definitely didn't want to stick out in this crowd for the wrong reasons. She wanted to stand out for her amazing conversing skills or be applauded for her harrowing jokes, but only time would tell how she would be remembered, if at all.

They entered the party with Thomas' hand firmly around Gweneviere's waist. It was clear he wasn't going to let her out of his sight for the entirety of the night.

"Thomas, how are you?" they heard from behind them.

They turned around to see a rather fetching gentlemen who was likely no more than ten years younger than Thomas, but he most definitely looked a damn sight better. He was tall, dark, and handsome – there was no attraction, however, as he soon reminded Gweneviere of her father. Though he wasn't as well built and filled out like her father, she couldn't help but notice how all the middle-aged women glared at him.

"Gerald! I'm brilliant. How are you?" Thomas replied, sticking out his hand to be shaken.

"No doubt better than you, you old sod," Gerald teased, accepting the shake before nudging his arm in jest. "And who do we have here? Thomas, you never told me you had a daughter."

"Piss off, you cheeky git, this is my *wife*, Gweneviere. Don't be rude because you're jealous, Gerald." Thomas gave his friend a smug grin.

"Ah, Thomas. What did you do to get this one, then? Hit her over the head and drag her to the bakery? And though my dear Gweneviere here is a beauty, I'm very much happy with my mature lady, Agatha. Agatha, honey, come over here," he called, waving over his wife from across the entrance hall that was bigger than Thomas' whole apartment.

Agatha was a rather pretty woman with long, thick, blonde

locks of hair that cascaded onto her shoulders. They met her stunning black ballroom dress that had the most intricate lacing against the bone corsetry before it ballooned out at the hip, hitting the floor and making it look like she was practically floating as she walked. Agatha was in her late thirties, though no one knew her true age, not even Gerald. It was extremely obvious that in her hay day Agatha would've been the belle of the ball, but it was clear, in the way she eyed Gweneviere up when no one was looking, that the lack of wrinkles and crow's feet adorning her face were beginning to make Agatha jealous of Gweneviere's flawless, youthful skin.

"You remember Thomas, don't you?" Gerald asked, looping his arm around his wife's waist in a much gentler, more caring way than Thomas ever did.

"Of course, I remember, I wasn't born yesterday, silly." She giggled, patting her husband's chest playfully.

"How did the two of you meet?" Gweneviere asked, having remained silent thus far.

"Oh, who's this sweet young thing?" Agatha asked.

"I'm Gweneviere," she answered for herself, sick of everyone talking about her as if she weren't stood right in front of them.

"Well, it's a pleasure to meet you, Gweneviere, and if I do recall correctly, this old man took my husband under his wing when he was just a boy," she began to explain.

"Yes, he was like a much, *much* older brother to me. He showed me how a real man takes what he wants from life, and I guess the student became the master. I'm more than ten times richer than him now." Gerald chuckled, thinking Thomas could take the joke.

Thomas could not take the joke, and Gweneviere could see in his face that he wasn't as happy to receive the condescension as he was to dish it out to Gweneviere.

"Though, I still owe it all to him in the end, that's why I invite him to my fancy parties, as a thank you," Gerald added, trying to stop Thomas from throwing a tantrum as he too began to see the embarrassment of his rosy cheeks.

"Anyway, Gwen. Can I call you Gwen?" Agatha asked, as she stood opposite Gweneviere.

"Yes, Gwen is fine," she nodded, having realised almost everyone was going to refer to her as 'Gwen' from now on.

"Great, well, *Gwen*, we shall have to make arrangements for you to come over one afternoon for some tea and we can get to know each other better," Agatha proposed.

"That sounds lovely, but I have far too many chores to find the time to do that," Gweneviere answered honestly.

"Nonsense! Thomas, do you have her under lock and key or something? Surely the poor girl can be allowed a day off to visit a lady friend?"

"Of course, provided she catches up the next day," Thomas replied, his cheeks once again becoming rosy red.

Gweneviere couldn't help but feel like she would be paying for that later.

"I wouldn't have it any other way," she said quickly, trying to placate her husband.

"It's settled then, I'll see you on Wednesday, at noon. Now, I hope you will excuse me and my husband as there are many guests here and we can't be seen to be having favourites, even if we have them." Agatha winked at Gweneviere before floating away to another rich London couple.

So far, the party was going Gweneviere's way. She was seemingly making acquaintances with one of the richest couples in London. After the gracious hosts were out of sight, however, Thomas tugged at Gweneviere's arm, pinching a chunk of her skin between his thumb and forefinger.

"Ow, what?" Gweneviere snapped.

"Don't embarrass me like that ever again. Making out like I'm some horrible tyrant of a husband who doesn't even let you shit in peace," he growled, quietly enough not to make a scene.

"Well, you are," she retaliated, thinking he wouldn't dare do anything with so many people around.

"Watch your tone, Gwen. Make no mistake, you will be punished for your insolence," he whispered into her ear, his grip on her tightening. "There's a lot of whores out there who would be much more appreciative to be by my side, so don't think for a second that you're not replaceable."

"Sorry," Gweneviere apologised, though she thought her husband must be delusional if he considered her to be lucky.

"Don't bother apologising, actions speak much louder than words. I know a much better way you can apologise with those lips rather than saying '*I'm sorry*'," he mocked.

Gweneviere shivered at the threat that he had painted all too clearly; she didn't want his genitals anywhere near her lips, or any part of her for that matter.

Gweneviere spent the last few hours of the party downing any drink she could get her hands on. If she was going to have to do unspeakable acts that made her feel worthless, she certainly didn't want to be conscious enough to remember it.

Fate wasn't that kind to Gweneviere, however, as the disgust and pain of Thomas' lust kept Gweneviere wide awake long after it was over. She once again laid there, in the aftermath of Thomas' deviant ways, feeling sorry for herself. It almost made her chuckle as she was now in a worse situation than a whore, a job she'd turned down all those months ago.

At least they were making their own money, she thought, torturing herself.

Gweneviere had to put her plan into action as swiftly as possible, starting with making a better connection with Agatha on Wednesday, because Gweneviere wasn't sure just how much more of life as the baker's wife she could take.

CHAPTER 5
The 'Friend'

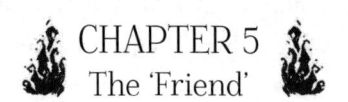

The day of Gweneviere and Agatha's 'play date' had arrived and Gweneviere had to behave and do her upmost to solidify their friendship.

Gweneviere, of course, was still required to carry out a few of her basic chores in the morning before she left, such as starting up the bakery and making some lunch ready for Thomas to have while she was out. God forbid he fed himself. The remaining, less prioritised, tasks, however, could wait until the following day.

As Gweneviere finished getting ready, Thomas appeared in the living room.

"Gwen, I have arranged for a carriage to take you to see Agatha," Thomas stated.

"Oh, thank yo—" Gweneviere began, as she thought it was rather sweet of him.

"We can't have you walking there, God knows what Gerald would think of me if he heard about that. No, *we* need to keep up with our reputation, so be on your best behaviour, understood?" Thomas added, making it clear that the gesture was more so for his benefit than it was hers. "Oh, and he will be back around three to pick you up. Just enough time for you to get back and get dinner on the table."

"Ah, yes, of course, I wouldn't have it any other way," Gweneviere said, with a hint of sarcasm, just subtle enough to go unnoticed.

"Here, take these with you." Thomas handed Gweneviere a cake box, which upon her sneaking a peek inside, was full of a range of pastries and sweet treats. "Now, don't go eating them on the way, they're a gift to take with you. I don't like fatties," he commented, grossly eyeing up Gweneviere's slim waist while licking his disgusting lips.

Gweneviere tried her best to let his distasteful words run off her like water off of a duck's back, but it was truly testing being married to a chauvinistic pig. She knew that one day she would have the last laugh over the creep when she had made a name for herself.

"Of course I won't eat any, I'm much too full after that mouthful of porridge I had for breakfast this morning," she snarked.

"I'll have less of that backchat, Gwen, or you'll be seeing a lot more of the back of my hand. Do you hear me?" he retaliated.

"Yes." Gweneviere sighed, biting her tongue.

It was so frustrating to Gweneviere knowing that, if she wanted to, she could light his greasy body alight with a single flick of her pinkie finger. The only problem with that was, how would she explain his death to the town without looking extremely suspicious. An eighteen-year-old woman marrying a gross old man with his own bakery who then mysteriously dies. Even if the Londoners weren't witty enough to work out that she was a witch, they would definitely catch onto foul play.

"Right, then, I should really be getting off now, shouldn't I? I wouldn't want to be tardy and make you look bad in the process."

"Yes, well, the carriage is outside waiting."

Gweneviere walked out of the door before Thomas had time to realise that his lunch had not been prepared.

"Wait, where's my lunch?!" he shouted as the door closed behind Gweneviere.

She heard him, but kept walking with a smirk on her face, acting as though she hadn't. It was the little things that kept her smiling and hopeful amidst a life of misery.

Gweneviere rather enjoyed her peaceful ride around London on her way to see Agatha. The journey was made much more comfortable by Thomas not being there, for numerous reasons. Number one was that the carriage didn't sink as low without his added weight, meaning that going over any bumps in the road was much smoother, and two, she didn't have his sausage fingers attempting to climb up her dress. Number three, and possibly most important, was that the limited amount of oxygen available in the carriage wasn't tainted by his toxic breath. Sure, oral hygiene wasn't great in general, back in those days, but even compared to their standards, Thomas' was something else.

She had arrived at Gerald and Agatha's house, which in the light of day was even more impressive than when she had seen it for the first time. Much grander than living in an apartment above a bakery.

Agatha must have spotted Gweneviere's arrival through one of her many large windows, as before she could grasp the decorative iron knocker in her hand, Agatha thrusted the heavy-duty door open with force.

"Gweneviere! You made it." Agatha looked just as glamorous as she had at the party. "It's so lovely to see you. Gosh, you look so... young, and full of life," she added, with a false and jealous tone to her voice.

"Thank you, you look beautiful yourself," Gweneviere complimented, not quite catching on to Agatha's bitterness.

"Well, of course I do. It's all the baby blood I use on my face each morning." She cackled at her own strange joke, to which Gweneviere just smiled awkwardly. "Oh, Gwen, I'm just jesting with you. Don't look so gaunt, you're going so pale that you look like you've seen a ghost."

"Oh, ha ha, that really tickled me," Gweneviere laughed stiffly with her hand covering her mouth, like she was taught back in her etiquette classes.

"Anyway, come on in. I'll have some tea ready in no time," Agatha proposed, as she fully opened the door and nodded her head inside.

"Okay."

Agatha walked Gweneviere into the main sitting room which was eclectically decorated with paintings, and other decorative ornaments that gave off a very *rich* vibe.

"Ah, what's that?" Agatha asked, as she noticed a box sticking out of Gweneviere's not so feminine satchel.

"Sorry, I almost forgot. Thomas gave me these for you and

Gerald – some of his finest cakes."

"Well, I'm sure they're absolutely delicious. Here, I'll take them into the kitchen and we can have some in a little while," Agatha said, heading off to the kitchen.

"Oh, no, they were for you and Gerald to enjoy. I don't need any," Gweneviere said, correcting the misunderstanding.

"Nonsense, Gwen, you are a guest, and I hadn't planned anything for us to eat, so it's only right that we share these together. Worry not, we will be sure to save one for Gerald," Agatha reassured her.

"Okay."

Gweneviere was actually rather glad that they would be sharing them, considering that there would apparently be no other food on offer and Gweneviere's stomach was already growling through her corset.

Agatha swiftly returned from the kitchen and sat across from Gweneviere. They both had a delightfully velvety cream sofa to themselves with a mahogany coffee table between them.

"So, Gweneviere. How does a pretty, young thing like you end up with a husband like, well... Thomas? I know he was good to my husband when they were younger, but make no mistake, I'm very aware of what a horrid man he can be."

"No, no, honestly, he isn't that bad," Gweneviere lied.

"Hmm, very well, but if you ever need anything, or he does anything to you, tell me, because Gerald and I would be the first to your aid, understand?" Agatha offered sincerely.

"Yes, I understand," Gweneviere spoke softly, as she contemplated telling Agatha what he had already done to her so far in their short marriage.

"Okay, good. Now then, enough talk about *him*, tell me more about yourself. I want to know just who Gweneviere Farriner is?"

Gweneviere opened her mouth, but as she was about to tell Agatha her life story, she remembered that much of it would have to be filtered to suit her mortal world. "Er... yes, well, I grew up on a small farmhouse with my parents. My mother was a..." Gweneviere paused as she thought of a quick lie. "... housekeeper, yes, a housekeeper," she exclaimed, just happy to not have blurted out 'magical healer', or worse 'witch'.

Agatha's head tilted slightly in confusion at Gweneviere's rambling.

"And my father was a blacksmith," Gweneviere quickly added, when she realised how strangely she was acting.

"A blacksmith? Oh, I do say, I've always had a soft spot for a man of manual labour. Sometimes I wish I had married a man who worked with his hands, like a blacksmith, someone who could be a little rough and ready in the bedroom." Agatha winked. "Oh God, I can just imagine it right now, a big muscular man with filthy hands throwing me around like a rag doll. But no, I went and married a prim and proper rich man. Though I suppose it's for the best, as I could hardly have lived the life of a blacksmith's wife. Poor as piss and having to possibly work myself? Nope, that was not the life I was meant to live." Agatha finished her fantasising, almost gagging at the thought of having to get a job like a common peasant. "Besides, Gerald isn't exactly ugly, is he?" Agatha chuckled to herself. "Anyway, never mind my deviant thoughts, you were saying about your parents?"

"Oh, yes. Erm, well, my mother sadly passed away some months back. My father wanted a fresh start for us, so we moved to London, but he too was sadly taken not long after. It was the plague that got him. Then I managed to find a nearby school for girls to house me. After graduation I met Thomas and, well, now I'm here." She tried to speak nonchalantly, but even Agatha could see the inconsolability in her eyes.

"Oh, my poor dear. What a devilish start to life you have had. You know, Gweneviere, you should really keep your options open, my dear. I mean, a girl like you could quite easily find yourself a husband much richer and far more handsome than *Thomas*, and, if you're lucky like I am, you won't have to do any chores either."

"Thank you, but I can barely stand courting with one man, let alone keeping an eye out for another suiter," Gweneviere joked.

"Very well. Though, the next party Gerald and I have, I will be surely parading you around for all the young bachelors, who are much more eligible than Thomas, to see."

Gweneviere smiled as she sat wondering to herself when the cakes would be eaten, or the tea drunk, that Agatha had promised to her what felt like forever ago, would arrive. To her surprise, Agatha voiced the same opinion.

"Where's the bloody tea?" Agatha pondered aloud, shaking her head.

Is she crazy, or having a stroke, Gweneviere wondered, seemingly confused by Agatha's question. *Am I supposed to be making it?* Gweneviere questioned herself, while looking at Agatha with a blank expression.

Agatha picked up a small bell on the coffee table between them. She rang it rather aggressively and, not long after, a tall, slim toned man with deep brown skin and a gaunt face entered the room. The man's skin was so dehydrated that it clung to his face, allowing his high cheek bones and square jawline to stick out far too much to be considered attractive anymore. Even his eye sockets were sunk deep into his skull. Gweneviere could see by the man's eyes that he was lifeless, but she had never come across such a person like this before.

Who is this man? Why is he in Agatha's house responding to a bell? Why does he look so frail for such an otherwise behemoth man? Gweneviere contemplated.

Having grown up in the countryside her entire life, where most townies were poor, Gweneviere had never really put two and two together about slavery. Most of the residents from her hometown wouldn't have been able to afford such a *luxury*. She remembered seeing the odd black man or woman working about the town, but it was only now that she was realising exactly what slavery was.

"Yes, Mistress?" the man, dressed in quite literally rags and an apron, said wearily.

"Where's my blooming tea, Jericho? We've been waiting bloody ages. We're absolutely parched, for Christ's sake!" Agatha shouted.

"Sorry, I will fetch it for you now." He slowly scuffled off to the screeching kettle that was sat, engulfed in flames, in the kitchen.

"I'm sorry for his insubordination, Gweneviere. I'm truly embarrassed. I would've had the butler do it but, apparently, he's *sick*. He'll be sick when I'm through with him, that's for sure," Agatha said, looking rather disgruntled.

"It's fine, I don't mind waiting. I hope he doesn't have the plague, or anything serious."

"Oh please, the little puff is probably faking it. Honestly, Gweneviere, don't give them the satisfaction of thinking that they're not replaceable because I assure you, they are. Take Jericho for instance, he *was* the best birthday present I'd ever had, but these days he's really not pulling his weight, so I've been hinting at Gerald all year for a new one."

"Sorry? A new... one?" Gweneviere asked, still attempting to understand the situation.

"Yes, Gweneviere, a new slave, keep up," Agatha said, hastily, fidgeting her hands, clearly still in a tizzy about the tea not being ready.

Gweneviere was silent. How could someone who had just shown so much care and worry for Gweneviere be so disgusting a person as to actually think of human beings as replaceable birthday presents that could simply be exchanged when they're not 'pulling their weight'?

And people think us witches are the monsters, Gweneviere thought to herself. She was truly in shock, but if she made a point of disagreeing with her now, it could throw off Gweneviere's entire plan, and not to mention it would anger Thomas even more than usual. Gweneviere reluctantly kept quiet about the situation, which made her feel equally as queasy as Agatha now did.

"He's just become so lazy and docile," Agatha added while Gweneviere was having an internal moral debate. "Speaking of which, where is he with that god forsaken tea? Jericho? Hurry up!" she shouted about the house, slamming her hands down beside her on the couch.

"I've never met a slave before," Gweneviere blurted, forgetting all knowledge of how to engage in normal conversation, not that there was anything 'normal' about the situation at hand.

"Well, we don't really like to use the word slave, more servant," Agatha informed.

"But you just said slave before," Gweneviere pointed out.

"It must have just slipped out." Agatha tried playing the mistake off as she noticed Gweneviere's not so subtle uneasiness.

"Do you pay him, then?" Gweneviere asked.

"What?" Agatha said, only to buy herself another second of thought before answering. "Well, no..."

"So, he *is* a slave."

"Honestly, Gweneviere! Save that witty little head of yours for the bachelors at my parties, not to interrogate me." Agatha chuckled, trying to play off her anger towards Gweneviere's forwardness. "Besides, he's lucky he ended up with a family like us. We have him doing much easier labouring than most have their sla– servants doing. Plus, it's not like he has to go down to the well himself and fetch the water for this GODDAMN TEA! We have the latest running water pipes about the house. Anyway, what else is a black man to do in London?" Agatha gestured to the room, expecting the question to be rhetorical.

"Oh, I don't know, maybe start a life for himself, learn a trade, create a family, or perhaps nothing, as he probably shouldn't have been dragged to London from his home in the first place."

"Really, Gweneviere, you're becoming quite tedious now, that's enough," Agatha said sternly.

"Yes, I'm sorry, you're right. I'm just being silly," Gweneviere backtracked, before she got herself kicked out.

Internally, she was still very much in disagreement with Agatha's views, but she desperately needed to make some powerful connections and so decided to bite her tongue going forward.

Jericho re-entered the room carrying a large silverware tray, on it balanced a tea pot with two cups, saucers, and a sugar bowl. He bent down and placed the tray on the coffee table, but before he could even reach an upright position again, Agatha huffed.

"Milk?" she shouted in his face, causing droplets of her spit to glisten on his bony cheeks. "It's the only thing they seem to respond to," Agatha bitched to Gweneviere, in front of Jericho.

"Oh... I see." Gweneviere was hardly able to even look Jericho in the face, she felt so guilty and embarrassed.

The poor man retrieved the milk without a second thought; he was clearly on autopilot to do as she said. Although Jericho's stature meant he could easily swat Agatha to the ground with one smack from his incredibly large hands, he knew he would only end up being sold to another even more gruesome family as a result or sentenced to death. Anyone who looked into his eyes could see he was a broken shell of a man. In some ways he was like the witches who faced the water test: if he ever tried to flee or hit back, he would soon be dead, and if he stayed and obeyed, he would slowly die of exhaustion and a lack of food and water. It would seem, though, that Jericho didn't have the mental capacity to make that decision for himself anymore. He was like Agatha's personal zombie; victim to some sick form of mind control. Though, if Agatha had been a witch, at least Gweneviere could do something to break the spell. Alas, the even sadder truth was that Agatha was simply another human who, due to her wealth and status, was afforded a godlike role over her earthly, gated grounds.

Jericho returned with the milk and Gweneviere made a point of thanking him.

"Hush, Gwen, you wouldn't thank a leech for letting your blood so *don't* thank him for doing his job either. It's his *purpose*."

Gweneviere grimaced internally at Agatha's remarks as she thought about how the world saw her own purpose as to stand behind a man and be a 'good wife'. Of course, she couldn't begin to imagine how Jericho must have felt, as people believed that *this* life of unruly servitude was his purpose.

Jericho, as quickly as his malnourished body could, ushered himself out of the room before he could be any more of a nuisance to his mistress.

"Now then, Gweneviere, when are you planning on having children?" Agatha pried, bluntly, as she poured both their teas.

Gweneviere choked on her own saliva as she watched her tea be made with anticipation. "Children?" she blurted. *I'm barely an adult yet, myself.*

"Yes, children. I really thought Thomas would have had

the conversation with you by now, especially considering what happened with his first wife." Agatha remained purposely elusive.

"What do you mean? What happened to his first wife?" Gweneviere asked.

"I really shouldn't say, it's not my place... but, well, they tried for years to have children, and one day she finally fell pregnant. Thomas was so excited to have an heir to his bakery, but his dreams were crushed when the baby was born," Agatha exclaimed, spilling the metaphorical tea as well as a little of the real tea onto the tray. She didn't seem bothered by the spillage, probably because she knew that she wouldn't be the one to clear it up.

"Oh no, was it stillborn?" Gweneviere asked, softly.

"Sugar?" Agatha crudely ignored her.

"What? Oh, er, yes please," Gweneviere answered, as she noticed Agatha hovering a spoon of it above her cup.

"And no, it wasn't stillborn, it simply wasn't his," Agatha gossiped, looking as though she was taking enjoyment in it.

"How did he find out?" Gweneviere asked, as she accepted her teacup from Agatha.

"She bloody admitted it, didn't she, and then ran off with her lover. Though, in all honesty, I think Thomas was more upset about the baby than the wife herself," Agatha explained, before taking a sip of her steaming tea.

Gweneviere almost felt sorry for Thomas, but that feeling only lasted a millisecond when she remembered everything he had already done to her to make her life hell. "Let me assure you that I will *not* be having children anytime soon, especially with *him*."

"Don't be too put off by them, Gwen, mine are a delight, *most* of the time."

Gweneviere almost spat out her tea as the wicked woman confessed to having offspring. "You have children?"

"Why of course I do."

"Might I ask where they are?"

"With the nanny, of course. Women of our status can't be expected to wipe bottoms and change soiled garments. No, no, simply not. Besides, they're much too noisy for my liking, it's far better this way. They're in the other wing of the house where I can't hear them."

"Oh, I see," Gweneviere replied, looking bewildered by the woman's lifestyle choices.

"Gweneviere, don't look at me like that. I fully vetted out the nanny beforehand, of course. Also, I actually enjoy sex with my husband, and he doesn't want me to be tuckered out at the end of each day from cooking, cleaning, and picking up after small humans."

Gweneviere plastered on a smile in response, as the thought of how Thomas had his way with her mulled over in her mind and sent shivers down her spine. Agatha continued to ramble, about what Gweneviere didn't know, as she was deep in the dreaded thought of bearing a child for Thomas. Gweneviere was brought out of her trance by hearing Agatha speak of food. Gweneviere was famished.

"Shall we have another cup of tea? And I'll break out those cakes you brought," Agatha suggested, not having quite finished her first cup. She was clearly that high maintenance that she needed a freshly brewed one to carry on her gossiping.

"Are you sure you don't mind me having one?" Gweneviere asked politely, while her stomach was almost screaming for food.

Please fucking say, 'Yes, I don't mind'. I'm starving, Gweneviere thought to herself, almost going crazy with hunger.

"Don't be silly, of course I don't mind, Gwen. I'll get Jericho to fetch everything. If he can be bothered, that is."

"Thank you," Gweneviere replied, still feeling awkward about the Jericho situation.

"Jericho?" Agatha called out, having not lifted a finger all morning.

"Yes, Mistress?" he asked, as he dragged himself into the room, looking weaker by the step.

"We're absolutely famished, bring in the cakes, will you? While you're at it, we could do with another pot of tea. Take the tray with you, it needs cleaning. You over filled the teapot, that's why tea has gotten everywhere. Do me a favour and get it right this time!" Agatha demanded, without a please.

Jericho simply nodded as he saved his dry lips the effort of stringing together any more words. Jericho picked up the tray and slipped back into the kitchen to fetch the cakes and second round of tea while Agatha kept gassing and boasting about her life to Gweneviere.

The poor man hadn't eaten anything substantial for days. Alas, the temptation was too much, and he finally caved as he placed the cakes onto a platter. There were many miniature cakes and pastries, a real variety, and so Jericho hoped that he might just be able to sneak one without Agatha noticing. The smell alone was causing his mouth to water; he couldn't not eat one, they practically called out to him. In a hunger trance that would put Gweneviere's to shame, Jericho slipped one of the pastries into his mouth without fully processing what he was doing. It was delicious. The specific flavour didn't matter to Jericho, he was just grateful to feel the buttery sweet pastry melt on his tongue. It was worth it just to taste something, anything, and for his stomach to finally stop howling at him morning, noon, and night. After taking a minute to fully digest the small bite of food, and draw it out for as long as possible, he finished setting up the tray and headed back into the room hoping he had gotten away with it – just in time too, as Agatha once again screamed out his name.

Jericho returned to the coffee table and placed the clean tray down. Upon it was a fresh tea pot and the cake platter. He turned on his heels before quickly trying to make a beeline for the exit, but Agatha stopped him in his tracks, calling his name. He took a deep breath and slowly turned to face her.

"There's something wrong with this tray, isn't there?"

"Is there?" Jericho asked innocently, with his hands quivering behind his back.

"Yes. There is," she stated.

Jericho's heart was pounding, almost hard enough for them to see it poking through his skinny chest, as he anticipated her next words.

"Sugar?" she said, bluntly.

"Sorry?" he replied, confused.

"There's no sugar for the tea, you idiot. I said we needed

more when I asked for the pot of tea," she added, knowing that she, of course, was the one who had forgotten to mention it.

"Right, yes, sorry. I shall get some more sugar right away," he said, with a sigh of relief.

Agatha was silent while she awaited her sugar, and Gweneviere could sense that there was still some tension in the air. She waited for the other shoe to drop. Jericho reached the table once more and placed the pot of sugar in front of Agatha as she poured herself some piping hot tea. She looked up slightly at Jericho's face as he bent over.

"Do you notice anything else wrong?" Agatha proposed, having had more time to examine the tray of goodies on the table.

"Erm, no," he answered, hoping it was a trick question.

"Very well, on your way," she granted.

But before Jericho could even turn around, Agatha slung her cup of boiling tea into his face. Jericho yelled in agony as he dropped to the floor and cradled his face.

"You fucking idiot, how stupid do you think I am? Of course I noticed that you ate one of *my* cakes, you greedy little fucker!" Agatha spat, before getting up to stand over him.

"No, I didn't, I promise," he pleaded, still on the floor.

It was unclear what was tears and what was tea that drenched his face.

"Where is it, then?"

"I dropped it onto the floor, and so I put it in the bin," he replied, shakily.

"Go get it, then," she demanded.

"What?" he rasped, barely able to converse as his whimpers

continued.

"Go. Get. It!"

"I... I can't," he cried.

"And why not? Oh, because you ate it!" she screeched furiously, kicking him in his hollow stomach before she grabbed the remaining pot of tea and began pouring it across his body.

Gweneviere, up until now, had kept quiet, but she couldn't any longer. The sound of Jericho's cries took her back to seeing her mother's death.

"STOP! Agatha, you're going to kill him!" she cried.

"Good, maybe in death, he will learn his lesson," Agatha said, ignoring her concern as she continued pouring the hot tea over Jericho's twisting, wriggling body. Each drop she waved over him caused his body to contort into another direction.

Fuck this, Gweneviere thought, no longer caring about her, or Thomas' reputation. Fuelled by her anger, the fireplace behind Agatha roared to life, blasting her across the room.

"Run. Go, Jericho," Gweneviere shouted, but he was too weak to even get up, let alone run anywhere.

"I can't," he muttered.

Gweneviere knelt beside him. He was breathing heavily and was blinded by the scalding hot liquid.

"I'm so sorry, Jericho. I should have stopped her sooner, I'm just so sorry."

"It's okay, my lady," he replied shakily.

"Please, call me Gwen," Gweneviere insisted, in a bid to give the dying man some dignity in his last breaths.

"It's okay, Gwen. I'm too weak to go on. To finally leave

this plane of existence will be a relief, but... please, would you do me a favour?"

"Yes, of course, anything," Gweneviere accepted, taking his scorched hands in her own.

"Take this," he mumbled, unfolding his hand in hers to reveal a crumpled piece of paper. "Please get this back to my home village..." Jericho took his last breath, before going limp in Gweneviere's hands.

Gweneviere opened up the paper to see a message in his native tongue with the name of the village written on the back. She stored it in her bosom and promised his corpse that she would get it there, it was the least that she could do.

As Agatha came to, Gweneviere explained that she had passed out, not mentioning of course the means in which it happened.

"Well, no wonder I passed out, the last thing I remember was *it* launching at me," Agatha said, feigning innocence.

Gweneviere resisted the urge to strangle her.

"Er, is *it* dead, then?" Agatha asked, as if Jericho was nothing but a cheap pet goldfish.

"Yes, *he* is," Gweneviere replied, her face reddened by the concoction of anger and sorrow that plagued her.

"Right, I suppose you should be leaving now then, seeing as I have this whole *mess* to deal with."

"Yes, I agree, I should really be getting off now," Gweneviere concurred, quite happy to get out of there before she punched the heartless bitch in the throat.

Agatha saw Gweneviere out as she exited the grounds of the house. She sat by the road and awaited her lift, though it still wasn't scheduled to arrive for at least another hour yet. The ordeal had brought their luncheon to an earlier end.

As Gweneviere sat there trying to unravel the events that had just taken place, she began to weep. Was she cursed? It seemed like everywhere she went death ensued; Gweneviere couldn't help but feel like it was somehow her fault. Maybe if she had never brought the cakes in the first place, none of this would have happened. Her mind ran wild, torturing herself with 'what ifs', but that wouldn't bring anyone back. All she could do now was try to honour those who had passed, starting with Jericho. She pulled out Jericho's letter and tried her best to flatten it out before refolding it into a size fitting of an envelope. She pulled one from her satchel along with a feather quill. A lesson she had learned in school was to always have a bag that was prepared for anything, thus, the quill she pulled from it was enchanted, meaning it needed no external ink supply – it self-filled when needed. She rewrote the address of the letter onto the envelope and sealed it, placing it back in her bag with the intention of posting it the next morning.

Although Gweneviere couldn't read Jericho's letter, as it was in his native tongue, she could certainly sense the love that it was written with, and it inspired her to write a letter of her own, for Poppy. She missed Poppy greatly and, after her attempt at making a new friend failed at the first hurdle, she needed someone to confide in. Maybe Gweneviere could even live vicariously through Poppy, as surely, what with her delicious husband, she'd be living a much grander life than Gweneviere was.

Dear Poppy (or should I say Lady Poppy Hammersmith),

I hope this letter finds you well. I must say that, first of all, I was indeed right, married life simply isn't for me. Thomas is an absolute arse, and I hate him with a vengeance. I also attempted to make a new friend, but that went south rather quickly and, before you roll your eyes, no, it wasn't my fault, I can assure you of that. Life really isn't the same since graduation and I miss you so much. I even kind of miss the twins. I'd sooner have them lurching around every corner than Thomas. I do hope that we might be able to see each other in person sooner rather than later, but for now, I hope you'll write back. I want to know everything so that I might enjoy listening to the fruits of your marriage rather than focusing on the failures of mine. Speak soon.

Much Love,
Gwen.

Her carriage arrived just as she sealed the envelope and placed it beside Jericho's in her bag. She swung her clunky satchel over her shoulder and hopped into the back of the carriage, where she was taken home. 'Home', however, was a rather loose term for the place in which she lived.

She opened the front door, dreading that Thomas would be awaiting her inside as he would've surely finished work by then. She just hoped that after her ordeal of a day that she might be lucky enough to escape his touch that night.

"I'm home," she called out softly, praying he would be sleeping.

"About time," he shouted back from the kitchen. "Come in here, I have a surprise for you."

A surprise? Gweneviere pondered. *A real surprise would be if he dropped dead of natural causes so that my plan could jump forward by a couple of years,* she hoped, but no, fate wouldn't be that kind to Gweneviere, or at least not in such a direct way.

Gweneviere walked into the kitchen to see Thomas' hefty body stood in front of the oven, staring back at her. There was seemingly some steam coming from behind him, and she could smell all kinds of deliciousness coming from his direction that was surely not his scent. Had he actually cooked her a meal? Surely not, he wasn't that kind or thoughtful a husband, was he?

"Welcome home, my love. Here is your surprise," Thomas exclaimed, as he moved out of the way of the oven to reveal...

CHAPTER 6
Kambili

... a beautiful young woman with a smooth, deep brown complexion and a short, untamed afro. Her lips were plump, and her large, open doe eyes stared at Gweneviere. As Gweneviere stared back, there was an instant unspoken spark between one another, which was quickly diminished when Thomas once again spoke.

"Well? How do you like your new slave?"

Gweneviere's mouth dropped open, and her eyes widened in shock.

"I bought her for you while you were at Gerald's house today. She's not much of a manual labourer, by the looks of her, but she can cook and clean, which should surely help you out and take some of the load off your shoulders," Thomas said.

Gweneviere was mute, still trying to wrap her head around the whole idea, while also being transfixed by the girl's beauty.

"God, don't thank me too quickly. Come on, what do you think?" he urged, nudging Gweneviere's arm.

"She's... amazing, thank you," Gweneviere replied, still

clearly entranced with the girl who couldn't have been more than a year younger than Gweneviere herself.

"You're welcome. Though, I'd be lying if I didn't say she was for my benefit as well, should you go cold on me again in the bedroom department. Afterall, she's quite the sight for sore eyes, isn't she? Well, if you ignore the fact she's a *darky,* I guess." He cackled to himself, almost choking on his phlegmy saliva. "Now then, I'll leave you two women to get acquainted and delegate the daily chores while I grab a whiskey and await my dinner."

Gweneviere hadn't stopped looking in the girl's direction since she first laid eyes on her, and it was beginning to feel a bit awkward as neither of them had spoken a word to the other.

"Hi, I'm Gweneviere, but you can call me Gwen." She smiled, holding out her hand for the girl to shake, but the girl simply stared at her blankly. "What's your name?" Gweneviere encouraged.

"My name is... Kambili," the girl stuttered in accented English, clearly unsure whether Gweneviere would be a kind mistress or not.

"It's nice to meet you, Kambili," Gweneviere said, gently taking Kambili's hand in hers.

Kambili's handshake was weak and fragile, giving Gweneviere flashbacks to just a few hours earlier when she watched a frail Jericho die. She couldn't let that happen to Kambili. She wouldn't.

"I'm sorry. Though it is nice to make your acquaintance, I am truly sorry that this is your life. If I were in charge of this stupid, rage filled country, I'd have never allowed such vile actions to be lawful. But I promise, I'll do my best to keep you well fed and safe for as long as you are here with me," Gweneviere promised sincerely.

"Safe?" Kambili questioned.

"Yes, mainly from that retched excuse for a man out there," Gweneviere replied, shooting a disgusted look through the wall at Thomas.

"But he is your husband? Is he not?" Kambili asked.

"Unfortunately, yes, but that's a long story, that will hopefully come to an even longer overdue end sooner rather than later."

"Maybe you could tell me that story one day," Kambili said softly, warming to Gweneviere.

"Yes, maybe." Gweneviere smiled. "I don't mean to be rude, but might I ask how your English is so good?"

"It's okay, I'm not easily offended. I'm a second-generation slave. My mother and father were slaves on a colossal estate. They fell in love and managed to keep their pregnancy secret, and even once they had me, they managed to keep me a secret for many years. I lived in one of the old, dusty attic bedrooms that the masters never seemed to use. My parents brought me what food they could, I had a window to look through, and some old toys that must've been forgotten about." Kambili described her childhood with a grateful look on her face, like she was in some way lucky to have what she did.

"So, you never went outside?"

"No, I didn't, but I knew my parents were doing the best they could by me. And to answer your original question, I could hear the masters and their children about the house and playing outside. I taught myself much better English than my parents had achieved through listening in on their conversations."

"So, how did you end up here, then?" Gweneviere asked.

Kambili answered while keeping an eye on dinner, making sure not to burn it. "Well, one day, one of the masters of the house had climbed up into the attic to retrieve an old family heirloom but instead found me, and then—" Kambili jolted as Thomas' raised voice bellowed throughout the apartment.

"I'm hearing a lot of chatting and not much cooking, I'm getting very hungry out here!"

Clearly Thomas was back to his usual ways after his pathetic attempt at being nice to Gweneviere. Somehow, in his twisted way of thinking, buying her a slave was a good thing. He'd obviously been listening to Gerald and Agatha too much.

"Sorry, Kambili, we should probably finish our conversation later, before his royal arse gets impatient," Gweneviere said, making Kambili chuckle.

Kambili began dishing up the food onto two plates, confusing Gweneviere.

"Where's the third?" she asked.

"Third? Sorry, Mistress, Thomas didn't tell me you were having company." Kambili cowered back to her shy ways – her knee jerk reaction to any form of confrontation from a master.

"Company? What? No, the third plate is for you," Gweneviere explained.

"Oh no, Mistress, I may not have been a working slave for very long, but still long enough to know that one doesn't include themselves in such meals."

"Well, I've been a decent human being long enough to say that stops now. From now on, you eat every meal that we do, understand?"

Kambili nodded with a shy smile.

"Oh, and please call me Gwen, I'm only, like, a year older than you, I'm certainly not your mistress."

The term 'Mistress' also reminded her of Agatha, and Gweneviere was nothing like Agatha. Speaking of whom, Gweneviere couldn't help but ponder what they had done with the poor man's corpse. Poor Jericho was probably tossed away into a plague pit. No one would've even batted an eyelid due to the colour of his skin. Gweneviere lost her train of thought for a moment as she began to spiral internally.

"Okay, *Gwen*," Kambili replied, pulling out a third plate.

As it clinked onto the table, it snapped Gweneviere out of her trance.

"Come on! There's two of you now, that's supposed to make things twice as fast," Thomas shouted from the comfort of his chair as he took another swig of whiskey.

"We're coming, now!" Gweneviere shouted back. "Right, let's go," she said hastily, as she turned back to Kambili.

Thomas sat at the head of the dining table awaiting his supper. There was a candelabra in the centre which Gweneviere had lit with a flick of her finger before Kambili entered. As Kambili walked in and placed the plate of food before Thomas, he licked his lips, appreciatively. It wasn't clear whether he was licking his chalky lips at the food or Kambili. Kambili inhaled deeply as she walked to an empty chair with the third plate of food. She looked over at Gweneviere to confirm that she was indeed allowed to sit and eat with them. Gweneviere nodded with a smile, and Thomas was too busy, already headfirst into his food, to notice. Thus, she took a seat and began her meal, albeit still warily. After a few minutes, the pig released himself from the trough of food to allow some oxygen to his brain, as well as a sip – or rather a gulp – of whiskey. As he wiped the food from his face, he noticed that Kambili was sat at the table.

"What do you think you're doing?" he said to Kambili, while bits of food spewed from his mouth.

"I said she could sit with us," Gweneviere spoke in her defence.

"And who do *you* think you are to tell this slave girl that she has any rights at all, let alone to sit with us at the table."

"I'm not going to treat her like a dog, Thomas!" Gweneviere said.

Everyone could sense the rising anger in her tone.

"And *I'm* not going to treat her as a respected young woman, *Gweneviere!*" he barked.

"Well, that's rich, as you don't respect any woman at all!" Gweneviere retaliated, slamming her fist on the table with her knife clutched within it.

"I respect Agatha. Now, she's a lady who knows how to carry herself and please her husband, you're just pathetic. Now, I'm not having her eat my hard-earned money."

"*Your* hard-earned money?" Gweneviere scoffed a laugh. "Thomas, I know how much extra you're making because of me and my magics. I've looked into the price of fuel for your ovens, and without me you'd barely be scraping a profit. So, I suggest you change your attitude towards Kambili, or I won't be lighting any fires anytime soon, let me assure you of that!"

"Are you sure you want to make threats like that, Gweneviere? I could always—" Thomas was cut off by Gweneviere.

"Could always what? Find another witch at the next graduation?"

"Yes, well—"

Gweneviere once again cut him off. "Good luck trying to find another pyrokinetic witch on such short notice. You see, when I attended the Crone's school, I was so kindly made aware, by a friend of mine, that I am indeed a rare breed. There's really not a lot of *me* out there. So, if it's all the same to you I would like a part of the money, that my powers provide, to go towards another plate of food, for Kambili, which is still half the size of your own, might I point out."

Thomas glared at Gweneviere; his face screwed up more as his anger grew. He huffed at them both, as he had no real retort to come back with. He stood up and, taking his food and whiskey with him, headed to his bedroom to finish it alone in peace. Though Gweneviere should've been glad that she stood up for herself, she knew the excuse wouldn't last, and it wouldn't be long before he reverted back to his usual, ignorant self. For now, though, Gweneviere was more than happy to enjoy the rest of her meal with Kambili and engage in a conversation where both parties were equally as interested in the other. They sat opposite each other on the sides of the table so that there was less distance between them, and Gweneviere popped open a sneaky bottle of wine from Thomas' stash.

"Do you mind if I move this to the side?" Kambili asked,

grasping the candelabra that was between them, making it hard to make any unbroken eye contact.

"Not at all," Gweneviere replied, as she poured their glasses almost full to the brim.

They said a cheers as they raised their glasses to one another, clinking them loud enough so that Thomas would surely hear, rubbing salt into the wound. Gweneviere felt Kambili's knuckles brush hers and as their eyes met, Gweneviere's soft cheeks flushed pink involuntarily. Gweneviere had always been attracted to both sexes but, in the day and age in which she lived, it was seen as a sign of the devil himself. No one would have accepted that two people of the same sex could entertain such feelings. So, Gweneviere tried to push the feelings of desire she had for Kambili down. After all, if she'd have had a husband like Poppy's, she might've been happy – that was a man worth suffering marriage for. Thomas, however, was just repulsive in every way; there wasn't a single redeeming quality about him.

Kambili, on the other hand, was, from what Gweneviere could tell so far, kind and very pretty, but Gweneviere also knew that the likelihood of Kambili reciprocating those feelings was near to zero, and thus she would have to try and ignore her desire for her. Kambili's youthful face was staring at Gweneviere's still, as she let out a little smirk at Gweneviere's blushing cheeks.

"Should I continue my story?" Kambili asked, waking Gweneviere from her enamoured trance.

"Huh?"

"My story?" Kambili reminded.

"Oh, erm, yes, please do," Gweneviere said awkwardly, as she tucked her hair behind her ear.

"Okay." Kambili smiled at Gweneviere's awkwardness. "Now, where was I?"

"Someone found you in the attic?"

"Oh, yeah, one of the masters of the house found me when I was about ten. Surprisingly, though, they weren't angry, they actually seemed rather glad. I think they liked the idea of a free slave that they could train from young to obey them. My parents begged and pleaded them to allow me to live a free life. Even more to their surprise, the lady of the house offered to raise me as her own and give me everything I could ever want in life. The catch was that I could never see my parents again. I couldn't be seen to have a slave mother and father on the property, it wouldn't have looked good, and the lady was sticking her neck out in the first place by offering to look after me. Her husband wasn't best pleased by the idea, though she seemed to enchant him with her beauty as he could never stay mad at her for very long. He was truly in love. My parents inevitably agreed, as they saw it to be the only chance, they'd have to give me a life better than theirs. And well, that's all any parent wants, right?"

Gweneviere nodded as she thought about her own parents, and reminded herself what she was living for and that she had to make them proud. At least by making something of her own life it might ease the guilt that she felt about failing them in the first place.

"Anyway, their plan for me worked for a few years. I ate amazing food, I bathed almost as often as I slept, and she taught me talents, like how to play the piano."

"Wow, I can't even play the spoons," Gweneviere interjected, causing them both to giggle. "So... where did it all go wrong?" Gweneviere shifted her tone in a bid to console Kambili.

"The lady of the house fell ill and eventually passed, and for some convoluted reason, her husband decided to blame me for her illness. He had always despised me, and I think he was probably jealous that she spent so much time with me. She really did treat me like I was her own. Once it was just me and him, he wasted no time in selling me off to the local slave tradesman. I didn't even get to attend the funeral. So, I've spent the last year being sold from one master to the next, as no one cared for a slave with intellect, they just wanted someone who could complete laboursome tasks, until Thomas purchased me this morning."

"I'm so sorry, Kambili."

"What do you have to be sorry for?" Kambili asked, confused.

"I'm sorry that you have to endure this way of life. You're *not* property that others should be able to buy, trade, or *possess*. You're priceless," Gweneviere said, reaching her hand across the table.

"It's okay, Gwen. Honestly, I've had a much better life so far than most slaves, I'm lucky, really."

"No, you're not. Luck isn't being spared torture, even though you're a woman, or black. Luck is supposed to be something that affects little things in life. It's bad luck if you slip in the street, it's good luck if you find an extra penny in your pocket, or on the ground. Luck isn't something that should be used to measure the amount of sorrow in a person's life. I promise, Kambili, you won't live an enslaved life forever. I *will* free you."

Kambili had kept silent during Gweneviere's passionate speech. Her eyes had slowly widened as she listened to every word that left Gweneviere's lips with as much enthusiasm as the last. It was truly captivating to watch Gweneviere talk about something so passionately.

"Thank you," Kambili said, letting out a smile as she clasped Gweneviere's hand in her own.

"What for?"

"For not being like everyone else. This world is full of sheep flowing from field to field, guided by one shepherd and his mutt, but you, you go against it all. You swim upstream, and it takes a strong person to do that."

"I'm not strong," Gweneviere said, shrugging off the compliment.

"Gweneviere, I haven't known you very long, well, only a few hours, really, but even I can already sense you're one of the strongest, kindest people that exists. You've survived living with that oaf, for God's sake. Gwen, you can do anything."

"Thanks." Gweneviere smiled, gripping Kambili's hand tighter.

"Oh, by the way, I couldn't help but notice you mentioned your powers earlier. You know, when you were putting Thomas in his place. Could I see them?" Kambili asked excitedly.

"Powers?" Gweneviere stopped as her eyes suddenly widened tenfold. "Er, I don't have powers, it was... it was a metaphor," she said, rather unconvincingly as she stumbled over her words.

"Gwen, relax, it's okay. Thomas told me you were a witch. I don't have a problem with it. Besides, my parents used to follow a voodoo queen back in their days of freedom in Africa. They'd tell me stories about her: a powerful mother figure that protected the people in their village. Well... I guess until she couldn't any longer. And though I've never personally practiced anything, I'm more than open to learning about your magic. So, don't worry, I know you're not some child snatching monster. I know much better than to listen to everything the biased town crier's cry."

"Okay, I suppose you have deemed yourself to be trustworthy," Gweneviere said playfully.

"I should hope so!"

"Blow the candle out," Gweneviere said.

"What?"

"You wanted to see my powers, didn't you?"

Kambili didn't say another word as she blew the candles, and now that the sun had set, it left them in complete darkness. Gweneviere had enjoyed watching Kambili's lips purse as she blew out the flame from across the table. Though they had been plunged into darkness, neither felt scared in the other's presence. It was more like a comforting sensory deprivation. Gweneviere relit the candles with nothing but a thought. As the wicks sparked back to life, light was restored to the room to reveal Gweneviere and Kambili gazing at each other once more.

"Wow, that was magical, literally," Kambili gasped in awe.

"That was nothing, you should see what I do in the bakery every morning."

"Can I?"

"Oh, yeah, sure. You can come with me in the morning." Gweneviere was surprised. She wasn't used to someone actually taking an interest in her. "Speaking of which, we should probably get to bed, it's getting quite late."

"Okay. Wait, what's that noise?" Kambili questioned, hearing a thick snarl from the other room.

"*That* would be Thomas' incessant snoring," Gweneviere answered.

They both chuckled and Gweneviere showed Kambili to the spare room before they bid each other a good night.

Gweneviere walked into the bedroom she shared with Thomas, though she wished she could've stayed with Kambili. Not even to do anything sinful, just to not have to sleep on the same lumpy mattress as *him*. At least this time he was already well into a deep slumber, meaning Gweneviere could get a somewhat peaceful night's sleep.

The next morning Gweneviere woke up to the smell of porridge in the air, which normally wouldn't do anything for her, but something about it just smelled amazing. She followed the warm caramelly oat scent into the living area to see that Kambili had just finished making breakfast and, of course, Thomas was sat in his chair, waiting to be served.

"Wow, Kambili, that smells amazing. What the hell did you

do to that porridge?" Gweneviere asked as she entered.

"It's a top-secret recipe," Kambili said, feeling much more comfortable thanks to Gweneviere's presence. "Thomas understands, right? What with being a baker," Kambili prompted, trying to be considerate and involve him.

The man hadn't earned the garnered attention, as he entered the conversation smugly with, "Gwen, shouldn't you be starting up the bakery?"

"Yes, I will in a minute, I would just like to partake in breakfast, if that's okay with you?" Gweneviere answered back.

"As a matter of fact, no, it's not. You can take your bowl of shite she seems to call porridge with you, now, go on," he barked.

Gweneviere was fuming. How could he be such an arse all the time? Though Gweneviere knew her standing up for herself wouldn't last long in his mind, she surely expected it to last longer than one night.

"Come on, Kambili, I'll show you the bakery."

"I don't think so," Thomas said.

"What? Why?" Gweneviere asked, looking puzzled.

"I don't want any customers seeing a *darky* in the bakery, it's bad for business. No one's going to want to buy my delicious pastries if they think that her filthy paws have been all over them," he spat, despite having another spoonful of the very girl's porridge ready to shovel into his mouth.

"My God, Thomas, it's five in the morning. Who would even be up at this time to see us? Besides, we're only going into the back room to start the ovens," Gweneviere said, trying to reason with him.

"I don't care! It's my bakery and the answer is no!"

I fucking hate you, you horrible piece of shit! Gweneviere screamed in her head to release her anger, for lack of wanting to subconsciously burn the house down with her magic. Gweneviere stormed off to the bakery, alone, with her bowl of porridge in hand. She shovelled it in with almost the amount of ferocity that Thomas used every time he ate. She began her spell as she kept munching sloppily on the delicious porridge.

"I forge this... fire, from eternal... flame." She swallowed, before spooning in another mouthful. "Let it... continue to blaze, until I speak thy name... Gweneviere Baxter!" she finished, angrily.

She swanned back into the house and headed straight to the pots that needed washing. The leftover porridge stuck to the bowls made it extra satisfying for her to take out her anger when scrubbing it off. Thomas came up from behind her and gave her a sloppy kiss on the neck, which she tried her best to wriggle out of, and a slap on the bum, which she gritted her teeth to endure.

"I think we'll make a baby tonight," he whispered in her ear, making her sick to the stomach and full of dread. He then strolled past Kambili, giving her a disgusted look up and down without so much as a thank you for breakfast.

He left the room and Kambili slowly walked over to Gweneviere, grabbing a cloth and drying the pots beside her.

"Hey, are you alright?" Kambili asked, keeping her hands busy by drying off a pan.

"Yeah, I'll be fine," she muttered, her anger now turning into sorrow.

"Is he always so...?" Kambili struggled to find the words.

"Yes, yes he is," Gweneviere replied, wiping the single tear that had been rolling down her cheek. "Right, come on, let's get on with some jobs and then get out of here for a bit. I need to post some letters and buy ingredients for dinner, anyway."

The two women got on with a few chores before making some lunch and leaving it on the table for Thomas, with a note explaining that they had gone out to run some errands.

They walked about the market to get some produce for dinner.

"What do you fancy?" Gweneviere asked.

"Erm, I don't know. I don't usually get a choice," Kambili answered.

"Well, now you do. So, what would you like? Bear in mind that my culinary skills only really go as far as stews," she joked, though she wasn't exactly lying.

"Stew it is, then."

They both giggled at that.

"What meat?"

"Er, lamb?" Kambili suggested, unsure of herself.

"Okay, money bags, lamb it is.".

"Oh no, sorry, I didn't know it was expensive," Kambili apologised.

"Relax, it's fine, we have enough," Gweneviere reassured her, though she did double check her draw string purse to see how much money they had left. Luckily, there was still enough for Gweneviere to save a little bit for her own secret pot.

They continued their way through the market, making sure to pick up some accompanying vegetables, not that Thomas cared which they chose. He only really ever cared about the meat – the vegetables were merely a vessel to bulk up the dish with.

As Gweneviere opened her satchel to place the vegetables inside, she noticed the letters. She had almost forgotten about them amongst all of the giggling with Kambili.

"Come on, we need to go send these letters and make it back in time to make dinner."

"Can't we do it tomorrow?" Kambili asked.

"No, I need to do it today, otherwise I'll forget again and again, and... I'll never send it, and I made a promise that I would..."

"Okay. Don't worry, we'll get them sent. Come on, we can make it if we run," Kambili reassured her.

After running down a few streets together, unknowingly holding hands, Gweneviere stopped them.

"It's no use, we'll never make it, it's on the other side of town. I'm going to try something."

Gweneviere pulled Kambili into a side street, not realising how closely she'd pulled her towards herself. There was only about an inch between their lips, but she had no time to fantasise about kissing Kambili – she had to post Jericho's letter.

"Try what?" Kambili asked, confused and a little flustered, having definitely noticed how closely they were stood together.

"*Magic*," Gweneviere said. "I created this teleportation spell when I was a kid because, well, I was lazy. Let's hope the old thing still works."

"Erm, Gwen, I don't know about this."

"Come on, have a little faith. Just hold my hands. You said you were more than open to magic."

"Okay, okay." Kambili gave in as she joined hands with Gweneviere, causing both their palms to tingle and become slightly clammy.

"Transport my vessel from here to there. To the image in my head, no matter where."

Kambili had closed her eyes during the spell, scared of what might happen, but she decided to open them as it seemed as though nothing was changing.

Kamibili looked at Gweneviere. "I don't think it wor—"

A gentle breeze fluttered beneath them, and Kambili gasped as they slowly turned into a magical dust, their bodies melting away. A mist of the very same dust appeared in a side street just next door to the post office, which soon re-materialised back into the girls.

"Oh my, I think I'm going to—" Kambili threw up against the building wall.

"Sorry, I probably should've warned you that might happen."

Gweneviere turned away to protect her nose from the pungent smell. Though she did kindly try to reach out a hand and rub Kambili's back in comfort.

"It's alright, you get those letters sent and I'll wait here for you," Kambili replied, still spitting out the last contents of her stomach.

"Thanks, I won't be long."

Gweneviere walked into the post office, which was extremely busy, what with it being the only one in the city at the time. Luckily, the queue that she had joined wasn't too long, so after about five minutes of waiting, she had made it to the front of the line.

"Next," the clerk called.

Gweneviere stepped forward and handed him the letters.

He quickly read the addresses on both and commented, "We won't send *that* one," before handing her back Jericho's envelope.

"What do you mean you won't send it?" Gweneviere asked.

"I mean we don't send letters to wherever *that* is," he reiterated, aggressively pointing his forefinger at the address of Jericho's home.

"It says very clearly where it needs to go. It states a country in Africa, and I'm sure they'll interpret and send it to the right village from there."

"Miss, I assure you, we don't send letters to that place, okay?" he said, becoming short with Gweneviere, who was in no mood to back down.

"Listen to me, clerk, and listen good. If we can take whole boat loads of people from said places to enslave them, then I'm pretty confident that we have the means available in this country to send one letter back, don't you? Oh, and if you need any more convincing, I'll quite happily wait for you to finish work and speak to you then."

The very real fiery glow in her eyes made the clerk rethink his answer.

"Fine, but it'll cost you double," the man took pleasure in saying.

Gweneviere pulled out her purse and counted what was

left, she would have no money left over to add to her savings should she post the letters, but she had made a promise and she wasn't going to break it. So she decided to give up her day's savings to send Jericho's letter. It was the very least that he deserved. Besides, she could always try and scrape back on costs another day. Gweneviere gave the petty man his money and watched him for a moment to ensure he did indeed sort them correctly.

Once satisfied, Gweneviere headed back to meet up with a still queasy Kambili. Luckily, she had managed to clean herself up.

"You alright?" Gweneviere asked, with a concerned look.

"Yeah, I'll survive," Kambili answered light-heartedly, wiping her mouth.

"Can you *survive* the spell back?"

"Sure," Kambili said, giving her an optimistic, albeit shaky, thumbs up.

Gweneviere teleported them back home, though she made sure to do it outside and a few doors down so that Kambili's inevitable vomit wouldn't be their problem to clean up. Clearly, it was going to take a fair few trips until Kambili had gained some sea legs when it came to teleportation. They returned to the house to begin dinner preparations when Kambili became curious about something.

"Gwen?" Kambili asked, peeling potatoes in a chair, still not quite well enough to be working at one hundred percent capacity, or on her feet.

"Yes?"

"Who were those letters for? And why were they so important?"

"Well, one of them was for my friend, and the other..." Gweneviere paused. "The other was for Jericho."

"Jericho?" Kambili repeated, unsure if she was supposed to know who Gweneviere was talking about.

"Yes, Jericho. I went to meet someone who I thought might be a new friend yesterday, but instead a horrible scene unfolded before me. You see, Jericho was her slave, and she was horrible to him. She..." Gweneviere paused once more as she caught her breath, trying to stop herself becoming emotional. "She tortured him right in front of me, and by the time I intervened to stop, it was too late, the damage was done, and he died beside me. He asked me of one favour, that I send his letter back to his home. I promised him that I would, and I just didn't want to forget or postpone it and then never get around to doing it."

"That's horrible. I'm sorry you had to witness that," Kambili sympathised.

"No, *I'm* sorry that it happened. If I had just reacted sooner to the situation, then maybe he wouldn't have..." Gweneviere burst out into tears.

Kambili jumped up to embrace her, holding her in her arms, stroking her soft, coppery, brown hair as she cried.

"It wasn't your fault," Kambili asserted, pulling Gweneviere from their embrace so she could look her in the eyes. She wiped away the tears from her face. "It sounds to me like Jericho wouldn't have had much time left as it was, but at least you were there to bring him some comfort in his last moments. You assured him that you would send that letter, and you have. I'm sure that wherever he is now, it is much more peaceful than being in *that* house."

"Thank you, Kambili." Gweneviere sniffed. "I promise that won't happen to you. I won't let it."

"I know, Gwen... I know." Kambili smiled softly, taking comfort in the fact that she felt safe in Gweneviere's presence.

CHAPTER 7
Sunday Dinner

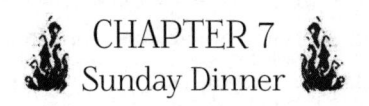

As Gweneviere and Kambili finished preparing the evening meal, Thomas burst through the door connecting the bakery to the home. They heard the door slam from the kitchen. Gweneviere simply rolled her eyes, assuming he was just having a hissy fit about one petty thing or another. What they couldn't see, however, was the vicious look on his face: he was foaming at the mouth like a rabid dog.

"Gwen!" he shouted from the living room.

"Dinner is almost ready, we'll be there in a second!" she called back, still not detecting anything unusual from his shouting, as he *always* shouted.

"I don't care about dinner! Get in here, now!"

Gweneviere did as he said. She knew something more concerning was wrong as he would never disregard food in such a way, the greedy pig that he was. Gweneviere entered the living room and Kambili hung back in the doorway to see what all the fuss was about.

"What did you do the other day, at Gerald's house, with Agatha?" he questioned.

"What? Nothing, why?" Gweneviere replied in confusion.

"What. Did. You. Do?" he reiterated, sounding out the question in a condescending manner.

"I. Don't. Know," Gweneviere replied, in the same tone.

"Gwen, I'm seriously not in the mood for your attitude right now. What the fuck did you do?" he raged, causing his foul mouth to secrete even more bubbles from the corners.

"We had tea and cakes and talked, Jesus Christ. What more do you want me to say?" she replied, avoiding mentioning the part where Jericho was murdered, and that she used her magic to try and help him.

"Well, I want you to tell me whatever you got up to that you're not telling me. You really upset Agatha. I've just had to take an earful of Gerald's crap about it, in front of the whole bakery, no less."

"Fine. She was treating Jericho horribly, so I—"

"Who the fuck is Jericho?" Thomas interrupted.

"Their slave, but she was—"

"Treating him like a slave?" Thomas once again butted in. "Jesus, Gwen, they're not your friends, nor part of the family. They're slaves, nothing more. We buy them, we sell them, we instruct them, and if they don't obey, we have every right to beat or dispose of them however we see fit."

"That's disgusting! They're people, just like me and you, well, not like you, I suppose, as you're a heartless bastard of a man," she screamed.

He scoffed at Gweneviere's insult. For Thomas to be truly insulted, he would first have to care about Gweneviere's opinion, which he certainly didn't. No, all Thomas wanted from a wife was a dolled-up show pony that did their chores, birthed him an heir to his business, and, most importantly of all, kept their mouth shut.

"No, Gweneviere, they're slaves. That's the way the world works, whether you like it or not, so grow up and deal with it."

"No, that's the way *your*, sick, twisted world works."

"Well, guess what, sugar tits, as long as you're my wife, and live under my roof, you do live in *my* world. Kambili!" he called out, looking to her shadow in the doorway. "That means no more sitting at the table and eating with us, and no more sleeping in the guest bedroom. You can eat the scraps off my plate, and you can sleep in the corner of the living room in a box, and you'll be grateful for both."

"That's barbaric! Besides, with an oaf like you around there's never any leftovers," Gweneviere spluttered through the tears that flowed down her face.

Thomas stormed across the room and grabbed Gweneviere by her throat. "Who are you trying to impress? This filth?" he asked, with a glance in Kambili's direction.

Gweneviere could barely breathe, let alone answer him. She flailed under his grip as it tightened on her neck and he pushed her up higher against the wall. Unfortunately for Gweneviere, her father couldn't rescue her this time. No one could.

"Stop it!" Kambili pleaded, tugging at his arm.

He swatted Kambili away like a fly, though he did loosen his grip slightly on Gweneviere. He didn't want to kill her, just maim and scare her, as deep down he knew she was all too right; it would be far too hard for him to find another pyrokinetic witch so soon.

He inched closer to her face and, as the smell of his rotten breath flew up her nostrils, he whispered, "This is your last chance," before turning back to his regular volume, "I've stuck my neck on the line for you and apologised on your behalf, but to solidify your remorse we're hosting a Sunday dinner at the weeks end. I expect you *both*..." he said, now turning to Kambili to make sure she could hear him too, "to rustle up the best meal of your lives and behave yourselves... or else." He finally released Gweneviere, leaving a large red handprint around her neck in the process.

He stepped out of the room and walked into the kitchen. Seeing the three equally sized plates of food, he scoffed, almost barking out a laugh before he grabbed one and slid all of its contents onto another plate. He took his now 'adequate' portion of food and went to sit at the table, alone, as he wolfed down the monster plate of dinner, leaving the girls one measly portion to share. Though, neither Gweneviere, nor Kambili, had much of an appetite after the ordeal.

"Are you okay?" Kambili asked, before instantly correcting herself. "Sorry, that's a dumb question."

Gweneviere nodded in reply as she held her throat, indicating to Kambili that it was too painful to speak. The girls returned to the kitchen and Kambili fetched Gweneviere a cup of water to ease her throat. Gweneviere insisted that Kambili eat the remaining plate of food by sliding it towards her. Neither of them knew when Kambili might get the opportunity again and Gweneviere could barely swallow her water, let alone solid food.

Kambili ate while stood in the kitchen beside Gweneviere,

as neither of them wanted to sit at the table and endure Thomas' company. Kambili reluctantly finished her dinner as Gweneviere merely watched. They went about tidying up the kitchen and once Thomas had left the table, they cleaned up the aftermath of that, too. He also asked Kambili to wipe him down, as the slathering beast had wasted the majority of the extra portion smearing it across his face and beard, matting it together. Still scared from his earlier outburst, Kambili agreed as she didn't dare do anything to irritate him even more. There was certainly a different atmosphere than the night before. It was as though Gweneviere's standing up for herself was completely erased from history. She even began to question whether it actually happened herself, or if it was just in her head.

Gweneviere and Kambili hung around in the kitchen after they had finished cleaning up, in the hopes that he would leave them be for the rest of the evening, but that was a mistake. Thomas waltzed into the kitchen and told Kambili she had missed a spot whilst cleaning him. There was a stain on his shirt that he pointed to, so, of course, Kambili nodded, grabbed a warm cloth, and applied it to area to try and clean it. As she finished cleaning up the mark and retreated her arm, Thomas grabbed her wrist and pressed her hand, and cloth, against his hot, sweaty crotch. He did it while staring Gweneviere in the eye, it was thrill for him to see her reaction as she became silently irate. Meanwhile, Kambili suffered, being a mere pawn in his cruel mental torture. Once he'd had his fill of teasing Gweneviere, he threw Kambili's hand back at her.

"I expect to see you in the boudoir in five minutes. Don't

keep me waiting," he said to Gweneviere with a malicious smile.

"W-why would I go anywhere near you?" Gweneviere wearily croaked, still caressing her throat.

"Because, if you don't, it'll be little *darky* here who gets it," he said, grabbing Kambili by her hair and holding her head grossly close to his face as he sniffed her and rolled his eyes back into is head.

Gweneviere saw the terrified look on Kambili's face. She couldn't let him touch her, Gweneviere was sadly used to it, she could take another night, especially if it meant keeping Kambili safe.

"Alright, alright, just leave her alone," she said, still struggling to speak.

"Atta girl." Thomas grinned as he released Kambili from his grip and left to prepare himself in the bedroom, which simply meant dropping his pants.

Kambili cradled the back of her head, where, without realising, Thomas had yanked a clump of her hair out.

"Are you alright? I guess I'm the one asking the dumb questions now," Gweneviere said.

"Yeah, I'll be fine. You don't have to go in there, you know. You don't have to protect me."

"Yes... I do." Gweneviere struggled to speak. "I promise, I won't let him soil your beauty and innocence the way he did mine." She placed her palms gently against Kambili's soft cheeks.

"But..."

"Shh," Gweneviere hushed her, placing her finger on

Kambili's lips. "It's okay," she whispered, as they gazed at one another.

"Gweneviere, why do you stay with him?" Kambili asked, wondering why anyone would willingly subject themselves to this.

"Because marriage wasn't really a choice for me at that point in time, but don't worry, I—"

"Gwen! Times up!" Thomas howled.

"I guess, I'll have to tell you my masterplan some other time."

Gweneviere smiled, trying to make light of the horrid situation that she was about to walk into. It was only now, as Gweneviere was leaving to head into the beast's pit, that she and Kambili realised that they had been holding hands with one another. Kambili's face was far from smirking as she watched Gweneviere walk away and felt her hand slip from her own. She felt such an overwhelming sense of sorrow and guilt. Kambili was the reason Gweneviere kept getting into trouble, or at least that's what she kept telling herself.

It's all my fault, Kambili internally sighed as she witnessed the bedroom door close behind Gweneviere.

Gweneviere entered the bedroom a broken woman. She gulped the saliva bouncing around her mouth from the anxiety, and began to undress. Thomas stood there with his manhood, not that he deserved it, hanging between his chunky, chafed thighs. Gweneviere allowed a solitary tear to flow from her cheek all the way down to her breasts as she prepared herself to be violated once more.

The following hour played out in a series of grunts from

Thomas and a mixture of silence and screams from Gweneviere, which pained her even more as her throat was still raw. Once the harrowing event was over, Gweneviere's body was left bruised and battered like a fallen peach. Of course, right on queue, no more than five minutes after he had concluded his deviant acts, the pathetic excuse for a man passed out, sleeping like a log in the middle of the bed.

Gweneviere was quite literally naked and afraid. It was the worst encounter she'd had with Thomas thus far, and it left her shaking. She couldn't bear to stay in the same room as him, let alone the same bed. So, she hobbled out into the living room, still stark naked, with her frail body on show. Kambili hadn't yet slept a wink in her corner as all she had heard was Gweneviere's cries for the past hour. Hearing the bedroom door creak, she jumped up to see Gweneviere's body in the doorway. Even in the darkness of night, the patches of blue, purple, and green were clear to see as they covered more skin than they left bare. As Gweneviere dragged herself towards the unlit fireplace, Kambili could see she was getting weaker by the second, like she could collapse at any moment. She raced over and caught Gweneviere just in the nick of time. Gweneviere's knees gave out, dropping her in Kambili's arms in front of the fireplace. Gweneviere was barely conscious as she mustered up the strength to wave her arm at the fireplace to spark it to life. Gweneviere laid her head across Kambili's lap and looked up at Kambili lovingly, though all Kambili could see as she looked back down at her was a girl in pain. She knew, by now, not to ask if she was okay – of course she wasn't okay – so Kambili just held Gweneviere in her arms, softly brushing her hair with her fingertips until she fell asleep.

Kambili slipped Gweneviere's sleeping head onto the rug and went to fetch a blanket to wrap around Gweneviere's exposed skin. As Kambili wrapped her up in the linens, she became flushed at the sight of Gweneviere's supple body; she could see past the bruises to the beauty underneath. She just couldn't begin to comprehend how someone could do this to another person, before remembering that someone was Thomas, and that he probably had no qualms about what he did to anyone. Gweneviere stirred awake as Kambili finished wrapping her up.

"Thank you," Gweneviere muttered, still half conscious.

"Come on, let's get you into the spare room," Kambili said, propping Gweneviere's arm onto her shoulder as they shuffled along.

Kambili tucked Gweneviere in and planted a tender kiss on her forehead.

"Goodnight, Gwen."

"Wait," Gweneviere croaked.

Kambili turned around in confusion. "What's wrong?"

"Will... will you stay with me? Please, I don't want to be alone."

"Always," Kambili said softly, climbing onto the bed and making herself comfortable on top of the covers.

She found Gweneviere beautiful, but knew that she would likely not feel the same way, and so she didn't want to tempt herself by being so close to Gweneviere's bare skin. Though, even with the covers between them, Gweneviere lovingly turned and rested her head on Kambili's chest, sending butterflies through her stomach. Not long after, they both fell soundly asleep in the comfort of each other's arms.

As the early blinding summer sun began to rise, a beam of its light crept into the spare room and hit Kambili's face. It was just in time to wake her up before Thomas was about to catch the two of them in bed together. He'd surely be angry enough as it was that Gweneviere had decided to depart to the spare room during the night, let alone the fact that Kambili, 'the slave', was in it with her. Kambili slipped out of bed, peeling Gweneviere's arms off her while trying not to wake her up. She began making breakfast when she felt the floorboards creak from Thomas weighing them down.

"Morning, Master Thomas," Kambili said meekly as he strolled straight over to the dining table to await his breakfast.

All she got was a grunt in reply. Though after a few minutes, he did pipe up, asking where Gweneviere was.

"Er, I believe she is still asleep, in the guest room," Kambili answered, awkwardly. She knew that he didn't know they had slept beside one another, yet she still felt guilty of a crime and acted as awkward, and suspicious, as a criminal being interrogated.

"Well, I don't know what she was doing in there when there is a perfectly good bed in our room. Nevertheless, go wake her up before I drag her lazy, good-for-nothing arse out of bed myself," he demanded, as Kambili dropped off his breakfast before him.

"Yes... sir." It wasn't worth the abuse of trying to defy him.

She entered the spare room to see Gweneviere still peacefully sleeping. Kambili only wished that she was special enough to possess Gweneviere's powers, at least that way she could take some of the pressure off. Alas, the only power that Kambili possessed was being able to make Gweneviere feel better. An ability that Kambili didn't realise she had, and that was far more special than being a witch.

She gently stroked Gweneviere's face and whispered her name until she awoke. Gweneviere softly woke to see Kambili's gorgeous face looking down over her. Through the haze of Gweneviere's glossy, not yet fully open, eyes, Kambili looked even more ethereal than Gweneviere thought she did every time she laid eyes upon her.

"Good morning." Gweneviere smiled sleepily.

"Good morning." Kambili smiled back, drawn in by Gweneviere's transcendent beauty. "Listen, we need to get you up before Thomas loses his rag."

"Okay." Gweneviere sighed. "Thank you, for waking me instead of him. And... thank you for last night, you're a real angel, Kambili."

"You promised to look after me and free me of this life, but Gwen, I'm not the only one trapped here, and I promise to return the favour to you. *We* will get out of here, together, okay?"

Kambili's words were like music to Gweneviere's ears, her smile stretched further across her face than should surely be possible. Gweneviere's smile slowly softened, however, as she awkwardly hinted that she needed help getting out of bed.

Her wounded body was still too weak to carry herself around with confidence. Kambili got Gweneviere onto her feet before turning around and allowing her to get dressed.

"Erm, Kambili?"

"Yes?" she replied, still facing away. Although she had certainly seen everything the night before, it was under much different circumstances, and Kambili didn't want to make the assumption that Gweneviere would be comfortable with Kambili watching her dress.

"I don't have any clothes in this room, please could you get me some out of my bedside drawer?" Gweneviere politely requested.

"Oh." Kambili blushed, unseen by Gweneviere. "Yes, I'll get some."

Kambili returned with a fresh pile of clothes for Gweneviere to adorn and, once she had, Kambili guided her into the dining room for some breakfast. Thomas, seeing the way Gweneviere hobbled in, allowed her to eat her porridge before heading down to the bakery, after all, he couldn't have her being too weak to use her magic.

After breakfast, the three of them went about their day in the most harmonious way possible. Gweneviere and Kambili were far too weak to start anymore fights with Thomas, and Thomas didn't want to push Gweneviere to the point of death. He knew she was right about finding another witch, but he would certainly not give her the satisfaction of allowing her to know that fact.

In the days leading up to the Sunday dinner party, or rather just a dinner to grovel to Gerald and Agatha, Thomas had seemingly calmed down, though that was mostly due to the fact that Gweneviere had become relatively quiet since *that* night. She had even been giving Kambili somewhat of a cold shoulder. Gweneviere knew she was developing feelings for Kambili. She got all tingly inside every time she heard her calming voice. Gweneviere also knew, however, that she was dreaming to think that she could have a life with Kambili. No one would take them seriously. Two women in a relationship, with one of them being black, no less. No, Gweneviere knew it was too dangerous a love to allow. Besides, Gweneviere still had no indication that Kambili felt the same way for her – even if it was obvious. So, she tried her best to keep her feelings at bay, but as the dinner party drew closer, Gweneviere's true feelings would surely show, as she dreaded how Kambili would be treated.

The day of the dinner party finally arrived. Gweneviere and Kambili had been busy all day preparing the evening's feast. Neither of them were looking forward to the evening ahead, as Gweneviere knew that she would have to play nice with Agatha, and that they would treat Kambili like crap.

As they set the table for dinner, Kambili could sense that Gweneviere had been acting different in the past few days and decided to check in.

"Hey, are you okay?"

"No, not really," a troubled looking Gweneviere replied.

"What's wrong?"

"I'm dreading tonight. I know what Agatha and Gerald are like. They're not nice people, Kambili, and I know how they'll treat you."

"It's okay, Gwen, I can handle being a waiter for one evening, I've survived much worse."

"Yes, but Agatha's last slave didn't survive, did he?" Gweneviere snapped, without meaning to.

"So you do see me as a slave?" Kambili paused and folded her arms.

"No! Kambili, that's not what I meant. I..."

"Just leave it, *Gweneviere*, I'll be fine. Now, you should probably go get ready for your evening. We wouldn't want to keep Agatha waiting, now, would we?" Kambili said coldly, as she ignored Gweneviere's lingering gaze and kept setting the table.

Kambili was hurt, of all the people she expected to refer to her as a slave, Gweneviere was at the bottom of that list.

Before Gweneviere could reiterate that her words didn't reflect what she was trying to say to Kambili, Thomas strode in.

"Are we all set?" he asked them, rubbing his calloused hands together.

"Yes, dinner is almost ready, and the table is set," Kambili answered, before placing the candelabra in the centre of the table, completing the layout.

Gweneviere just looked over at Kambili as she pined for her

forgiveness, but there was no time for such yearning, as Agatha and Gerald were due to arrive at any moment.

"Grand, I'll go get us a bottle of fancy wine from the stash, and Gwen, bloody get ready, will you? They'll be here soon, and you still look a mess," he said, not that she needed reminding.

"Okay."

Gweneviere sighed as she lit the candles with an unenthusiastic, limp flick of her finger and left to adorn her evening dress. As she finished tying her own corset with an enchantment she'd learnt in class, she heard the front door knock. What came after was a very loud Agatha on the other side of it.

"Thomas? We're here!" Her annoying voice pitched through the door.

Gweneviere re-entered the living room to see Gerald and Agatha dressed to the nines, far fancier than herself and Thomas. They had clearly done it to try and make Gweneviere and Thomas feel inferior, but that was the last thing that was on Gweneviere's mind. All she could think about was how she could make things right with Kambili. Gweneviere hated the thought of hurting Kambili, especially when Gweneviere only wanted the best for her.

"Gwen, get over here." Thomas grinned, with a demanding undertone that signalled there would be consequences if she didn't do as he asked.

"Agatha," Gweneviere exclaimed, slapping on a fake smile.

"*Gweneviere*," she replied, rather coldly.

"I'm ever so sorry for our last encounter, I honestly didn't mean to offend you in any way."

"Thank you, Gweneviere, let's just put that day behind us, shall we? Start fresh?" Agatha proposed.

"Agreed." Gweneviere smiled, falsely.

"Oh, my, it's lovely to see you and Thomas finally took Gerald's advice," Agatha praised.

"Sorry?" Gweneviere asked in confusion.

"The slave," Agatha replied, pointing to Kambili stood in the doorway. "Maybe now you won't be so jealous next time you come around to my house," she snarked playing it off as joke, like a true socialite.

"Nice to see the ladies getting along again," a clueless Gerald observed.

"Yes, happy wife, happy life, as I always say." Thomas grinned, seemingly pleased with Gweneviere's performance so far. Not that any wife of Thomas' would ever experience true happiness.

Kambili finally opened her mouth, now that Agatha had drawn everyone's attention to her.

"Dinner is ready," she politely informed the room.

"Very well, we shall be there in a minute," Thomas replied.

They all flowed into the dining room and took up a chair; the two men were at either head of the table, and the women were on each side, with nothing but a metre of table and a candelabra between them. With everyone seated and the wine poured, by Thomas as he deemed it to be far too expensive to entrust a slave to pour it, Kambili began to roll out the starters.

It was a simple, but delicious, leek and potato soup. She served the guests first, as she thought it would help keep her on their good side, before moving on to Thomas and then, finally, Gweneviere. Partly because she knew, out of everyone there, that Gweneviere would be least bothered about being served last, but also because she was still angry. She practically ignored Gweneviere's upward glance as she dumped the soup in front of her, causing it to sway about the bowl.

Gerald's eyes had been transfixed on Kambili the whole time, and it most definitely did not go unnoticed by Agatha as she watched him like a hawk. Gweneviere could feel the tension brewing across the table and tried to distract Agatha with some small talk and flattery.

"So... Agatha, how have you been? You look beautiful tonight, I must say," Gweneviere complimented her.

"Huh? Oh yes, I'm fine, thanks," she replied, briefly, before refocusing her glare on her husband, not that he had noticed.

"How's business, Thomas? Must be good if you can finally afford to buy an, albeit weak, slave, after all these years," he chuckled to himself.

"Yes, business is great. I've managed to double my profit margins, actually," he bragged smugly, as Gerald's attempt to embarrass him failed.

Yeah, thanks to me! Gweneviere thought to herself. *Why do they even entertain each other, it's so obvious that they all hate one another and are just trying to outdo each other. I guess I'll never understand being a true socialite.* Gweneviere's eyes darted back and forth between Thomas and Gerald as they continued to chat on about nonsense that Gweneviere had tuned out.

The awkward conversations were few and far between, meaning that they, at least, were all eating much faster and, hopefully, the dinner could end much sooner. They zoomed through the rest of their starters and quickly devoured their main course of roasted pheasant, with a rich salty jus, and vegetables that Kambili had somehow made taste just as amazing as the pheasant itself.

As Kambili came around to collect plates, practically everyone's was already clean, a real sign of Kambili's culinary magic. All except Agatha's, that was, as she left a considerable amount behind. It was clearly in protest to Gerald's ongoing infatuation with Kambili. Something Agatha would surely later regret when her stomach would inevitably rumble, though she'd probably have one of her many servants whip something up if needed.

"Is everyone ready for dessert?" Kambili asked the table.

Most of them quietly nodded, which would have been the normal response, Gerald, however, decided to make it very clear he wanted dessert.

"Oh, I'm ready for *dessert*, alright," he answered, practically eye-fucking an innocent Kambili in front of the whole table.

Agatha's ears began to pour with steam; it was only a matter of time before the pressurised anger within her blew. Gweneviere also wasn't too happy about the remark.

"For God's sake, Gweneviere. Do you always let your slave behave like such a whore?" Agatha suddenly shouted across the table.

"Excuse me?" Gweneviere replied, moving the candelabra to the side ready in case she needed to smack some sense into the bitch.

"Well, she's obviously been trying to seduce my poor

Gerald all night. He's a man, he can't ignore it, it's not his fault," Agatha said, of course, ignoring any wrongdoing by Gerald. No, of course, *he* wasn't the problem, *he* was innocent. "I mean look at her, for Christ's sake, it's like having dinner in a brothel," Agatha continued, as if Kambili wasn't stood there hearing every word.

"Oh, do calm yourself, dear, it's my prerogative as a man to enjoy the fruits on show to me." Gerald stepped in, not helping the conversation move along at all.

"Oh, shut up, Gerald, the point is, that that *thing* shouldn't have any *fruits* on show!" Agatha raged, pointing at Kambili. "I bet Gweneviere planned it, didn't you? You bunch of trollops," she added, rambling so ferociously that her spit was flying everywhere.

Thomas, showing his true selfish and cowardice self, didn't utter a word as he didn't deem either Gweneviere or Kambili as worthy of defending. Gweneviere, on the other hand, was becoming angrier by the second. She wasn't going to make the same mistake as she did with Jericho and wait around for Agatha to become more aggressive. No, Gweneviere had had enough.

"Firstly, her name is Kambili, and she may wear whatever she damn well pleases. And secondly, it's not our fault that your husband has a wandering eye," Gweneviere spat back across the table.

"Right! That's it. Come on, Gerald, we're going."

Agatha stood up and hurled what red wine was left in her glass, which wasn't much, in Gweneviere's face. It took every ounce of strength that Gweneviere had not to singe her hair down to the scalp as they left.

As soon as the door closed behind them, a furious Thomas marched over to Gweneviere. He began rolling up his sleeves, ready to beat her to within an inch of her life, but as he raised his arm, Gweneviere conjured up two fireballs in her hands, causing him to step back.

"Stop pissing around, Gwen, you've already ruined the evening, now take your punishment."

"No!"

"What did you just say?"

"I said, no! I am your wife in name only, now listen to me, and listen good. You are not to lay a finger on me or Kambili again, or I'll light your fat, greasy arse on fire before you can even say my name."

"You can't speak to me like that," he said, stepping closer to Gweneviere.

"What's stopping me?" she asked, also taking a step closer, and enlarging the balls of fire in her palms to show her strength.

Thomas' cheeks began to redden, and his forehead formed beads of sweat as he was gently reminded that, if she wanted to, Gweneviere possessed the power to kill him at any moment.

"I'm going to bed, hopefully some sleep will get some sense into you. Now, clean this shit up," he huffed, before slamming the bedroom door. He knew he wouldn't win that fight.

Gweneviere turned to Kambili, who had stayed silent throughout the whole ordeal. Kambili smiled, forgivingly, she knew that, deep down, Gweneviere didn't mean what she said earlier in the day. Her outburst at Agatha and Thomas proved that.

No, Gweneviere was definitely team Kambili.

CHAPTER 8
A Potion's Brewing

Gweneviere and Kambili were cleaning up the dining room and kitchen when Kambili noticed that Gweneviere still had a slosh of dried red wine on her cheek. She walked up to Gweneviere, with a damp cloth in hand, and gently brushed the side of her face. She managed to clear the red mark away, but the inevitable blushing on Gweneviere's face caused her cheeks to look just as rosy as when the wine had been there, though a little more inviting, now that they were clean.

"Thanks," Kambili spoke softly as she finished cleaning up Gweneviere's face.

"What for? You're the one mopping up my face."

"Everything," Kambili answered sincerely.

"You don't need to thank me for doing what any decent human being should do. Besides, it's the least I can do after what I said earlier. I hope you know that I never meant to refer to you as a slave, not that anyone should be referred to as a slave. Urgh! I just wish it didn't exist," Gweneviere continued rambling, exasperated with the world they lived in.

Kambili grabbed Gweneviere's flapping hands and held

them in her own. "Shh, it's okay, Gwen. It's okay," she said, calming her as they became lost in one another's eyes.

Being so close to Kambili's face, and more importantly, lips, was hypnotising to Gweneviere. She couldn't help but feel herself pulling in closer and closer. Gweneviere's senses were firing on all cylinders, she couldn't deny herself her feelings any longer. Screw what anyone else thinks. They were already a witch and a slave; how could a simple kiss make their lives any worse, and surely the feeling of each other's love would make it all worthwhile.

I can't believe I'm about to do this, Gweneviere thought to herself as she contemplated planting her lips on Kambili's, but before she could, Kambili made the first move.

Kambili's hands left Gweneviere's so that she could wrap them around her waist and pull her in closer, before gently pressing her own lips against Gweneviere's. As their eyes closed and their lips met, they felt as though they had been transported to another realm: a beautiful place, where everyone was free to be anyone. A place where fireworks sounded each night, lighting up the sky, and meadows of flowers bloomed without need for the sorrow of rain. A magical place where they could be together, forever. The rest of reality seemingly melted away in that moment, as their kiss became more and more passionate with the exchanging of tongues. They were now holding each other more tightly than ever before and neither wanted to be the first to let go in case it could never happen again. It was a much overdue kiss, as Gweneviere could have quite happily dropped a kiss on her lips upon first laying eyes on Kambili, if the circumstances had allowed it.

As they heard Thomas' snores, they didn't hesitate to continue their rendezvous, climbing onto the dining table, sweeping any clutter to the side. They undressed each other in quick succession as their flushed bodies lusted and longed for one another. With Gweneviere's back against the table and Kambili laid over her, Kambili danced her fore and middle finger down Gweneviere's stomach. Gweneviere hadn't quite noticed her doing so in the midst of their French kissing, but as Kambili worked her way down Gweneviere's body, a stream of dark, heavy flashbacks of Thomas' wicked touch raced through Gweneviere's mind. She tried to hide it, but when Kambili softly slipped her fore finger an inch inside of Gweneviere, she jolted in discomfort. This time, however, it was far too obvious for Kambili not to see.

"Gwen? Are you okay? Am I hurting you?" Kambili asked, worried, as that was the last thing she wanted to do.

"Yes, I mean no... Er, I'm sorry, I just can't do this." Gweneviere sighed, slowly pulling herself away and sitting up in front of Kambili on the table.

"I'm sorry, Gwen, I didn't mean to hurt you," Kambili apologised sincerely. She was mortified to think that she had ruined their first precious moment together by being too hasty.

"No, no. It's not your fault, and I know that, of course, you didn't mean to hurt me. I just need some time to recover, mentally and physically, from what he did," Gweneviere confessed, covering herself up with her clothes that were spread across the table.

"Oh... God, I hate him even more now, and I didn't think that could be possible," Kambili spat with anger as her gaze turned to the door to his bedroom.

"I know, *he* should be the one apologising, but I think pigs would sooner fly before that happens. Though, my friend Poppy could technically make that happen," Gweneviere joked, in a solemn attempt to lighten the mood, not that it did, as Kambili asked her a serious follow up question.

"What are you going to do the next time he tries to... you know? After all, doesn't he want you to birth him a child?"

"I don't know yet, but I promise you, I won't let it happen again. I will certainly not bring a poor child into this world, and by the hands of him, no less."

"That's great, Gwen, but that sounds like a promise that you need to make to yourself more than anyone else."

"Yeah... I understand what you're saying. Thanks for being patient with me."

"Hey, I've waited this long for you, I can wait a bit longer, because you're worth it, Gwen, in every way."

Kambili leaned in for a brief kiss on the lips, which Gweneviere happily reciprocated.

They finished cleaning up the mess from dinner and headed to the spare room. Beforehand, Gweneviere snuck back into Thomas' room for some nightwear, when a voice came from within Gweneviere's mind, whispering her name. She turned to Thomas sprawled across the bed, snoring, not leaving any room for Gweneviere, even if she had wanted to sleep in it. Clearly, he hadn't said her name, but she was still unsure if she had even heard it in the first place. As she continued to scour her drawer for some pyjamas, she heard another unintelligible whisper.

Come closer, she made out in her head. This time the voice in her mind seemed to have come from a specific direction. Gweneviere turned to where she believed the sound to be coming from. As she edged closer to the voice, she realised that it was emanating from one of the bags that she had never fully unpacked when she moved in. As she dug her way into it and passed the eclectic objects that apparently hadn't made the cut of being worthy to unpack, she found her mother's old spell book. It was the one that almost helped Gweneviere save her father's life. She didn't know whether she could trust picking it up again and risk failing someone else with it. The voice in her head started to become clearer as it called her name, and she realised it was her mother's. Quite possibly the only voice that could have convinced her, in that moment, to pick up the book.

As she bit the bullet and pulled the dusty book from her bag, it came to life in her hands, with the pages fluttering around. It was so noisy that she tried to close it, for not wanting to wake Thomas, but it wouldn't allow her to. It forced itself back open and once again flipped through each page until it landed on a spell. The page was titled 'The Libido Tamer'. It must have been the potion that her mother used for the local women, including the very one that ended up getting her mother caught in the first place. If this was indeed a message from her mother from the afterlife, how could Gweneviere ignore it? Gweneviere took a brief look at the spell, which caused her eyes to widen with hope – it could be the answer she had been looking for! She closed the book with her finger jammed into it as a bookmarker, grabbed her clothes under her other arm, and headed back to the spare room, making sure to quietly shuffle past Thomas' lump of a body.

She entered the spare room where Kambili awaited. Gweneviere was happy to be walking in with a plan to share with her, but first, she was showered with another round of smooches.

As they gently pulled away from each other's lips, Gweneviere whispered, "I have something to show you."

"What is it?" Kambili smiled, hazily, still entranced by their kiss.

"It's one of my mother's old spell books, it spoke to me, or rather, she did," Gweneviere answered, wary of trying not to sound crazy.

"What did it... she, say?"

"Well, it's not so much what it said, but what it did."

"Well, what did it do, then?" Kambili asked, playfully rubbing her legs against Gweneviere's under the covers to keep warm.

"It opened up by itself and landed on this page, which has a potion that should stop Thomas from ever laying his filthy hands on me again," Gweneviere explained, as she passed Kambili the book, turned to the libido spell page.

"I don't see anything," Kambili said, after examining the page greatly, in case she had missed something. Alas, to her, it was a blank page.

"What?" Gweneviere asked in shock. She turned the book back to herself to confirm that the spell was indeed still there. "It's right here," Gweneviere said, pointing out the title and showing Kambili.

"Gwen, I'm sorry, but I don't see anything, on any page," Kambili answered, flicking through all of the pages. She felt guilty that she couldn't corroborate Gweneviere's claim, and she didn't want Gweneviere to think that she wasn't being supportive, but she couldn't lie.

Gweneviere sat back for a second as she flicked through the book, the first half was covered in spells, and the second was blank, so Gweneviere decided to test a theory. She quickly sneaked back into Thomas' room to fetch her magic quill. Upon returning to Kambili, she went to one of the pages that they both saw as blank and wrote a simple sentence which, to Gweneviere, was as clear as day. She passed it to Kambili to see if she could indeed see it.

"Nope, nothing, sorry," Kambili replied.

"Huh." Gweneviere paused as she thought for a second. "You try and write something, just here," she encouraged, pointing at just below where she had written her own sentence.

Kambili took the book and quill and attempted to write a sentence where Gweneviere had instructed. "Ugh, this quill has run out of ink."

"Wait, so nothing is happening when you try to write?" Gweneviere questioned, to confirm her theory.

"Yeah, it's not working, look."

"That's a magic quill, it doesn't run out of ink," Gweneviere said.

"So why isn't it working?" a confused Kambili asked.

"Because I think the book is also enchanted, by my mother. She probably did it so that only her, or in this case someone of her blood, like me, can read and write in it. To keep her spells secret and safe from prying eyes. It's rather clever, really," Gweneviere explained.

"Oh, wow, that is quite ingenious. Go Gwen's mother! Maybe she left half the book blank for you to write some spells of your own? Like your teleportation spell you came up with as a child, I'm sure that'd make a great addition."

"Yeah, maybe."

In reality, her mother probably intended on living a much longer life, filling in a lot more of those blank pages herself, though Gweneviere did find the idea of continuing her mother's legacy comforting.

"Anyway, how does this spell, potion thing, even work?" Kambili asked, with genuine interest.

"Well, it's actually rather like a recipe, so you'll probably be better at it than me. It says that once we've cooked it up, we just drop a bit into his evening meal every day. The recipe says it makes enough for a couple weeks," Gweneviere explained, reading the invisible page to Kambili.

"That's great! What do you we need? Eye of newt?" Kambili joked.

"No, though, it does mention blood from a new-born baby," Gweneviere said sombrely.

"Wait, what?" Kambili raised her eyebrows, eyes wide.

Gweneviere looked back at her with a blank expression, which quickly cracked as she couldn't help herself from bursting into laughter.

"Oh, ha-ha, very funny," Kambili said, nudging Gweneviere in the arm and rolling her eyes.

"I'm sorry, it was just too easy. Though, on a serious note, most of these ingredients we can pick up from the market. Although, there is one that you definitely won't find at the local herb and veg stall."

"What is it?"

"It says here that we need werewolf hair, specifically that of an alpha wolf. It says the spell works in that it makes the recipient a 'beta', and less sexually driven," Gweneviere attempted to decipher.

"Werewolves? How in the hell are we going to get werewolf hair?"

"Er... Yes, and I don't know."

"Gwen, come on, be serious. You've got a lot riding on this."

"I know, I know. Just let me think for a second. My mum, I'm assuming, got the hair from the enchanted woods behind our old house, but that'd take too long... Oh, my old school might have some. The Crone is an avid witch, I remember in potion class there were walls full of magical ingredients, she must have some that I can borrow."

"Okay, great. First thing tomorrow, you go get everything we need, and I'll take care of the household chores. Then, when you're back, we can brew it and sneak it into Thomas' dinner before he can even get a whiff of what we're doing."

"I think you're enjoying this witchcraft stuff a little too much," Gweneviere chuckled.

"Hey, after what he's done, he's lucky we're only taking his sex drive away, he deserves a lot worse."

"Touché," Gweneviere agreed, tipping her imaginary hat to Kambili before leaning in for another kiss, and then another, and another.

They were like giddy schoolgirls making out for the first time, and to be fair, they weren't far off that. It was only the tragedies they had both faced so early on in life that caused them to grow up so fast. This was the first time in, well, forever, that they could be the loved-up, giggling teenagers that they were meant to be.

The presence of each other's bodies being intertwined with one another brought about a relaxing atmosphere that allowed them to sleep like logs all night.

The next morning, the girls woke up spooning one another, though who the big spoon was can stay their secret. They made sure to get up and ready before Thomas could awaken and have a chance to catch them together. They went about their morning as usual, as to not raise any suspicions about their plan. Not that Thomas would've had the brain capacity at five in the morning to work out that they were planning to make a potion to take away his libido. It was quite the obscure plot, and quite frankly only a fellow witch would be able to decipher it. He certainly was not a witch, nor Sherlock Holmes, as he went to work as clueless as always.

Once Thomas was out of the way, Gweneviere grabbed her satchel and was ready to head out.

"Hey, you're forgetting something," Kambili called out, as Gweneviere's hand grasped the doorknob.

"What?" Gweneviere turned around, puzzled. She checked

her bag, before looking back at Kambili; she was sure she had everything.

"This." Kambili smiled with a raised eyebrow as she waltzed over to Gweneviere and planted a kiss on her lips.

"Ah, yes, how could I forget." Gweneviere smiled back as their lips slowly separated.

"Right, you are free to go now," Kambili said, reluctantly, as she smacked her lips together, lovingly savouring their kiss. She could still taste the honey on Gweneviere's lips from her porridge, and it was deliciously sweet. "Oh, and don't forget to pick up dinner ingredients, too!" Kambili shouted, as Gweneviere closed the door, just managing to hear her on her way out.

Gweneviere left the house with an uncontrollable grin slapped across her face that stretched from ear to ear. For a moment, she felt like she was living her dream life. After all, if Thomas hadn't existed, this would be the life that she'd be living with Kambili. With cute goodbye kisses every morning as both of them went to work. At least that day would be another step closer, if the potion worked, that was.

Gwenevicre headed out on her mission to source some alpha werewolf fur, or hair – she wasn't sure what the correct term was – from the Crone's school. She hadn't seen the Crone since graduation, and she was rather dubious of how their encounter would go. It was no surprise that Gweneviere wasn't exactly happy with the husband that graduation had lumbered her with and felt resentment towards the Crone for reassuring her that everything would be okay. Though, Gweneviere also had no idea how kindly the Crone would take to lending her the ingredient if she knew what Gweneviere was planning to do to one of the Crone's chosen men of London. Nevertheless, it was the only option Gweneviere had, as she didn't have time to go back to the enchanted woods. Not to mention that the last time she was there was when her father brutally murdered another werewolf, so it wasn't exactly a happy place for Gweneviere to return to. Besides, she probably would have gotten lost trying to find a tuft of magical fur amongst a whole forest full of strange and dangerous creatures. Even if she did muster up the courage to go back, Thomas would never allow her to go on such a trip without any good reason. No, it would seem that the Crone was inevitably, and annoyingly, her only option.

As Gweneviere neared the Crone's school, she had almost forgotten that the streets surrounding it were full of dirty men looking for a good time. As she passed the old tavern she used to work at, a rebellious tear left her eye. She couldn't help but think back to the day her dad saved her from that grotesque man, Robbie.

If only he saw who I'm with now, Gweneviere pondered, as she shuddered at the thought of Thomas' touch. He would have surely never let a sleaze ball like Thomas lay a finger on his daughter. She'd have given anything to have her overbearing father back in her life, even if just for a day. She'd hug him so tight that he would practically die all over again, and she'd tell him how much she missed him and her mother, and that she was sorry she failed them both. Gweneviere, whether for hours at a time or just a few fleeting minutes, thought about it every day; she was almost drowning in guilt. They both died under

Gweneviere's watch, not that it should have ever fallen on her to be their saviours in the first place, alas, it did, and she felt like she failed them. A future with Kambili was the only thing keeping her afloat. Gweneviere couldn't wait for a new, kinder world to arise where they could live their lives authentically and unapologetically, and for the dark, rotted one in which they purely existed in, to perish.

Arriving at the school doors, Gweneviere knocked, and just as quickly as she did, a young girl answered. She was so rapid to respond that it was almost as if she was just waiting by the door for the next person to knock. Or perhaps she knew of Gweneviere's arrival, but that couldn't be possible, could it? It was a pretty, blonde girl who reminded Gweneviere of Poppy, but much younger.

"What do you want, then?" the girl asked, abruptly, with no regard for who Gweneviere was.

Gweneviere was slightly taken back as she liked to think that her fire abilities had given her a little fame amongst the pupils of the school. Even Gweneviere was sure that she'd seen the young girl about the school before, but clearly the girl had no more a memory of Gweneviere than she did of what she had for dinner last week.

"My name is Gweneviere, and I've come to see the Crone. I'm an *ex*-pupil," Gweneviere stated.

"Hmm, wait here, then," the young Londoner replied, as she slammed the door in Gweneviere's face.

Gweneviere waited patiently until she began to hear an unintelligible whisper coming from behind the door. It was clear this time that it wasn't her mother's voice she was hearing, and it *wasn't* in her head. She edged closer, pressing her left ear to the door to try and make out any words that were being conversed, but she simply couldn't hear them well enough to put together anything of use. Suddenly the door handle jiggled, and Gweneviere popped back into her position, just in time, to not look like she was eavesdropping. The young girl reappeared, only opening the door ajar, giving Gweneviere a dodgy look up and down with squinted, judging eyes, before confirming to Gweneviere that the Crone wasn't home.

"You want me to pass on a message?" the girl asked, clearly not interested in whatever it was that Gweneviere had to say.

"Er, no, it's okay, there might be someone else who can help me. Any of the teachers or senior students, actually, I just need a potion ingredient. Some alpha werewolf fur, or hair, whatever the correct term is."

"It's fur, and I'll go check if we can lend you any."

The girl rolled her eyes at Gweneviere's lack of potion brewing knowledge. Though Gweneviere had taken potion classes, she had never exactly been one of the top students. Her potion brewing skills went alongside nicely with her non-existent cooking skills. Thankfully, Kambili would be there to assist in any culinary expertise needed for the potion.

"Than—" Gweneviere attempted, before the door was once again slammed in her face. The loud slamming was starting to warrant unsolicited attention from the local inebriated men, thus Gweneviere was hoping to get out rather shortly. If not, she'd be obliged to set some alcohol-soaked men alight like a Molotov cocktail.

The girl popped out once more. "Here you are, then."

Gweneviere was busy keeping an eye on the zombie-like alcoholics walking about the street, when she heard the girls voice. The girl handed Gweneviere a vial with a large tuft of fur pressing up against the sides.

"Oh, thank you..." Gweneviere paused with a raised eyebrow, hinting at the girl to reveal her name, but clearly the girl had no time for Gweneviere's nuisance politeness as she closed the door and Gweneviere heard the many locks click.

Well, that was weird. Clearly she hasn't begun her etiquette classes yet, Gweneviere thought, as she walked down the street, weaving in and out of the drunken men like they were gates in a ski slalom. What Gweneviere didn't know, however, was that the Crone was indeed in. *She* was the second voice that Gweneviere couldn't quite make out behind the door. Oblivious to that fact, Gweneviere carried on her day as she made her way to the market, closer to home, and away from all the estranged men.

After filling her satchel with food for dinner and the remaining herbs needed for the potion, Gweneviere headed home. She had only managed to get mutton for their evening meal, as she had to spend so much more money on the potion ingredients. Kambili would have to really put her cooking abilities to the test to make a meal that Thomas would deem as decent enough for him to eat.

As Gweneviere arrived home, she opened the front door and called out for Kambili. Kambili popped her head around the kitchen doorway like a meerkat, though she was looking for something far sweeter than a predator. She was on the lookout for Gweneviere, her unofficial girlfriend.

"That was quicker than I thought," Kambili exclaimed, upon seeing Gweneviere's radiant face.

"Hey, I can go out for a few more hours, if you want?" Gweneviere teased.

"Shut up and get over here," Kambili said, grinning playfully.

"In all honesty, I didn't get to spend as much time at the school as I thought. In fact, they didn't even let me through the door. But I got everything we need, so I'll take that as a win. Also, you've not got much to work with for dinner, so I'm going to need you to work some magic of your own on that, too."

"Well, I guess it's a good job that's my area of expertise. Now, come on, I want to get my witch on," Kambili exclaimed, making Gweneviere chuckle at her inherent cuteness.

Gweneviere followed an excitable Kambili into the kitchen, where she had already laid out all the equipment needed for the potion. There was a large pot with the correctly premeasured amount of water in it, along with some of the herbs they already had in the pantry bedside it. The final ingredient was also there: a hair from one of Thomas' undergarments, which Kambili had reluctantly retrieved. Gweneviere had only told her about it that morning in bed. Not quite the pillow talk that one looks forward to. It was also quite the daring task for Kambili to carry out. It was bad enough she had to wash his clothes on a regular basis, especially when he clearly didn't know how to wipe himself after using the toilet, but to then have to source out a pubic hair, amongst all of the sweat and literal shit, was another level of torture. Though, if it helped

Gweneviere stay clear of his sexual deviances, then Kambili definitely knew it was worth it.

"Oh, wow, you're really prepared, aren't you?" Gweneviere said, amazed.

"Mmhmm."

"Right, well then, let's get started."

Gweneviere began by summoning fire beneath the large pot to get the water to a roaring boil. They then started adding the ingredients one by one: a cracking of black pepper, a pinch of cloves, a sprinkling of dried hemlock petals, and a handful of mint to disguise the otherwise vile flavour. The pot became unruly as a foggy mist began to spill over the sides. Kambili's eyes were wide open, loving every second of it. The final ingredients were the werewolf fur and Thomas' pubic hair.

"Would you care to do the honours?" Gweneviere offered.

"I'd love to," Kambili answered ecstatically, until she remembered that she'd have to touch Thomas' hair again. "Hey, you just didn't want to touch this, did you?" she said, waving around the curly strand.

Gweneviere kept quiet and averted her eyes suspiciously, playing into the mischief. Kambili waved it closer to Gweneviere's face, causing her to flinch and Kambili to laugh.

"Okay, I'm sorry, I just really didn't want to touch it."

"It's fine." Kambili smiled, lovingly rolling her eyes.

As Kambili dropped the remaining ingredients into the pot, a plume of green smoke rose from it like a baby mushroom cloud. Gweneviere checked back in the book to see if that was supposed to happen; low and behold, it was, and it signified that the spell was complete. They began to decant the potion, filling up an empty wine bottle from the night before, and hid it at the back of the cleaning cupboard in the kitchen, somewhere that Thomas would definitely never look.

Later that evening, Thomas arrived home from work and the girls were applying the finishing touches to dinner, especially Thomas' portion. Although the recipe had specified only to use a single drop in each meal, Gweneviere didn't want to be a guinea pig as to whether her magics would pay off or not, especially knowing the consequences if it didn't work. So, she decided to add a generous glug to the dish. It was enough to make a catholic rabbit, the size of an elephant, celibate. They placed the meal before him and awkwardly watched as he began to tuck in with no hesitation. However, not long after he started, he pulled a face.

Oh god, I put too much in, he can tell something's wrong! Shit, what am I going to do? Gweneviere rambled to herself.

"What meat is this?" he asked.

"Mutton, sorry, it's all they had left at the market," Gweneviere lied.

"Hmm, very well, make sure you get there earlier next time, then. I don't work long, hard hours for this shit," he spat, before digging straight back into his meal.

Clearly Kambili had indeed worked some magic of her own to make the meal still edible for him, which was lucky, as if he hadn't eaten it, then the potion would've become redundant altogether.

"Yes, of course, sorry again," Gweneviere apologised, laying it on thick as to not distract him from eating.

After that, it didn't take him long to wolf down the rest of his dinner without any further suspicions. Now Gweneviere just had to hope that the potion had done the trick.

After dinner, while the girls were tidying up the table, Thomas was sat in his chair with a whiskey in hand. This was usually when the catcalling would begin, as he would be slightly drunk and carelessly groping Gweneviere until she submitted to him. To their surprise, however, he simply bade the girls a good night before heading to his bedroom, alone, without even so much as a disgruntled look.

It, of course, could've been a fluke, but as they proceeded to spike his dinner for the following weeks, it continued to work. It seemed that he no longer had any interest in pawing after Gweneviere's body. With the lack of sexual frustration rattling around in Thomas' brain, he had somehow become nicer in general, still not nice by a normal human's standards, just less of a piece of human trash.

The weeks of peace in the evenings meant that Gweneviere could finally begin to heal. Her and Kambili would enjoy late nights together with wine and cheese after Thomas was abed. They got to know each other on a deeper level, with Gweneviere confessing to Kambili the guilt she felt about her parents passing, as well as sharing her happy memories of them. Kambili loved hearing the tales of Gweneviere's old family life, it was comforting, in a way, as she'd never had the classic family dynamic herself. Gweneviere kept trying to ready herself to slowly become more intimate with Kambili again, until one night she was indeed ready.

After a usual evening meal Thomas retired to bed early. Gweneviere placed an enchantment on the remainder of the cleaning up and dragged Kambili to what they now referred to as their room. They had both been dreaming of the moment that they could finally enjoy each other's bodies after so long, and now that Gweneviere was ready, there was no holding back. They quickly ripped off layers of each other's garments and ridiculous corsets until there was nothing left but the beauty of Gweneviere's ivory complexion, and Kambili's deep ebony skin. Gweneviere's body had finally freed itself of the bruising that Thomas had caused, meaning that there was no longer a physical reminder of his touch. They climbed onto the bed and playfully threw the covers over their heads, kissing each other in the darkness, often missing their lips and butting noses. Their hands glided along each other's curves, both gently grasping one another in their hands.

It was everything Gweneviere had imagined sex should feel like – sweet, tender, and loving. Nothing like what Thomas did, which was selfish and cruel.

With her eyes closed, Gweneviere went in for another kiss but missed Kambili completely this time. She opened her eyes to see Kambili's face level with her breasts. Kambili dropped her lips onto them as she softly nuzzled her face against them before slowly working her way down Gweneviere's body with nothing but her tongue. Kambili reached between Gweneviere's thighs and kissed her, making her whole body shiver and tingle. Gweneviere lightly placed her hand on the top of Kambili's head to let her know she was doing all the right things – Kambili already knew that, from the moans that emanated from Gweneviere's mouth. Kambili dipped her tongue inside Gweneviere and began flickering it faster than a candle flame in the wind. She was hitting just the right spot, and Gweneviere was getting hot and sweaty to the touch as her body thrashed about in pleasure. Kambili gently covered Gweneviere's mouth as her *pleasure* might've been loud enough to wake Thomas. Gweneviere certainly didn't mind having Kambili's soft fingers covering her lips. Kambili used her other hand to pleasure herself, slipping her fingers inside. She became in rhythm with Gweneviere, and she brought them both to a harmonious climax. Gweneviere was in a euphoric state, they both were. Neither of them had experienced anything like it. Kambili had some experience pleasuring herself before, but even she had no idea that she was capable of doing that for them both. Gweneviere was extremely grateful as Kambili arose from beneath the sheets to greet Gweneviere's face once more.

"That was incredible," Gweneviere panted, almost out of breath.

"*You're* incredible." Kambili smiled back, also breathless.

The two of them fell asleep wrapped up in each other's arms. It was the best night sleep either of them had ever had.

CHAPTER 9
The Poppy Predicament

The next morning Gweneviere woke to the cute sound of Kambili's snoring. As she laid there watching Kambili's face squished against the pillow, Gweneviere knew she was falling for her. Not even the high-pitched steam train whistle emanating from her nostril could put Gweneviere off. Gweneviere didn't want their blossoming love to be forever in the shadow of Thomas, and knew she needed to come up with a plan to get out soon. They deserved to be free. They deserved each other.

Gweneviere woke Kambili by showering her exposed cheek with kisses, then softly whispering her name into her ear. Kambili rubbed her eyes awake and began shivering a little. Even though it was summertime, Kambili seemed to be one of those people who was always a little cold. Gweneviere noticed Kambili's wincing, chilly face and pulled her in for hug. Due to her powers, Gweneviere was like a human radiator, therefore their bodies complimented each other rather nicely.

They stayed in the warmth of their embrace until one of them heard Thomas coughing himself awake – probably choking on his own drool. As they heard him begin to shuffle about his room, they sighed, knowing that it was time for Kambili to leave and pretend like nothing had happened. It was truly the worst part of their day, but they knew it had to be done not to raise any suspicions.

The rest of the day played out rather normally, Thomas went off to work in the bakery, and the girls went to the market for the day's dinner and completed all their chores. Upon completing their errands, there was a knock on the front door. Neither of them was expecting anyone, especially not Kambili, as being a slave meant she had no means of making any friends of her own.

Gweneviere crept up to the door and tried to peer through the keyhole. At first, all she could see was a man in shorts, but as he impatiently wriggled around and knocked once more, Gweneviere caught a glimpse of his hand. She saw a letter in it. Gweneviere opened the door and smiled at the postman, who wasn't keen on the fact he'd been kept waiting.

"Hello," Gweneviere exclaimed.

"Special letter delivery for a Mrs Gweneviere Farriner," the postman said.

"Yes... I am she." Gweneviere smiled back, though she hated the fact that her letters had to be addressed to her as Gweneviere *Farriner*. That'd be the first thing she'd change once they'd escaped Thomas.

"Great, here you go," he mumbled, handing Gweneviere the letter and turning on his heels before she could even say thank you. Clearly, he was a very busy postman, unless he was just rude.

"What is it, Gwen?" Kambili called out.

"A letter for me, I think it's from Poppy," she replied, closing and locking the door behind her.

"Oh, your old school friend, right?" Kambili asked, remembering her name in one of the stories that Gweneviere had shared with her during their pillow talk.

"Yeah," Gweneviere answered, wasting no time in tearing open the envelope.

Dear Gwen,

I assure you there is no need to refer to me as anything but Poppy. The whole 'Lady Hammersmith' title is really rather dramatic, though, it does make me sound like a princess sometimes, and I do like that.

I'm truly sorry married life hasn't gone well for you thus far, and that Thomas does sound like a right knob. I wish I could tell you that my life is but a mirror of your own and that I hate it, alas, my husband has indeed been amazing. He treats me so kindly and really values my opinions, which is hard to come by. He also treats me like a very naughty girl when he needs to, if you catch my drift.

Anyway, enough about that, I'm so glad you wrote to me. I had been debating sending you a letter for a while, but I just didn't know where to start, so thank you for making the brave first step.

Now then, I have spoken to my husband and discussed your situation with him, and he has graciously agreed that you can come stay with us anytime you like. Whenever you need a break from him, just come on down, and we will put you up in one the guest bedrooms. So, please don't suffer alone, and come see me soon. I really do miss you, Gwen, some days I'd give anything to have another night in our dormitory together playing tricks with the twins. Besides, none of my new fancy friends are as fun as you are.

Lots of love,
Poppy

P.S. You are welcome anytime except between the 10th and 17th of August, as were swanning off to Cornwall. How exciting!

"What does it say?" Kambili asked, as Gweneviere had silently read it at least twice by now.

"It just says that she's really happy and that I should go visit her. Though, I obviously won't be able to do that." Gweneviere tried to hide her disappointment.

"Why not?"

"Well, I can't leave you alone with *him*," Gweneviere answered, with a deathly look to the door joining the house to the bakery.

"Gwen, I'll be fine. I can handle a few days' worth of chores on my own. In regard to *him,* I'll just make sure that I keep him topped up on our little potion until you're back," Kambili said, in a bid to reassure Gweneviere. After everything she'd been through, she deserved it.

"Are you sure? I don't want you to do this just to be nice to me," Gweneviere asked.

"Of course, I'm only doing it for you. I mean, no one in their right mind actually wants to be alone with Thomas, but the point is you do stuff like that for your *girlfriend.*" Kambili smiled.

"Girlfriend, huh?"

"Yeah," Kambili replied, confidently.

"I didn't know that you were ready to be my *girlfriend*," Gweneviere teased.

"Hey, you're the one who's still got a husband," Kambili joked, causing them both to laugh.

"Yes, well, I promise that after my visit to Poppy, that will all change."

Kambili simply responded with a hopeful smile. Of course, she wanted nothing more than to live with Gweneviere somewhere far, far away from there, but she also didn't want to set her hopes on dreams and fairytales that may never come true. Though, she did live in a world where magic existed, so anything was possible.

When Thomas returned home from work, Gweneviere filled him in on her plan to take a trip to see Poppy. She didn't leave much room for questions, and had already explained that Kambili was happy to take on the extra workload for a few days, but Thomas did have one major question in an attempt to throw a spanner in the works.

"Who is going to start up the bakery while you're gone? Kambili's a half decent cook and cleaner but she's no witch! I need my bakery operational," he said with a smug grin, thinking he had foiled Gweneviere's plan.

Gweneviere paused for a moment before realising the answer was much simpler than she had imagined. "Easy, I'll just leave the spell active, it should last for a few days, as long as you don't put it out manually," she responded, with a rather smug look of her own as she stood, folding her arms and dropping her hip, contently knowing she'd answered his only query.

"Fine," he grunted, crossing his arms in frustration.

Later that night, Gweneviere packed a bag and was ready to set off on her journey come sunrise. She had arranged a carriage to take her all the way to Poppy's estate using Thomas' extra profits, which he couldn't have made without her, of course.

Gweneviere laid beside Kambili in bed and double checked that she was going to be okay without her.

"Are you sure you don't mind me going? It's not too late, I won't go if you don't want me to, just say the word."

"Gwen, shh. It's okay. I'll miss you, obviously, but it's only a couple of days. I'll survive," Kambili assured her, calming Gweneviere's slight frantic state. Kambili was great at that.

"Yeah... I know. Oh, by the way, I found this spell in my mother's book that you can use to contact me if anything happens while I'm away."

"Ooh, more spells. You know, I could really get used to this whole having-a-witch-for-a-girlfriend thing. We may have to start a coven together," Kambili joked. Though, on a more serious note, she would've actually been open to the idea.

"Okay," Gweneviere chuckled. "One day we will start our own coven. Now then, I copied this symbol from my mum's book so that you can actually see it. All you have to do is draw the symbol on your palm with your finger and think clearly of me when you do it."

"What will that do?"

"It's like an emergency calling. When you do it, it will sear a raised rash into my palm in the design of the rune. Then I'll know you're in trouble," Gweneviere explained, showing Kambili the rune drawn onto a piece of parchment.

"Oh, so it's a one and done kind of thing, not for sending cute goodnight messages," Kambili said, in jest. "Also, that sounds like it's going to be painful for you. Why can't it just burn something into Thomas' hand instead, surely you'd be able to smell the searing bacon even from Poppy's house," Kambili said, almost causing Gweneviere to wail in laughter. "But seriously, won't it hurt you?" Kambili asked, once the laughter had died down to a cute smile on both their faces.

"Well, it wouldn't come close to the pain of losing you, so in the grand scheme of things it's most definitely worth it." Gweneviere smiled, gazing lovingly into Kambili's eyes.

"Aw, that's so sweet," Kambili teased, giving Gweneviere a swift kiss on the cheek.

"Alright, alright, now, come on, we need to test it out to make sure it works. Draw the rune on your palm and concentrate on me when you do it."

"Okay," Kambili agreed, enthusiastically.

Kambili began slowly drawing the symbol on her palm, making sure to meticulously match every stroke. Once she had completed it, they waited a minute or two and watched Gweneviere's hands – nothing appeared. Her hands remained unscathed, signifying that the spell hadn't worked. Kambili had a slight look of worry on her face as she realised that she had failed. Noticing it, Gweneviere reassured her.

"Hey, it's okay, there's plenty of spells that don't work the first time for me, and I'm an actual witch. Now that you know the symbol, try and close your eyes as you finish it and clear your mind of all thoughts except those of me. Let your mind express its desire to see me," Gweneviere explained, feeling extremely cheesy as she said it.

"Okay, I'll try." Kambili once again drew the symbol on her palm, following the exact path she did before. This time, however, as she came to the last few strokes, she closed her eyes and thought of all the happy moments they had shared together. Keeping those in the forefront of her mind and imagining seeing Gweneviere's return from her trip, she completed the rune. After a mere few seconds, she heard Gweneviere wince in pain. Opening her eyes, she saw Gweneviere's palm searing with a red bubbling rash raising from her skin. It was truly disturbing to look at, but Gweneviere assured Kambili she was okay; it was worth it to know that the spell worked.

"Gwen, are you sure you're okay?"

"Yeah, I'll be all right, the main thing is that it worked. Promise me you won't hesitate to use it if something happens. Now, I'm not teleporting there because, well, I don't know where it is, and I need to at least have an idea of where I'm going to use the teleportation spell. But I can certainly use it to come back in a jiffy if anything happens to you," Gweneviere professed, seriously.

"Yes, I promise, though I'm quite sure I'll be fine." Kambili smiled, stroking the side of Gweneviere's cheek to once again calm her. Taking her calming touch a step further, Kambili took Gweneviere's searing palm and sensually kissed it. The tender touch sent Gweneviere's eyes rolling into the back of her head. Kambili carried on kissing it gently in order to not hurt her. She glided her tongue up one of Gweneviere's fingers before sliding it into her mouth. She released it, only to do the same to the next finger along. Gweneviere couldn't resist the playful teasing any longer as she pulled Kambili in for a passionate kiss. They became, once again, intertwined in one another's bodies, and spent the following hours reaching climax after climax. Their hands trailed across each other, as did their lips, making the most of their last night together – for a couple of days, at least – though you'd have thought it was their last night on earth. They pleasured each other deep into the night until finally they passed out, with Kambili folding up nicely in Gweneviere's arms, which kept her warm.

The morning of Gweneviere's departure had arrived, and she started up the bakery hoping that her theory was right and that it would stay alight for next few days. Upon returning to the house, Thomas brushed past her as he headed into the bakery without so much as a goodbye, not that she expected anything more. Kambili, on the other hand, stood with her arms wide open, ready to receive a lasting hug from Gweneviere.

"Hey, we could always say *goodbye* in the bedroom," Kambili suggested, with a sultry wink as Gweneviere edged closer to her open arms.

"God, Kambili, don't tempt me. You know my carriage is already outside waiting."

"I know," Kambili sighed, with a forlorn expression on her face.

Gweneviere finally reached her and embraced Kambili tightly. "I'm going to miss you."

"I'm going to miss you too," Kambili exclaimed, pulling out of the hug so that she could plant her lips against Gweneviere's.

Gweneviere ended the kiss with a smile, rubbing Kambili's arms for reassurance. "I'll see you in a couple days, okay?"

"Yeah, okay. Have fun, and have some fun for me, too."

"I will, and I promise everything will be different soon," Gweneviere vowed, with a peck on Kambili's forehead before heading out on her trip.

Gweneviere set off in the back of her carriage, where she would journey for just over four hours to Poppy's house. Not far from the outskirts of London, Gweneviere couldn't help but notice the beautiful meadows that littered the land. She made sure to take a mental note of where they were, as it would surely make the most romantic place for a picnic with Kambili upon her return. She could imagine it so vividly: both of them sitting together, with a wicker basket on a checked tablecloth amongst the plumes of multi-coloured wildflowers. She'd lived in the grey, cramped city streets for so long by that point that she hardly remembered what life was like back in the country. Though the people were no better, she did miss being amongst the wildlife and nature. She could quite happily see herself and Kambili in a farmhouse, much like her parent's, but hopefully without the hateful, incompetent men waltzing about the town. No, Gweneviere would definitely try take her father's advice and live somewhere even further from a town, unlike her mother. Gweneviere didn't need pesky locals ruining everything. She was more than happy for it to just be her and Kambili for miles around.

The rest of Gweneviere's journey was pretty boring; she even nodded off at times. After all, she didn't exactly get a lot of sleep the night before, but not for the same reasons as her many sleepless nights in Thomas' bed.

The carriage came to an abrupt stop as they arrived, waking Gweneviere from her snooze as she was thrown across the carriage, almost headbutting the other side. Luckily for the driver, Gweneviere wasn't like most socialite ladies, who would have probably had him fired for such insolence. She dusted herself off and sat back up to see Poppy through the carriage window. Coincidentally, Poppy was just by the front door, attending to some flowerbeds full of precious little petunias at the entrance. Once she noticed the carriage she jumped up with excitement. She couldn't have officially known it was Gweneviere, but she could sense it. Gweneviere descended the two deep steps coming from the carriage door, and landed on her feet amongst the gravel driveway.

"Gwen!" Poppy exclaimed, wiping her soil-covered hands against her pink floral dress.

"Poppy!"

They ran towards each other like the giddy schoolgirls that they had so recently been.

"I've missed you so much," Poppy mumbled into Gweneviere's ear as they hugged. "I'm so glad you took me up on my offer."

"I hope you don't think I've come too early, it's just as soon as I read your letter, I arranged travel for the next day, I was too excited to wait." Gweneviere laughed awkwardly.

"No, of course not! I'm more than happy to see you so soon, and I'm sure we already have a lot more to tell each other since we wrote those letters."

"Well, I definitely have some exciting news to tell you."

"Ooh, I can't wait. I'll show you to your room and let you settle in while I finish up a couple of personal errands and my gardening. Then, we can have a proper catch up with a cuppa."

"Sounds great," Gweneviere said, lugging her bag through the gravel.

"Oh, come here, I'll take that, don't worry," Poppy offered, and with a wave of her hand the bag floated on behind her with ease.

Poppy guided Gweneviere through the mansion, which could easily put even Gerald and Agatha's to shame.

"Wow, this house is amazing, Poppy. You've really landed on your feet, huh?"

"Yeah... I, er, got lucky, I guess," Poppy said, with less chipperness in her voice than usual.

"Are you alright?" Gweneviere asked, having noticed the shift in Poppy's tone. She wondered if Poppy perhaps felt guilty for rubbing her luxurious lifestyle in her face. But she was only there due to luck, right? If things at graduation had played out differently, then Poppy could've ended up with Thomas. Gweneviere shuddered at the thought.

"Yes. Yes, of course, I can't wait to have a proper chat later," Poppy chirped, trying to fill her voice with joy once more.

They ascended a grand spiralling staircase inside one of the many turrets of the manor house and began walking down a long and wide hall that seemed to go on forever. As they reached one of the doors, quite far down, Poppy opened it and let them in.

"Well, here we are, your humble abode for the foreseeable. I hope it's to your liking."

"To my liking? It's practically a bloody palace! Yes, I can safely say that this will do very nicely. Thanks again," Gweneviere said as she slowly spun around, trying to take in every inch of the room.

There was a huge four corner post bed with ridiculous amounts of plush pink blankets, duvets, and cushions, far more than any one person could need. It was clear that Poppy had designed this room; pink was her favourite. There was a darling little dresser table, and even the ceiling was adorned with a cornice, wrapping around every edge, carved meticulously to look like growing vines and flowers. Yes, this would do indeed.

"Right, well, I'll go finish my errands and I'll meet you in the drawing room around three-ish?" Poppy proposed to a still dazzled Gweneviere.

"Yeah, sure. If I can find the drawing room, that is," Gweneviere joked.

"Don't worry, it's not hiding." Poppy laughed, awkwardly, then headed back downstairs to finish her gardening, leaving Gweneviere to get acquainted with her room.

Gweneviere leapt onto the cloud-like bed, which almost enveloped her as she did so. The mattress was much nicer than any at Thomas' house – especially his own, as it had large dent in it where his lump of a body slept. Though, all Gweneviere could think about as she let herself get swallowed up by the bed, was how amazing it would be if Kambili was there too. They could surely get up to a lot more *fun* on a bed like this.

Gweneviere didn't see the point in unpacking, she would only be there for two days, and so decided to just lay her bag out on the floor. She also wanted to be prepared to make a fast exit, should Kambili use the emergency palm spell, something that Gweneviere couldn't help but find herself keep checking for. Although she knew the pain alone would be enough to draw her attention to it, she didn't want to risk missing anything, even the slightest blemish that might occur from a possible failed attempt. She had one last look before trying to ease her mind for a little while. Gweneviere knew Kambili could look after herself for a couple days and that she definitely wouldn't have wanted Gweneviere to spend her whole time away worrying.

After an hour or two passed by, it was almost three o'clock. Gweneviere had spent most of her time wandering about the grounds of the house, enjoying the beautiful gardens that Poppy had so lovingly tended to. She came to a central area with a handmade bench, that she could only assume Poppy's perfect husband had made with his bare hands. Sadly, she hadn't seen him around yet; hopefully he'd be there at dinner, as it would be a nice change to have a bit of eye candy in the guise of a man. She still cared for Kambili, of course, and would never act upon such lusts, but it was still nice to do a little 'window shopping', as Gweneviere would often think to herself.

She sat basking in the afternoon summer sun – most pale

Londoners would've already cowered into the shade, as they were used to the smog covered skies of London protecting them from the sun's UV rays. Gweneviere, on the other hand, could more than take the heat. She lived for it, and it didn't take much to give her skin a healthy glow and tan, though apparently pale was all the rage at the time. Gweneviere's tan would've probably been seen more as a sign of poverty, not that Gweneviere cared.

Soon enough, teatime came around and Gweneviere left the gardens for the house, where she began exploring all the rooms in search for her destination. There were rooms full of portraits, rooms full of taxidermy, and even a room with a singular piano in the centre. Eventually, Gweneviere found her way to the drawing room, at least she assumed it was the drawing room, where she awaited Poppy's company. Shortly after, Poppy arrived, with a floating tea set beside her.

"Do you not have a butler?" Gweneviere asked, intrigued.

"Yes, but I'm still not quite used to the whole being-waited-on thing. Besides, who needs a butler when I can do this?" Poppy smirked, pointing towards her floating tea set.

"Speaking of which, do the staff know you're a witch?" Gweneviere asked, assuming surely someone about the house would have seen Poppy's floating inanimate objects.

"Yes, they do. I'm rather lucky in that respect, too. My husband sourced out decent, open-minded human beings to work for us."

"Are they paid?" Gweneviere asked, testing the waters.

"Why of course they are, silly. What else would they... Oh, you wanted to know if we had any slaves. Thankfully, no.

He's too kind of a man to enforce anything as barbaric as that. No, each of our staff have a complimentary bedroom onsite, for when they need it, and are all paid rather decently, if I do say so myself, so that they can support their families," Poppy explained.

"Well, I must admit, that is refreshing to hear. I wish everyone with a bit of money was as classy as the *Hammersmiths*," she teased.

"Yes, well, enough about me, come on, what's this exciting news you have for me?" Poppy sweetly demanded.

"To cut a long story short, I'm in love. Her name's Kambili, and she's just wonderful. I love everything about her. She's kind, beautiful, funny, and strong-minded..." Gweneviere's face lit up uncontrollably as she described Kambili.

"Wow... that is certainly not what I was expecting. I mean, I knew about your preferences but... I guess I just didn't think you'd ever follow through with it."

"Are you not happy for me?"

"No, of course I'm happy for you. I just don't want to see you get hurt, is all. Besides, she sounds a lot like you, so I suppose you're rather well matched. I bet even I'd struggle to get a word in edge ways with the two of you," Poppy joked, reassuring Gweneviere that she was indeed supportive.

"Oh shush," Gweneviere chuckled.

"But, in all honesty, if she makes you happy, then I'm really happy for you, Gwen." Poppy smiled.

"Thanks... though there is once slight hitch," Gweneviere added, knowing it was more of a tree in the road rather than a slight hitch.

"Have you not told her that you're a witch?" Poppy asked, with wide eyes, before taking a sip of her piping hot tea.

"No, no, it's not that. To be honest, I think she enjoys that I'm a witch a little too much." Gweneviere smiled to herself as she thought of how excited Kambili always seemed about her magic.

"What's is it, then?"

"She's Thomas' slave," Gweneviere confessed.

Poppy's face froze for a second as she tried to digest the information. "Oh, I see... that is quite the predicament. Still, Gwen, if you love this girl, then you need to follow your heart! Do whatever it takes to be with her. Sod Thomas and his backwards views," Poppy insisted.

"Thanks. You know... I really think she's the one. I've been managing to put some money aside for myself and save up. As soon as I have enough, I'm going to take her and get out of there for good."

"I really hope it works out for you."

"Are you going to cry? You big softy," Gweneviere chuckled, though she was beginning to feel rather emotional herself.

Poppy remained silent as they leant into a hug.

"Well, it's nice to see that some things never change," Gweneviere added, twiddling the pink-checked cloth tying back Poppy's hair.

Poppy smiled, still a little teary eyed. "Yes... it is."

Later in the evening, Gweneviere spent the night around

the dining table with Poppy and her extremely handsome husband. They ate, drank, and played silly dinner party games. Gweneviere was enjoying herself so much, but when she caught a glimpse of her open palm clear from any rash, she soured slightly, as she wished that Kambili was also there to enjoy it with her. Poppy's husband brought Gweneviere out of her pitying trance as he offered her and Kambili a place to stay should they ever need it. Poppy had told him of Gweneviere's predicament and, of course, being the perfect, kind, open man he was, he had no qualms with offering Gweneviere salvation. She thanked him greatly, though hoped they'd be able to make a life for themselves without the charitable help. Gweneviere, in that regard, was rather stubborn, taking after both parents. She didn't think she deserved help after letting her parents down, but she *was* determined to get her and Kambili's life on track.

Gweneviere stayed one more day to try and make the most of her visit, before heading back home. She couldn't bring herself to be apart from Kambili any longer, especially knowing she was alone with Thomas.

"Thank you for the last two days, Poppy, I've really needed them. I'm so happy that you got your happy ending with your *delicious* husband. I hope that soon I can live my dream with Kambili."

"No, thank you for coming, Gweneviere. I hope that for you, too," Poppy said, looking slightly deflated. "I'll be sure to come visit you too at some point," she added, trying to perk herself up.

"Oh god, don't bother. It's a dump compared to this place. I definitely don't mind being the one to travel," Gweneviere said, causing them both to chuckle.

"Well, I guess it's goodbye, for now." Poppy smiled.

"Yeah, I guess so."

They embraced one last time and pecked one another on the cheek, before Poppy used her magic to help load Gweneviere's bag into the carriage. She returned to the doorsteps of her mansion and waved the carriage off.

Once Gweneviere was too far away to make out, another figure appeared beside Poppy. They had slipped through the door and waited beside her patiently, until Poppy turned and jolted in surprise at the Crone's sudden appearance.

"Well?" the Crone croaked.

"Well, what?" Poppy huffed.

"Don't talk back to me, young lady. This nice life I have given you can just as easily be taken away from you," the Crone wickedly reminded. "Now, is she on the right track?"

Poppy sighed. "Yes, I believe so."

"Very good. You know what you have to do next."

"Do we really have to do it? Hasn't she suffered enough already?"

"No! My vision was very clear, she needs to go through this to tip her over the edge in order to see in the new world."

"But even you, yourself, say that visions of the future can't always be trusted completely."

"You can't go back now, girl, we've come too far to risk it

not happening."

"Ugh, fine! When exactly do I need to do it again?" Poppy asked, through gritted teeth.

"The first of September," the Crone answered.

"Jesus, that's only three and a half weeks away. Can we not afford her happiness a little longer?" Poppy pleaded.

"No! My visions have made it very clear. It has to be that day, otherwise a butterfly effect could completely change the future that I have foreseen. Now, no more hesitations. Put the plans in motion and play your part, or else you can kiss being Mrs Hammersmith goodbye. Oh, and the fate of the world's future will be blood spilled on your hands."

The old hag began hobbling down the driveway until her body slowly melted away with the wind, teleporting herself back to the safety of her school. Poppy dropped to the sandstone step beneath her and cried. She hated the deal that she had made, she hated what she was going to have to do Gweneviere, and she hated herself.

CHAPTER 10
The Meadow

A few days had passed since Gweneviere's return home, and all had seemingly gone well while she was away. Thomas was calm enough, and Kambili had managed to keep him on his new 'diet' meaning that she didn't have to experience his wicked touch. Though, simply being in his presence was still enough to make anyone queasy. Kambili was relieved, to say the least, about Gweneviere's return. She had missed her deeply, even if it had only been about three days without her.

As they laid in bed together, after yet another successful *dishing up* of dinner, Kambili poured her heart out to Gweneviere.

"I really missed you, you know," Kambili whispered, her lips a mere inch away from Gweneviere's face as they laid on their sides facing one another.

"Hmm, really? You know, I had no idea, considering you've told me almost every hour for the last few days," Gweneviere joked lovingly.

Kambili soured in jest at Gweneviere's cheeky grin.

"But, for the record, I obviously missed you too, very much

so." Gweneviere smiled, before breathing a sigh of relief. "In all honesty, I'm just glad that you were safe while I was away. I'd never forgive myself if I let something happen to you."

"Hey, don't be so hard on yourself," Kambili said, brushing her fingers through Gweneviere's hair. "I know you blame yourself for your parent's deaths, which you shouldn't, but I definitely won't let you think like that about me. If *I* do something that gets myself killed, then that's not your fault, understand?"

"Why would you even joke about that?" Gweneviere asked.

"Okay, maybe that wasn't the right way to word it, but my point still stands. You can't hold yourself solely responsible for actions that are out of your hands. You couldn't stop a whole town from trialling your mother, and you couldn't stop a nationwide plague..."

"Thanks for reminding me of all the things I can't stop," Gweneviere mumbled, rolling her eyes.

Kambili smiled, cupping Gweneviere's cheeks in her hands. "If you'd let me finish, I was about to say that what you can do, and are good at, is making me happy until the day that I do die."

"Okay, I guess that is good, but you still could've worded it better."

Deep inside, Gweneviere knew she couldn't change the way she felt about death. How could she not be responsible? After all, she was there for both events when her parents died, not to mention she let her own father kill that poor wolf pup. It seemed that death followed her wherever she went, and Gweneviere couldn't help but think that she might bring death to Kambili's door next. Gweneviere tried to snap herself out of her depressive state as she listened to Kambili's words, and focused on keeping her happy in the here and now.

"Hey, I have a surprise for you, by the way," Gweneviere said, moving even closer to Kambili's face while swiftly changing the subject of conversation.

"What?" Kambili asked, as she nuzzled her nose against Gweneviere's.

"I'm taking you out tomorrow, just the two of us."

"Gweneviere Baxter, are you courting me?" Kambili teased.

"I believe I am, yes," she answered, delicately teasing Kambili's lips with her own. She hovered her lips so close to Kambili's that she could feel the heat from her fiery skin. She gave a seductive look towards her before continuing. "When I visited Poppy I saw these beautiful meadows just outside of the city, and now that I know where they are, I can teleport us there. We can even take a *picnic*."

"That sounds delightful. But what's a picnic?" Kambili asked, having not heard of the activity.

"Oh, it's wonderful, you pack some lunchtime favourites into a wicker basket, with a blanket, and you take it with you to beautiful parts of countryside. Apparently Poppy and her husband go on them all the time."

"Well, I must admit, that does sound rather fun, and it would be nice to eat lunch somewhere other than that depressing dining table," Kambili said, flicking her eyes in the direction of the dining area.

"Yes, it will be much nicer, I can't wait!"

"Me neither, I..." Kambili wanted to tell Gweneviere that

she loved her, but hearing about the amazing day they had planned tomorrow, she thought it best to save the moment until then. Somewhere where the surroundings were almost as beautiful as the two of them. Little did Kambili know, however, that Gweneviere had very much the same feelings, and had planned to profess the same thing at the picnic.

"What were you going to say?" Gweneviere asked.

"Nothing," Kambili whispered, leaning in for a kiss.

Fed up with Gweneviere's teases, Kambili snuck her arm under Gweneviere's waist and pulled her in. As they tasted each other's lips again and again, it wasn't long before they threw the sheets over themselves, and their bodies became intertwined. They twisted and contorted their bodies to each other's pleasure all through the night, like they had every night since Gweneviere's return. Clearly, they were making up for lost time.

The next morning, Gweneviere and Kambili wasted no time in getting their daily chores done. They completed them in record time so that they could spend the best part of the day in the sun, amongst the billowing, bountiful, wild meadows.

Gweneviere used her teleportation spell, that she had now officially transcribed into her mother's spell book, to whisk herself, Kambili, and their picnic basket to the meadows. Surprisingly, as they materialised into the field full of wildflowers, Kambili didn't vomit on impact. She even managed to swivel around in circles several times to try and take in the beauty. Having spent most of her childhood locked away in an attic bedroom, she'd never seen or experienced anything as naturally stunning. Gweneviere, on the other hand, was used to the countryside; her mother would often take her on long walks through meadows just like the one she was in now. Seeing the blanket of emerald, green, and a plethora of rainbow-coloured wildflowers popping out of every inch, made Gweneviere reminiscent of her mother and their walks together, both of which she missed dearly.

Bees and butterflies scoured the low skies as they dipped in out of flowers, feasting on the buffet of pollen that was on offer. Kambili was wary of them at first, but as Gweneviere showed her that there was nothing to worry about, she soon relaxed. Embracing the wild as much as she could, Kambili decided to kick her shoes off and allow herself to feel the soft blades of grass between her toes. Gweneviere could see the radiant glow of merriment on Kambili's face which, in turn, brought out the same look on Gweneviere's, unbeknown to her.

"Come on," Gweneviere said, nudging Kambili.

As Kambili turned to Gweneviere, she grabbed her hand and held the picnic basket in the other, before leading their frolicking through the knee-high fields. They were in search of the best place to settle down and enjoy the fruitful labours of Kambili's culinary skills. Gweneviere spotted a large willow tree atop a raised hill in the centre of the meadow. It was truly picturesque, and almost too good to be true. Thankfully, in their crazy world, this one magnificent tree was indeed real. They reached it just in time for a bit of shade, as even Gweneviere was starting to feel a bit flustered in the blazing

August sunshine. The drooping limbs of the tree provided the perfect mix of shady cover and sunshine, as the broken rays filtered through the leafy branches.

Many hedge witches believed that different trees were symbolic: each channelling their own unique blend of energies. A willow tree just so happens to represent love and happiness. It also represented grief, which seemingly coincided with Gweneviere's feelings perfectly. Perhaps it was all myth, but it couldn't hurt Gweneviere to sit beneath a tree with her true love, could it?

As they laid beneath the grand willow atop their tartan blanket, the sun lit them in small, golden, illuminative spots of light in the shape of crystals. It was a truly magical and romantic setting.

They unpacked the picnic that the all-so-talented Kambili had brilliantly prepared. Gweneviere, in particular, was famished due to the energy expulsion caused by her teleportation spell. They began tucking into their luncheon feast, though Gweneviere attacked it with considerably more ferocity than Kambili. Gweneviere groaned appreciatively as she became ingulfed in the orgasmic food.

"Oh God, Kambili, this food is amazing." Gweneviere moaned again as she took another mouthful of food.

Kambili couldn't help but chuckle at Gweneviere's over the top reaction, although her food *was* phenomenal, if Kambili did say so herself. It often reminded Gweneviere of her mother's cooking, which she found comforting.

"Hey, save some for me," Kambili said, half in jest and half deadly serious as Gweneviere shovelled another pastry parcel into her mouth.

"Do I have to?" Gweneviere joked, as she lovingly taunted Kambili by dangling the last pastry above her mouth.

"Right, that's it. Give me that, before I starve." Kambili launched herself at Gweneviere, tackling her to the ground and stuffing the parcel into her mouth. "Ha! I win," Kambili mumbled through her mouthful of food.

As Kambili swallowed, she realised what a precarious position she was in, with her body arched over Gweneviere's. Their eyes locked and Kambili dropped down to Gweneviere's level, all feelings of hunger quickly dissipated as a new hunger set in.

Kambili took Gweneviere's breath away as she kissed her. They began sliding each other's hands up and down their bodies, before tossing and turning as they pleasured each other. As they became more careless and intense with one another, they found themselves rolling off the blanket and amongst the grass and bugs. Neither of them cared, though, as they were much too engrossed in their relations to be bothered by the leaves and twigs that netted up in their hair.

"What was that?" Kambili jolted, hearing a rustle in the hedge by the edge of the meadow – a natural border separating it from the local farmers fields.

"Nothing, it's probably foxes," Gweneviere reassured her, though she was very much preoccupied by the fact that they were both inside one another, with their fingers edging each other closer and closer to the point of heavenly climax.

Kambili quickly agreed to shake it off as being nothing more than a fox, for she was also too engrossed in their *activities*.

Once they had reached the pinnacle of their lovemaking, they laid together, with Kambili nestled into Gweneviere's chest, both panting and having completely forgotten about the pesky fox that had tried to interrupt their lovemaking.

"Hey, I have something to tell you," Gweneviere whispered to Kambili as she squeezed her in even closer.

"Pray tell, beautiful," Kambili replied, repositioning herself so that she was sat up looking at Gweneviere.

"I have a plan, a plan for us to get out from beneath Thomas' crusty thumb."

"Well, you definitely have captured my interest. So... what's the plan?"

"Since I started living with Thomas, I've been saving some money for myself in a secret stash, and—"

"How? Where'd you get the money from?" Kambili interrupted, her voice shaking with excitement.

"Each day, when at the market, I keep track of how much I'm spending, and I always spend a little under budget so that I can stash the remaining amount away for myself. I just can't keep too much, as it would show through in the quality and quantity of food I buy," Gweneviere explained.

"That is very cunning indeed. Where do you keep it?"

"Never you mind."

"After all this time you don't even trust me?" Kambili feigned being insulted.

Gweneviere laughed. "Ugh, fine. I used to keep it just laying around in my bag, but after rediscovering my mother's grimoire, I found a rather useful spell that allows you to hide something within a physical object, but outside of this realm."

"Huh?" Kambili sounded confused.

"It's in Thomas' bedpan, but the enchantment allows it to exist in the bedpan in an alternate plane, where his piss isn't."

"So, it's there, but it's not there?"

"Yes, for me it's there, but for anyone else it's just a pot of piss. It's really a rather amazing spell." Gweneviere smiled softly as she thought about her magnificent mother who had created it.

"It is truly amazing, just like you."

Gweneviere turned back to Kambili, becoming lost in her lover's eyes. Now seemed like the perfect time to profess her love. As she opened her mouth to utter the words, more powerful than any magic spell, Kambili did the same.

"I love you," they both said.

Kambili's face lit up. "I've wanted to say that for quite a while."

Gweneviere grinned back. "Me too. And we're only a couple more weeks away from saving enough money to get out of here for good. We can start a new life, just you and me, anywhere you want. We could get a small farmhouse and live off the land, just like my father always wanted. Far away from any Agathas or Geralds, and especially Thomases. Just you, me, and occasionally Poppy and her husband."

It sounded like a dream to Kambili as Gweneviere described the potential for their new life together. It was so close that Kambili could taste it. A free life.

"That sounds like paradise," Kambili replied, doe eyed. "But don't forget our coven, too!" Kambili wanted to make it clear that she was very open to learning whatever magic she could.

"Of course, how could I forget? We can practice magic whenever you want. We can even try and source some voodoo material if you're interested in learning about your native magical beliefs."

"That sounds incredible." Kambili smiled lovingly as she listened to Gweneviere speak so passionately about their new life. The last time Kambili remembered someone caring that much for her future was when her parents begged their masters to let her be free.

Gweneviere noticed Kambili's adoring gaze. "Why are you looking at me like that?" she asked.

"Because... you're perfect," Kambili answered.

"Yeah, well, you chew too loud," Gweneviere joked, not being able to handle the honest admission of Kambili's love for her.

"How rude!" Kambili feigned seriousness, before pouncing on Gweneviere and once again making love to her, long into the afternoon.

Now that Kambili was in on Gweneviere's escape plan, they spent the next few weeks saving every last penny that they could. They also needed to produce one more batch of the libido potion to keep Thomas at bay. They were too close to freedom to risk any hiccups in their plan, like Thomas becoming sexually aggressive again.

Although they were busy preparing for their departure and keeping one step ahead of Thomas at all times, they made sure to still have some quality time with each other. They regularly teleported themselves to the meadows for picnics, and to keep reliving the magic of their first 'I love you'. It became a haven for the two of them; somewhere where they could be safe and secluded, well, other than when the odd pesky fox made itself known by a rustling in the hedges. They must have used the hedges to sneak into the nearby chicken fields, though, being the illusive creatures that they were, Gweneviere and Kambili never managed to catch a glimpse of them.

On their last visit to the meadows, Kambili couldn't shake the feeling that they were being watched or followed, but she decided to put it down to paranoia. She'd become very paranoid in those past few days as they edged closer and closer to their intended escape date – the second of September – just two days away. They planned on leaving during the early hours of the morning, while Thomas was still fast asleep.

They returned home to find a letter awaiting them on the doorstep. It was for Gweneviere, from Poppy. The letter was dated a mere few days after Gweneviere left her in the first place. Perhaps it was to tell Gweneviere that she had left something behind, though Gweneviere hadn't noticed anything missing.

Dear Gwen,

I know it may seem a little soon, but I couldn't dare let us wait as long as we did the first time around to see each other again. So, I have arranged to come to you this time, just for a day.

I'm taking you on a day out, there are still so many amazing things in London that you haven't experienced yet. Then, we can have dinner at the most delectable establishment that Mr Hammersmith told me about. Oh, and don't worry, it's my treat, you won't need to spend a penny.

I'll pick you up in my carriage say around ten, on the first of September. It's a date!

Love always,
Poppy

"It's from Poppy," Gweneviere told Kambili, after prying the envelope open and reading the letter in its entirety.

"Poppy? Already? That seems rather soon," Kambili noted, a little surprised.

"Yes, she said she didn't want to wait as long to meet up again, so, she's visiting tomorrow to take me out for the day, apparently," Gweneviere answered, regurgitating the letter's contents.

"Oh, that's nice, I'm glad you have a friend who cares for you that much."

"I don't have to go, if you think it's too close to our leaving day?" Gweneviere offered, noticing Kambili's look of worry.

"Don't be silly, of course you can go."

Kambili pasted a smile across her face that wasn't convincing in the slightest. Her hands were hidden behind her back, anxiously fiddling with each other as she thought about everything that the next few days entailed. There was no room for error, but she couldn't bring herself to stop Gweneviere from seeing her friend after everything that she had done for her. Gweneviere was about to carve out a new life for them both. Kambili knew she was just overthinking and took a deep breath to reply with more confidence to Gweneviere's follow up question.

"Are you sure?"

"Yes, don't worry about me, go enjoy yourself. Knowing that it will be the last day I have to be here will make the day go by much quicker, anyway."

There was just enough brightness in Kambili's eyes for Gweneviere to believe her. Though, Kambili knew, she was lying to them both.

Later that night, at dinner, Gweneviere informed Thomas of Poppy's plans to take her out for the day. Much to her and Kambili's surprise, there was no fight back. Instead, he seemed very nonchalant about the whole situation, which was strange to say the least. The old Thomas wouldn't have even allowed Gweneviere to entertain the idea, let alone go without any resistance. He'd surprisingly been rather quiet in general over the past few weeks. Gweneviere wondered if maybe she had made the potion too strong, and whether it may possibly be affecting his personality. That wouldn't have been such a bad thing, if that was indeed the case, as his personality certainly left a lot to be desired. At least a toned-down version of Thomas would surely make their escape that much easier.

After finishing his meal, Thomas retreated to his room and the girls began tidying up the aftermath. Although his attitude had improved, his sloppy table manners hadn't budged from being resemblant to that of a hog. As Gweneviere finished wiping down the dining table, she called to Kambili, offering to put an enchantment on the rest of the cleaning, so that they could head to bed, especially since Gweneviere was getting much better at it. Originally, the spell had created more mess than they started with, but with some practice and fine-tuning, Gweneviere had perfected her execution of the enchantment. Kambili didn't reply to Gweneviere's offer, as she stood staring deep into the water, looking as though in harrowing thought. She scrubbed the cooking pot over and over, long after the stain had been removed. She hadn't noticed, as the paranoia had once again kicked in.

"What's wrong?" Gweneviere asked, walking into the kitchen and noticing Kambili's pot-washing trance.

"Huh? Oh, sorry," Kambili answered, as her absent mind snapped back into reality. "I don't know what's wrong, I just have this horrible feeling, in the pit of my stomach, that we're missing something, like something could go wrong."

"What are you talking about? Everything's been going great. We've saved enough money and, after tomorrow, we'll be out of here."

"Yes, *after* tomorrow, but what if something happens? I feel like we've been getting complacent lately, relying too much on that potion working, but what if he knows we've been drugging him? What if he knows about our plan? What if—"

"Kambili! Calm down," Gweneviere exclaimed, as she placed her hands on Kambili's shoulders to keep her from acting frantically. "He doesn't know, and he's not going to know until we're long gone, okay? You're being paranoid, and that's okay and understandable. You're not used to something actually going right, and neither am I. So, of course, your brain is trying to create problems that aren't there because it can't believe that we're actually doing it."

"I get what you're saying, but I still can't shake this bad feeling. Can't we just leave tonight instead? We already have everything we need!" Kambili hoped that the distress in her eyes and broken voice would be enough to convince Gweneviere to accept her proposition.

"But I've got my day out with Poppy. Look, Kambili, I promise I won't let anything happen to you. Just twenty-four hours and we're out of here, forever, okay?"

Gweneviere was so busy being excited about seeing Poppy and enjoying herself that she couldn't see past that to notice just how scared Kambili was.

"Okay... yeah, I'm sure you're right," Kambili answered, accepting defeat.

"Great, now come on, we need to go to bed. It's getting late, and we'll need a good night's sleep considering this time tomorrow we will be packing up and shipping out for good."

"Yeah, I'll go get into bed."

"Okay, I'll be there soon, I'll just enchant the kitchen and I'll be there in a minute."

As Gweneviere left the kitchen, the pots and a cloth danced about through the air until they were clean and dry before floating back to where they were stored.

Gweneviere entered the bedroom to see Kambili already fast asleep on her side. Clearly she was tired and drained from a long day of work and overthinking. Gweneviere knew deep down how Kambili felt, a part of Gweneviere felt it too. That niggle in the back of her mind that the plan was indeed too good to be true. After everything that Gweneviere had been through, however, she pushed that feeling down, as she knew she deserved happiness.

She lifted the covers gently, not to disturb Kambili, as she climbed into the bed and snuggled up behind her. As Gweneviere wrapped her arm warmly around Kambili's waist, Kambili's eyes gently flickered awake. Feeling Gweneviere's touch made everything seem like it would be okay. She trusted Gweneviere to keep her safe. Her paranoia melted away under the heat of Gweneviere's body and she relaxed into her arms, falling back sound asleep.

They must have been dreaming about their new life together as they looked happy in their peaceful slumber, but what they didn't know was that there was indeed reason to be paranoid. After all, there hadn't been any foxes in the meadows all year. The local poultry farmers were sick of their stock being eaten and had carried out a mass culling earlier in the spring.

So, what could it have been stalking them in the bushes? A werewolf, perhaps? Or a fellow witch? Or another magical creature?

No.

It was something far more dangerous, and crueller than any magical creature known to exist. It was a woman with a tongue sharper than her bite, and a God complex.

Yes, Kambili was right, they were being stalked, by an... Agatha.

CHAPTER 11
The 1ˢᵗ of September

Gweneviere's eyes groggily awoke to the sight of Kambili beside her. Kambili was still asleep, and Gweneviere thought that she looked just as adorable as she did when she was awake. Gweneviere watched her beloved sleep. There was something soothing about watching the person you love in such a peaceful state. Soon Gweneviere and Kambili would be living together, and Gweneviere would get to savour those moments much longer every morning. Without, that is, the looming pressure of making sure they were both up before Thomas.

Gweneviere had wondered, as their escape lured closer, whether Thomas would try to find them once they'd fled. She didn't worry herself too much, however, as if push came to shove, and he did follow them, she could always put him six feet under. If they hadn't have lived in the bustling streets of London, she probably would've done it a lot sooner. Alas, the overpopulated and nosey streets had kept Thomas alive, for now.

Kambili awoke just in time so that Gweneviere wouldn't have to wake her. It would seem that the constant paranoia of waking up after Thomas and the risk of him finding them in bed together had now accustomed Kambili's mind to wake up earlier. Kambili looked even more tired than usual; the bags under her eyes were practically suitcases. As she yawned, stretched, and rubbed the sleep from her eyes, Gweneviere inched closer.

"How did you sleep?" she asked.

"Er, not great," Kambili replied, as another yawn took control of her mouth. She'd woken up repeatedly in the night, still worrying about the day ahead and whether everything would go to plan, but she couldn't bring herself to burden Gweneviere with that information again.

"Oh, I'm sorry. But hey, we did it! That's the last sleep ever in this house, with *him* next door," Gweneviere said excitedly.

"Yeah, I suppose that is true," Kambili replied, clearly still not feeling present enough to be joyous with Gweneviere about their escape.

"So, once I'm home from my trip with Poppy, we'll have dinner, and then once Thomas is in bed, we'll pack our things and leave. I'll arrange a cart to take us out of London. Sorry we can't splurge on a carriage. We'll need to be fruitful with what we have until we can set up a new home, but once we're out of London we can go wherever you want, okay?"

"Yeah," Kambili said, with slightly more enthusiasm. After all, hearing Gweneviere talk about them being out of London was like music to Kambili's ears. "Ugh, do you hear that?" Kambili asked, knowing what she heard was Thomas' lump of a body falling flat onto the bedroom floor.

"Great, the fat bastard must've rolled off again," Gweneviere surmised, rolling her eyes.

Kambili sighed. "I'll go make breakfast."

"For the last time," Gweneviere reminded her.

"So, you're going to make breakfast every day when we live together alone?" Kambili asked, teasingly.

"Ha-ha, you know what I mean." Gweneviere smiled. "Hey." She stopped Kambili again, before she could leave the room.

"Yeah?" Kambili turned back to Gweneviere.

"I love you," Gweneviere whispered.

"Love you too," Kambili whispered back, blowing her a kiss with her hand. That was the beauty of Gweneviere, even when she didn't notice that Kambili was struggling, just being herself managed to cheer Kambili up.

The early hours of the morning passed, and Gweneviere started up the bakery one last time, which she was glad of. The first thing she planned on doing when she left with Kambili was to have a lie in. She wasn't lazy, she just wanted to remember how it felt to wake up after sunrise.

Thomas was once again unconfrontational at breakfast. Gweneviere saw this as a positive as it meant herself and Kambili would be able to slip away much easier. Kambili didn't feel the same though. There was something eerie about Thomas' attitude lately, and she still couldn't shake the feeling that all wasn't as it seemed.

Once he had left for work, Gweneviere filled in the lull

before Poppy's arrival by helping Kambili with some of the household chores. Kambili had slapped a smile on her face as the inevitable return of her paranoia rooted its way back into her thoughts. Kambili had never been a pessimistic person, but lately, with the stress of everything, she couldn't control how she felt. Of course, she was excited and couldn't wait to start her new life with Gweneviere. She was happy and felt loved by Gweneviere, but that didn't make up for the fact that there was another feeling eating away at her. As Kambili bent down to sweep up the ashes from the fire place, she began to cry, silently, in a bid to hide it from Gweneviere. As a few droplets escaped her cheeks and dropped onto the ash, clumping it together, she stood up, wiping the remaining tears with the back of her wrists. She swiftly turned to pass Gweneviere and dump the ashes into a bin, but she didn't quite make it under Gweneviere's radar.

"What's wrong?" Gweneviere asked, stopping Kambili by gently holding her arm.

"Nothing, why?"

"Er, because your eyes are bloodshot and you have a stroke of ash on your cheeks. You've clearly been crying, Kambili. What's wrong? You know you can tell me anything."

"It's nothing that I haven't already told you, I just wish we could go now."

"But Poppy will be here any minute..."

Gweneviere considered their options for a second. She hated seeing Kambili like this, but she was also excited to see Poppy again. With them leaving London, who knew how long it would take for them to settle down somewhere before they could reach out to friends again.

"What about if you come with us on the day trip?" Gweneviere suggested, wiping the ash from Kambili's cheek. "Would that make you feel more at ease?"

"I'd still rather go... but yeah, I'd feel better not being separated from you," Kambili agreed.

There was a knock on the door.

"That'll be her now." Gweneviere smiled, giving Kambili a reassuring look before rushing over to the door. "Poppy!" Gweneviere beamed as she opened it.

"Gwen!" Poppy attempted to mirror Gweneviere's energy the second the door flung open to reveal her face. "Are you ready to go?"

"Er, yeah, pretty much. I was just wondering if Kambili could join us?" Gweneviere asked, moving to the side to reveal a glum looking Kambili stood a few meters behind, shyly waving.

It was the first time Kambili and Poppy had ever met, though from all of Gweneviere's stories, they probably knew more about each other than they realised.

"Oh my, this is the famous Kambili you've told me so much about? She's as pretty as a picture, just as you described, Gwen," Poppy said, walking up to Kambili and smiling brightly. "It's lovely to meet you," she added, holding out her expertly manicured hand.

"Thank you, it's great to meet you too," Kambili answered, meeting Poppy's hand with her own.

"So... about Kambili coming with us?" Gweneviere gently nudged Poppy to remind her.

"Oh, yes... I'm ever so sorry, Kambili, but I only booked for the two of us, I'm afraid. Honestly, I'm so ditsy sometimes, I really should've thought ahead and included you. I'm ever so sorry. I would say you could tag along, but it usually takes months to be able to get a table at where were going, and it's only because the owner owes my husband a favour that I wangled a table in the first place. Please, forgive me, I promise to make sure I include you next time."

"Of course, I understand, I'll be alright," Kambili said, reassuring them both.

"Right, shall we head off then?" Poppy proposed, not giving Gweneviere any time to change her mind.

"Er, yeah, sure," Gweneviere replied, taking one last glance at Kambili to see if she was indeed okay.

Kambili noticed Gweneviere's concerned look and decided not to make her feel any guiltier than she probably already did. So she simply nodded with a soft smile, to indicate that she'd be all right.

As the pair of them left, they both felt guilty, but for different reasons. Gweneviere knew she should have stayed, and even more so, that she should've just left when Kambili wanted to. Poppy knew that she should never have accepted the Crone's deal.

Nevertheless, as they walked out onto the street and headed towards Poppy's carriage, it was much too late for such regrets. The carriage was, for some reason, a few doors down from the house and so they had to pass the bakery store front – another thing that Gweneviere would be glad to see the back of. As they passed it, however, Gweneviere spotted something rather odd.

"Is that Agatha…" she muttered, squinting her eyes before being dragged aside by Poppy.

"Oh, come on, Gwen, we'll be late for everything that I have planned for us," Poppy said, pulling Gweneviere swiftly away from the bakery window and guiding her to the carriage. "We're starting with our lunch booking. Honestly, it's so fancy, apparently even King Charles II dines there on occasion."

"What? Wait, I think I just saw Agatha. What's *she* doing at the bakery?" Gweneviere asked, to which Poppy just shrugged.

"Gwen, who cares what Agatha's doing there? She's probably just called in to see Thomas, I mean, surely him and Gerald are still friends. She probably there to talk about that. Anyway, I brought you out to get away from all that drama. So, come on, relax and enjoy the finer things in life."

"Yeah, you're right, this is me-time."

Gweneviere exhaled deeply before finally looking in the direction of the carriage. It was stunning. Poppy's husband must surely have been related to royalty as Gweneviere felt like a queen when she climbed into the carriage. It was a huge, handcrafted cabin with a rather handsome driver and two snow-white horses pulling it. It probably cost more than Thomas' house. Yes, the finer things in life were already distracting Gweneviere from what she thought she saw. She allowed the vision of Agatha to slip into the back of her mind as she sat back, leaning into the carriage's seats. Poppy accompanied her in the cabin after taking one last suspicious look around the street.

"Wow, this is luxurious, to say the least," Gweneviere complimented, amazed by the grandness of her ride. The cart she had arranged for herself and Kambili to escape on was used for hauling hay, so it didn't even have proper seats, and even the carriage in which she travelled to Poppy's house in was nowhere near as extravagant.

"Yes, it is pretty magnificent, isn't it?" Poppy said, looking around and admiring the interior.

"You're not kidding. Where are we going again?" Gweneviere asked, having not been listening to a single thing Poppy was babbling on about before.

"I told you already, to a fancy lunch."

"Oh, yeah, sorry, I was distracted," Gweneviere replied, as she began to think about how Kambili was doing.

"It's okay, I understand you miss her," Poppy sympathised.

Gweneviere sighed. "It's not just that, it's because tonight, or rather the early hours of tomorrow, is when we're planning to leave. She wanted to go early, and I said no, and now I wish I'd just gone."

Poppy remained silent for a little while as she felt guilty herself, and struggled to see how she could console Gweneviere in the moment.

"So, if I hadn't come today, you guys would've probably already been out of London?" Poppy asked.

"Yeah, probably, but hey, it's not your fault, and I am grateful for all this." Gweneviere smiled, taking her hand in thanks.

Poppy sighed. *You shouldn't be,* she thought to herself.

A few hours had passed and Gweneviere had been managing to enjoy her day out, for the most part. Lunch was divine, and they'd been horse riding. Poppy was truly spoiling Gweneviere, even planning to treat her to dinner as well. Gweneviere did, however, feel a little bad, as she had planned to have dinner back home with Kambili. Though, at least she could give the majority of her portion back home to Kambili instead.

As they sat on a two-seater table in another tavern, that was, apparently, also approved by no less than the King himself, Poppy looked over to Gweneviere, noticing a discerned look upon her face.

"You okay?" Poppy asked out of guilt, knowing she'd stolen her away from Kambili.

"Yeah, I just really need to get back to Kambili soon. She'll be wondering where I am," Gweneviere admitted.

"I understand. I'm almost finished, and then we can head back, okay?" Poppy reassured her, knowing that the least she could do was scoff her food down a little quicker.

"Yeah, okay."

As she tried to quickly finish her meal, Poppy continued to watch Gweneviere's face slip into a more and more anguished state. Poppy couldn't hold it in anymore; watching what was happening to Gweneviere was like torture, and Poppy knew that this was only the beginning of what was to come.

Fuck the Crone, I can't lie to her anymore. She's my friend, she deserves to know, Poppy thought to herself, as she finally told Gweneviere the start of the truth.

"Gwen... I'm sorry."

"What? What for?" Gweneviere asked, looking at Poppy with a puzzled face.

"For what's about to happen, but if you go now, you might be able to stop it," Poppy vaguely explained.

"What are you talking about, Poppy? What's going on?" Gweneviere asked again, becoming distressed.

"The Crone, she made me take you out today, specifically to fulfil her visions; her prophecy for you. She thinks that you're the new witch messiah, or something, who's meant to bring about a new world, a happier world, for women and witches. She said that you need to go through this to push you over the edge... to do what has to be done."

"Jesus, Poppy! What the fuck are you talking about?"

"I'm sorry, she didn't give me a choice!" Poppy became teary eyed as she prepared herself to finally admit to Gweneviere what was happening.

"Didn't give you a choice about what?" Gweneviere shouted, causing the whole room's attention to turn to their table, though Gweneviere certainly didn't care in the moment.

"Kambili," Poppy muttered, shamefully, and as she did, Gweneviere felt a tingle on her palm.

Gweneviere turned her hand over on the table and watched as the rune began to sear a raised, bubbling rash into her skin. Gweneviere's eyes widened as she only now heard Poppy's last word and realised that Kambili was in trouble.

"What have you done?" Gweneviere gasped, slamming her hands onto the table to propel her out of her chair.

"I'm sorry," Poppy shakily muttered again as floods of tears rolled down her cheeks. "I didn't have a choice."

"There's always a choice, Poppy, you just made the wrong one." With that, Gweneviere didn't waste another second on Poppy as she ran out of the tavern to the next alley over in order to teleport home.

Gweneviere was understandably furious with Poppy, but that would have to wait. The only thing that mattered in that moment was Kambili. Gweneviere needed to find her and protect her. She stood in the alley with her anger present in her clenched hands, her nails dug into her palms, and she performed the spell.

"Transport my vessel from here to there. To the image in my head, no matter where."

She turned into dust and was one with the wind. She almost simultaneously rematerialized back inside the house. As she appeared, there wasn't a single light on: none of the lanterns, candles, or even fireplace, were lit. Gweneviere called out Kambili's name over and over, but there was no answer. She scoured every inch of the house with a globe of fire floating in her palm acting as a search light. She'd checked the entire house, even in the bakery, but Kambili was nowhere to be found. She became overcome with a mixture of fear and anxiety, but most of all, anger. Her eyes were frantically darting about, looking for any signs or clues to where she might be.

"Kambili!" she screamed, almost choking on her tears.

After finally accepting that there was no one home, Gweneviere took to the streets She had no idea where Kambili was, but she'd search every street and alleyway until she found her.

It was seemingly quiet at first outside. *Where is everyone?* Gweneviere wondered. It was like a ghost town. Gweneviere began to wander further afield, down the road from the bakery, calling once again for Kambili, no longer caring who heard her cries. The further she went, she began to notice a few people passing her from the opposite direction. She ventured past the closed markets and headed closer to the centre of town, where some more people passed her, and then even more. The increased amount of foot traffic coming towards Gweneviere's direction caused her to get constantly bumped and knocked until a big bruiser of a man, without realising, knocked her onto the floor.

What the hell is going on? Gweneviere internally panicked, as she struggled to get back up amongst the crowd. There were never masses of people like that. It was like when everyone in a theatre left at the same time, but Gweneviere was sure there wasn't any nearby plays on that night. The sheer amount of people was giving Gweneviere a darkening sense of déjà vu, but she couldn't quite put her finger on it. Where had she been where she had experienced so many commoners congregating in one place before?

As Gweneviere got to her feet, she began to tune in to the conversations going on around her, hearing bits and pieces.

"What a waste."

"I'd have had her."

"That's darkies for you."

"Witch scum."

The déjà vu that plagued Gweneviere's mind finally made sense: the last time she experienced the same situation was when her mother was trialled and murdered.

"Kambili!" Gweneviere cried, breaking into a sprint as she pushed her way through the mob that crashed like a current against her. Shoulders nudged and bumped her once again, but this time she was the one knocking them over.

Nothing was going to stop her from getting to Kambili. *Nothing*.

She eventually pushed her way through the thickest part of the herd, where she could see a clearing up ahead in the square. An exhausted Gweneviere pushed past one last person to get to the clearing. She hunched over for a few seconds trying to catch her breath, but as she arose, she saw a body hanging in the near distance. Gweneviere didn't need to take a step closer to know whose body that was.

It was Kambili.

She couldn't allow herself to believe it. How would she ever live with herself if it was indeed true? As she inched closer to the body, however, it slowly turned to reveal Kambili's face. The small part of doubt that was in Gweneviere's mind slowly shrank into an abyss of misery.

Gweneviere was disgusted, angry, outraged, inconsolably sad, but most of all, Gweneviere was sorry.

It took all the strength in her, but Gweneviere slowly lowered the rope until Kambili's limp body was softly laid onto the ground. Gweneviere nervously walked over to face her love. She sat beside her and scooped her up in her arms. She untangled her from the noose around her neck and threw it to the side, lighting the torturous device with a click of her fingers. She wept into Kambili's chest, screaming her name in agony in the hopes that she could perhaps wake them both from this living nightmare. Sadly, the scene was all too real, and she looked down to see there was no response from Kambili. Her face was dull and lifeless; her once bright beautiful eyes were blank and vacant.

The Kambili that Gweneviere had known and loved was gone.

Gweneviere's eyes burned with salty tears, she once again buried her face into Kambili, praying in hushed tones through her own snotty lips. Praying to everyone, anyone, that could save her, but alas, no one answered Gweneviere's prayers. She was alone, as usual, as she caressed Kambili in her arms.

She brought Kambili's face to her own and gently leant their foreheads against one another.

"I love you, Kambili. Please wake up," Gweneviere sobbed.

Of course, there was again no one to answer Gweneviere. She finally began to accept that her fate was sealed. She kicked her legs back on the cobbles and held Kambili between them, wrapped up in her arms. She stroked Kambili's hair as she apologised.

"I'm so sorry. I'm so, so sorry, my beautiful girl. You were right, and I should have listened to you. We should have gone, and none of this would have happened. I'm just so sorry, Kambili. I love you so much, I promised to keep you safe, and I've failed. I've failed you." Gweneviere continued to sob as she blamed herself. "You deserved to be happy, you deserved the world, and I was supposed to give that to you. I'm so sorry, my darling."

Gweneviere laid there on the ashy grey cobbles in the

middle of the square for hours, cradling Kambili in her arms. She couldn't bear to leave her side. A couple of chancing men took a shot at Gweneviere, but no longer having any restraint, she didn't hesitate to send them packing with a literal fiery behind.

When she finally ran out of tears to cry, Gweneviere's face slowly dried, and she felt a presence. She couldn't see or hear anything, but she could feel some kind of omnipotence. Though, she couldn't be sure of what, or who, it was, she hoped that they had carried Kambili's soul to her place in paradise.

The omnipotent being that Gweneviere could sense was Papa Legba, the voodoo deity in charge of the passing over of the spirits, of whom were worshippers of voodoo, and keeping guard of the spiritual realms. He took Kambili's soul, but due to her tragic death and having been unable to say her goodbyes to Gweneviere, she couldn't pass over into paradise, and rather had to stay in Limbo for all eternity. Limbo was the realm between realms, where all the souls were either damned, or lost, seeking to enact their unfinished business in the earthly realm.

Sensing that Kambili was no longer attached to her earthly vessel, Gweneviere knew it was time to leave, but she couldn't just leave her body lying there in the street for any perverted man to fondle over. Or just as bad, she could've been thrown into a mass grave along with all of the plague victims, like she regretted having to do to her father. No, Gweneviere couldn't allow either scenario to happen, but she also wasn't strong enough to bring her body anywhere to bury her herself. Nevertheless, Gweneviere thought hard until she had an epiphany. She could create a new spell, something that tied in with her natural abilities. A spell to cremate Kambili.

"Fiery warm sun, crisp cold mars. Allow this vessel to be at one with the moon and stars."

Gweneviere had never been great with the wording of spells, but she always backed them with power and intent, which was enough to pull through. She stood up and held her hands out, with her palms facing down towards Kambili. She recited the spell slowly, over and over, until finally, Kambili's body was engulfed in bright orange flames. Before Gweneviere knew it, Kambili was nothing but a slurry of smouldering embers that were carried up into the night sky by the summer evening breeze, disappearing into the stars.

"I'll always love you," Gweneviere whispered. She looked up and watched as her one and only true love was taken away from her far too soon.

Now that Gweneviere had given Kambili the best send-off that she could, given the circumstances, it was time to enact her revenge. Gweneviere was already a powerful witch not to be trifled with.

But now, she was a witch scorned.

CHAPTER 12
A Witch Scorned

It was the early hours of the next morning and Gweneviere wiped the solitary tear that managed to squeeze out of her otherwise dehydrated eyes. She made her way back to the bakery in search of Thomas. By then, any previous feelings had been suppressed to make room for the surging anger within her. As she stormed her way through the streets, her eyes and hair came to life as fire encompassed them. Red, orange, and yellow flames weaved in between the strands of her hair and caused her eyes to glow. This time no man passing her so much as chanced a look in her direction. Even from just the corner of their eyes, they could see an unhinged witch, and not one they fancied their chances with in a fight.

Gweneviere reached the shopfront door. Melting the handles clean off, she kicked the door open. Unbeknown to a smug Thomas, who was snugly tucked away in bed, Gweneviere set the bakery ablaze. As she walked through the shop with her palms out to the side, a hellish inferno followed them. By the time she'd reached the door joining the apartment to the bakery, every inch of the room behind her was on fire.

It would only be a matter of time before it spread up into the apartment and neighbouring buildings.

Gweneviere entered the apartment. She expected that Thomas would be in bed, but to be sure she silently checked every other room of the apartment first. As her search came to an end, she found herself outside of Thomas' door, and it would seem that her instincts were right, as she could hear his snoring vibrating through it.

Without making a sound, she opened the door to reveal Thomas' monstrous body snoring away without a care in the world. Gweneviere took it upon herself to wake him. She picked up the bedpan, from beneath his rotten and sunken side of the bed, that was brimmingly full of warm piss. She first reached inside to pull out her pouch of money that was hidden. Thanks to her mother's spell, Gweneviere didn't actually reach into the puddle of orange urine, but rather into an empty bedpan where her savings awaited. Once her money was secure, the bedpan reverted back to its earthly contents, which she then tipped over Thomas' slumbering body, causing him to become soaked in his own waste.

How could he have the audacity to be so sound asleep in the first place? After having, only a few hours earlier, committed such an atrocity. He had taken away the only thing left in Gweneviere's life that she loved, without seemingly an ounce of remorse.

No, not today, Satan, Gweneviere thought, as she watched, waiting for him to wake up.

As the lukewarm urine drenched his face, he woke up in a panicked state, thrashing around, causing the taste of it to hit his tongue. Gweneviere rather enjoyed watching that, but that was just the start of his torture. He wiped his face with a blanket before seeing a fiery Gweneviere stood at the foot of *their* bed, though Gweneviere hadn't ever really thought of it as theirs. Surprisingly, he didn't seem scared of her new look, like the men on the streets were, even though he should've been. Instead, he had a smug grin on his face as he looked at her calmy.

"What's wrong, Gwen?"

They both knew full well what was wrong, thus Gweneviere didn't want to play into his little games.

She didn't dignify him with an answer, but rather a simple question of her own. "Why did you do it?"

His menacing grin turned more wicked, into a smile that was so intense it looked like his reddened, chubby cheeks could implode at any second.

"*Because*, Gweneviere, you belong to me, and she is, or should I say was..." he sniggered disrespectfully, "my property. So, I have every right to do what I would with her, even if that means I wanted to dispose of her because she was no longer of any use to me."

Gweneviere found herself grinding her teeth, almost into dust, and digging her nails into her clenched palms once again as she had to restrain herself from roasting him on the spot.

"You found out that we were together, didn't you?"

"Yes, your dear friend Agatha thought that I ought to know what you had been up to behind my back. She came to me in the bakery yesterday morning while you were off galivanting with Poppy. She told me of the first time she spotted you in the meadows, groping each other like a couple of whores. From then on she kept tabs on you by sending one of her new slaves to watch you from the bushes. Truly, it's disgusting and sinful what you did, Gweneviere. But to think, if you had only thought to invite *me* on one of your little rendezvous and involved me in your sexually deviant activities, then perhaps this could have all been avoided, and I wouldn't have had to hang the poor cow."

Gweneviere was disgusted by the egotistical man, who would go so far as to murder somebody out of jealousy and spite just because he wasn't included in the lovemaking of someone else's relationship. He was a sick, deluded man, and Gweneviere had to put a stop to him so that he could never lay a finger on another woman again.

"You're vile," she spat. "And if you think that any woman would ever willingly touch you, then you're also stupid," she added, to agitate him as much as he was clearly doing to her. Though, of course, the difference was that in order to rile up Gweneviere, you'd have to disrespect those she loved, but to do the same to Thomas, all she had to do was belittle him, as there was no one he loved more than himself.

"That's life for you, Gweneviere, it's a cruel, vile place. Oh, and it was all too easy to convince the locals that *my* dirty slave, *your* darkie lover was using her black magics against me and the town. She even threatened to increase the plague's ability to spread and infect thousands more... or so I fabricated." He flaunted another wicked smile in Gweneviere's direction. "Yes, after that tale, the local lads were more than happy to drag her, kicking and screaming, and scream she did. They took her out of the house and down the street, which, of course, attracted an audience. By the time they'd made it all the way to the platform, she was knackered, by the looks of it. That didn't stop her, though. I really must commend her, she put on quite the show. She kept screaming your name and scrawling some dumb pattern onto her hands, until, of course, she needed them to try and ease the rough rope around her neck. You see, she didn't even die with a snapped neck like so many do. No, she really provided entertainment. I should've pulled up a chair. It took a fair few minutes of wriggling and flouncing around on the end of the rope before she choked to death, and the light was snuffed from her eyes."

Gweneviere's palms became full of blood, her nails now a centimetre deep within them, dripping blood onto the floor. Though Gweneviere could have quite easily sobbed at Thomas' grim retelling of events, that wouldn't help avenge Kambili. Gweneviere had to stay in a state of pure fury and rage to be able to finish the job. Hearing Kambili try to use the palm spell in her desperate last moments truly broke Gweneviere to the core. She knew exactly what she was going to do to Thomas to make him pay for his sins. He was going to suffer for as long as he lived.

"Thomas Farriner, you are an evil, demented man, and I will forever despise you. But it only seems fair that I take an eye for an eye, a life for a life. So, my dear husband, I bid you farewell."

Thomas was bewildered by Gweneviere's speech, but as she grabbed her satchel, she teleported out of the bedroom, this time not even speaking the spell. She was somehow powerful enough to not need the words, rather her thought and intent was all that was needed. As she dematerialised in front of Thomas' very eyes, he could then see the bedroom door in which she was stood in front of, and it was only then that Thomas had noticed there was a steady stream of billowing smoke seeping through the door frame. He raced over to the door to try and escape, but as he grasped the doorknob, it seared his palm on impact. Thomas yelled as he peeled his molten flesh off of the handle and his skin pulled like it was melted cheese. Not long after his failed attempt, the door became ablaze itself, as the fire began to fully take over the house.

Gweneviere had teleported herself to the street just outside, where she had the perfect view of the apartment. She watched through their bedroom window as a blinding sunset orange light cast a silhouette of Thomas' wide figure.

Thomas ran to the window and tried to jimmy it open, but it wouldn't budge, and though Thomas was a petty, horrible man, he was surely strong enough to open a window. It was if some invisible force was working against him, keeping the window tightly closed.

Low and behold, arising out of the darkness of the side street behind Gweneviere, was Poppy. She had one hand held out in the direction of the window, clearly using her telekinetic abilities to keep it shut and Thomas trapped.

"I'm sorry, Gwen," Poppy said shamefully, as she came up beside Gweneviere. "You were right, I did have a choice, and I did choose the wrong one. I can't tell you how sorry I am for that, and I know you'll probably never forgive me, but just know that if you ever need anything, I'm here for you. You know where I live, and you'll always be welcome."

A part of Poppy hoped they could still have a fairy-tale ending, where Gweneviere would indeed forgive her, and they could stay friends. Poppy was surely deluded to think it, she had been a contributing factor to the death of Gweneviere's one and only true love. Of course, there wasn't going to be a sweet reunion and a hug. She should've counted herself lucky to have not met the same fate as Thomas.

"Poppy, once upon a time, you were a good friend to me when I needed you, so for that, you are afforded your life. But make no mistake, even if I don't see you again until the afterlife, it would still be too soon." Gweneviere's tone was harsh and unforgiving. "Now, release the window and leave. I want to see him fall onto the cobbles and break."

Gweneviere's cruel but honest words ripped through Poppy's entire body. She felt ashamed and guilty for what she had done, but most of all sorry that she ever went along with it in the first place. Not only did she aid in the death of a young, innocent woman, but she also broke her best friend's heart in the process. Gweneviere was broken beyond repair; she would never be the same again and the fact that Poppy knew she'd played a part in that would gnaw away at her for the rest of her life. Nevertheless, the only thing left that she could do was respect Gweneviere's decision. So, she walked away, releasing her magical grip on the window, knowing that she had ruined quite possibly the only real friendship she'd ever had.

A half-roasted Thomas finally prized the window open. He had almost given up but, having the survival instincts of a street rat, he gave it one last go just as Poppy's magics released.

Thomas shimmied himself through the window and toppled out, smacking onto the cobbled ground below with a low thud and blood curdling scream. He then continued to groan intensely as his body was engulfed in a stupendous amount of pain.

Gweneviere walked over to him, and as he laid there, barely able to flinch a movement, he muttered, "You witch, you're an evil witch."

The majority of his body was exposed and burned to a crisp, though there were also parts where the searing heat had instead grafted his clothes to his body. Gweneviere took pleasure in peeling some away; the gummy flesh resembled someone pulling the first slice out of a Chicago deep pan pizza. Thomas cried out in pain, but it was mostly silent as his lungs could barely keep up.

"What was it you said?" She smirked, towering over him. "Oh yes, *that's life.*"

Gweneviere knew, looking at him, that he didn't deserve to die yet. He hadn't even come close to the amount of pain that he had inflicted on women over the years. Death would be too kind for Thomas, he needed to suffer for a *long* time.

To Gweneviere, he represented every disgusting man who had caused pain in a woman's life, and he was going to pay for them all. He would pay for the men like those who'd burned her mother, men like Robbie, who tried to molest her, men like Gerald, who thought status meant entitlement, and men like Thomas himself, who in many ways was a sickening combination of them all. Gweneviere couldn't single handedly take down every wrongdoing man in the world, but she could certainly make a start with Thomas. Even if he stayed in this painstaking state for the rest of his sad life, it wouldn't be enough to compare to the daily suffering women went through, though, it did give Gweneviere an idea for a place to begin.

Gweneviere then created a new spell, one that she may well never use again, as it was made especially for Thomas.

"Roses are red. Violets are blue. Let this pain stead, till death becomes you."

There was no instant reaction in Thomas' body, but that was intended, Gweneviere knew exactly what she was doing.

"My dear Thomas, may you spend the rest of your life wallowing in this pain, and remember that it was I, Gweneviere *Baxter*, who put your reign of terror to an end."

Gweneviere turned on her heels and began walking up the street that was roaring in fire around her. People had just begun waking up and fleeing their homes, trampling on Thomas in the process. No one would come for him, but if Gweneviere's spell could help it, he would surely last a few more years in pain.

"You fucking whore," he began, before spluttering from his smoke-filled lungs. "Wait until the Crone hears about this!" he screamed, using the last of his voice, from beneath the crowd of fleeing citizens, in a last-ditch desperate attempt to grab her attention.

Gweneviere stopped and turned her head slightly, just enough so that he could see her lips move as she said softly, "Where do you think I'm heading next?"

With that, she teleported once more, into the night sky, where she would next find herself at the Crone's school.

A lonely, helpless Thomas laid on the cobbled street as

he watched the swarms of people around him fly by. No one stopped to help. Did they think he was already dead? Or did they simply not care? It didn't matter much as they both had the same outcome, which was Thomas being in copious amounts of pain as he watched his bakery, everything he had worked for and the only real thing he cared about, turn to ashes before his very eyes.

Gweneviere had transported herself into the dining hall of the Crone's school, instinctively, her brain began to reminisce about her days there with Poppy and all the fun memories they had together. Gweneviere couldn't allow herself to think such things – Poppy was as good as dead to her now. She wasn't there to reminisce.

She was there to get revenge.

Gweneviere made her way through the school until she was outside the Crone's office, where the Crone was seemingly awaiting her arrival.

"Come in," she called from her office, sensing Gweneviere's presence just outside the door.

Gweneviere walked into the small room with every intention of turning the deluded witch into a charred corpse, but before she could even begin to express her anger, the Crone had a monologue of her own.

"Now, I know you're angry."

"Seething." Gweneviere was furious; how dare the Crone try to condescend her feelings.

"But, you see, it all had to happen like this. I had a series of visions last year, in my dreams, that must have been sent by the great witch Goddess Hecate herself. She told me of a maiden, a young pyrokinetic witch with longevity, that would outlive us all and see in a new world where witches and women were respected and had the same rights as men. However, that future could only exist if you went through a specific series of events. Events painful enough to motivate you and ignite a deeper, more powerful spark in your magics. You are the key to the future, Gweneviere, you always have been."

"Oh, so losing my parents wasn't enough?" Gweneviere snapped, unmoved by the Crone's attempt at explaining herself.

"Oh, grow up, Gweneviere, half of the girls here don't have any parents. So no, that wasn't enough. The visions clearly stated you were to fall in love and have it ripped away from you. *That* would be the ultimate factor that pushes you to your greatness, to usher in the new world. Don't you see what magnificent things you can do now? I can, I've been watching you grow, I even felt the two spells that you created this very night. You are one of the most powerful beings on the planet. This is your duty, and though I'm sorry that this is the way it had to be done, you must understand it was essential. Besides, none of the other girls could've survived being married to that oaf."

"What's that supposed to mean?"

"Oh, it was a compliment, dear, learn to take one," the Crone scoffed.

"No, you said no one else could've survived him. Graduation was rigged from the start, wasn't it?" Gweneviere always knew that something wasn't right about that night. She couldn't have been that unlucky.

"Well, of course it was. I knew you wouldn't fall in love with any of my men, which I did find worrying, but then Hecate came to me, again, in a dream, to say that if I paired you with Thomas, you'd find a love of your own. You did, and then we were right back on track to fulfil your prophecy. Besides, you needed someone to fight back against, you'd never have reached your full potential with a soft husband like Poppy's."

Gweneviere was becoming infuriated by the Crone; she couldn't believe how the Crone tried justifying what she had done. "How dare you dictate my life according to a hallucination that you had before you even met me. You're delusional, and I can assure you your *prophecy* will never come true now. Who do you think you are? You have no idea what I've gone through in these past months, the horrors that I've experienced, the—"

"I have every idea! I told you, I've been watching you; I've seen everything you've been through, and I've experienced it myself, when I was but a young witch, probably even younger than you are now. But did anyone come and save me? NO! I had to pull myself out of the gutter alone. I created this place from nothing so that I could provide a place for ungrateful bitches like you. When I had the visions at first, I was torn, because I know, better than anyone else, what you've been through. I know how disgusting and gut wrenchingly painful it is, and *I KNOW* that you'd rather die than crawl back into *his* bed, and... I know that you'll never look at yourself the same way again. So don't lecture me on what *you've* been through, little girl, because I'm the epitome of making it out the other side. Now, if my visions meant that one witch had to go through all that so that generations of witches in the future wouldn't have to suffer, then, to me, that was worth it."

A shocked Gweneviere took a moment to compose herself. "I'm sorry that happened to you, I truly am. But you are not God, and I am not a puppet to be strung along to act out your prophecy. You took the only thing I had left in the world away from me. So, though you may have deemed it to be worth it, funnily enough, I don't. I've freed myself of Thomas and now I'm freeing myself of you. I'm sorry, but I will never be the witch that you want me to be."

"We shall see," the Crone replied threateningly.

But Gweneviere wasn't threatened, she had nothing left to lose. "No, you won't…"

Gweneviere's eyes and hair became once again encompassed by flames. She conjured two orbs of fire in her palms and, as she prepared herself to deal the final blow, there was a quiet knock on the door followed by a squeaky voice.

"Hello?" the voice muttered.

Gweneviere's head flinched towards the door, hearing the young voice. She instantly extinguished the flames in her hands, hair, and eyes before opening the door to reveal a young girl, barely seven years old.

"I heard shouting," the timid, redheaded girl said, gripping her blanket tightly.

As Gweneviere looked into the young girl's deep brown eyes, she saw an even younger version of herself. She knew in that moment she couldn't kill the Crone. Though the Crone may have ruined Gweneviere's life, she did still play a part in housing young girls that, like Gweneviere, had nowhere else to go. If she killed the Crone, she'd effectively be kicking forty or more girls out onto the streets, where they'd either suffer the same fate as Gweneviere or, perhaps worse, be trialled and killed for being a witch.

"Hey, I'm sorry for shouting. Everything's alright, go on back to sleep, okay?" Gweneviere reassured the girl, softly tapping her on the nose with her forefinger.

"Okay," she giggled in reply, before nodding and heading back to her dormitory.

Gweneviere slowly turned back to the Crone. "I'm not going to kill you..."

"Than—"

"I'm not finished," Gweneviere continued. "I'm not going to kill you because these girls need you. They need someone to look out for them, but from now on, you don't play any idiotic games of chance with their futures. You do right by them, *and* if I find out otherwise, then I will come back to finish you off."

"I understand. In return, will you consider my visions?" the Crone asked.

"No, there will be no exchange. This is me giving you a second chance. Maybe if you had told me, before all of this began, that I was prophesised to do such things, then we could have found another way, but you didn't. Blindly following the ignorance of your own visions was the biggest mistake of your life. Goodbye, Matriarch."

Gweneviere walked out of the office, out of the school, and eventually out of London.

As Gweneviere left London, making her way through the neighbouring towns, she heard news travelling alongside her of a great fire in London. Gweneviere never meant to cause such damage, but in the heat of the moment she was blinded by her rage for Thomas. She'd never expected it to reach such a vast area, though as time went on, there were tales told that the great fire had somewhat helped to snuff out the plague that killed her father. She took some peace in that.

One person that Gweneviere had forgotten to deal justice to in her eventful last night in London was Agatha, and typically, the great fire didn't reach Agatha's mansion. That didn't prove much a of a problem to Gweneviere, though, as a few days later she teleported herself within the mansion's walls and set it alight while Agatha slept. She guided the staff, slaves and children out of the building before allowing the house to burn down to a few crumbs of rubble, taking Agatha with it. Agatha wasn't worth wasting time on to ask such questions as why she did it. The answer was simple: Agatha was a vicious and ignorant wretch of a woman, and Gweneviere didn't want to hear anymore disrespectful drivel about Kambili. No, she was quite happy in knowing that Agatha was baked alive – rather fitting, really. Gerald, on the other hand, being the lucky, entitled sod that he was, was away on a business trip, meaning that he didn't die. He, of course, did lose Agatha and the house, but it was never clear which one he mourned for more.

Thomas became paralysed from the neck down and, without any means of funding a life for himself, spent his last few years in an asylum. The smoke damage on his lungs left him mute, too, which was truly a gift to the world. The asylum was a rather dilapidated building full of criminally insane people who tormented Thomas on a daily basis, until he drew his last shallow breath some ten years later.

In the following years, Gweneviere became somewhat of a hermit. Using the money she had saved from the bakery, she managed to buy the kind of small farmhouse that she and Kambili had always dreamed of. She stayed there for a hundred years or so, alone, living off the land and working on her magics. By the industrial revolution, Gweneviere had almost filled the latter half of her mother's spell book, but there was still another thirty or so pages left for her next chapter in life.

Slowly, as time passed, more and more houses were built, until finally Gweneviere's farmhouse was practically among a cul de sac. Feeling that she had finally made some progress in moving on from Kambili, she decided to re-join society. She sold her farmhouse and made a name for herself, without the need of a man. Gweneviere was still a very smart woman, and had spent many of her lonely years studying. She had denied fulfilling any of the Crone's key points in time, but eventually started up many businesses, employing mainly women to provide them with a safe place to work. Though the Crone would've argued that Gweneviere had done it much too late.

By the twentieth century, Gweneviere was living in Manchester. She had never returned to London, even after all the time that had passed, it was still too painful a place to be.

She started her own coven in Manchester, just like Kambili had always wanted, though it wasn't quite the loving environment that Kambili had envisioned. The coven was strictly a business partnership, and Gweneviere invited the most prestigious witches in Manchester to join. Some, like Gweneviere, joined for their own self gain, while others joined to boost their husband's status. They did all, however, also look out for the local witches of Manchester, in case any rampant witch hunters with outdated ideologies were around. It would seem that even in the modern world there were still people of old rich blood lines – usually that of the old pastors – that sought to put a stop to all witches. Thankfully, they were the minority now, and rarely ever actually mustered up the courage to attack.

Though witches were looked after, mortals, on the other hand, were free game. Gweneviere didn't trust mortals, not after her long history with them. They were never to be trusted, and, on occasion, a mortal was born to two witches, otherwise known as a Marcidus. Marcidus' were born with no innate magical talents, and had no means of spellcasting or potion brewing. Gweneviere greatly encouraged any said parents to unburden themselves and get rid.

Over the years, Gweneviere became more and more cold and ruthless with her rules. Her Manchester sisters were becoming sick of Gweneviere's tyrant rule, and she had even adopted the term Matriarch from the Crone. By the 1980s, they'd had enough, and shunned Gweneviere out of the very coven she founded.

Feeling she had no reason left to stay in Manchester, or England at all, for that matter, Gweneviere decided to migrate across the pond to New York City. She started a new coven, inflicting the same rules on them, but no witch in America could match her power, so they fell in line, like the sheep they were.

Yes, Gweneviere was indeed enjoying her new life where her word was final, the power seemingly going to her head in her old age. Gweneviere became weaker over time. Her powers began to wane and her once beautiful auburn locks were now snow-white and thinning. Her cruel position on Marcidus' also came back around to bite her in the bum. When a certain Marcidus infiltrated the coven to take their revenge, Gweneviere just about escaped with her life, though she had to leave the coven behind.

Since that day, Gweneviere was, once again, alone, and had deteriorated to the point where she was an old, struggling woman with an arched back that no one would ever suspect was once the most powerful witch on earth.

Even though Gweneviere had distracted herself over the centuries with farms, businesses, and covens, she had to admit to herself that she hadn't found peace.

She never got over the death of her great love, Kambili.

EPILOGUE
A New, Old Friend

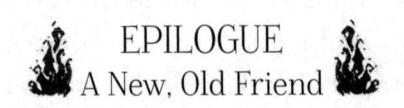

2026

Three hundred and sixty years after the death of Kambili, the world compared to then was a much better place in many regards, what with the women's rights movement and the abolition of slavery. However, the new world still echoed many heavy undertones of the past. Women had rights, and domestic abuse was no longer tolerated, but it still occurred far too often. The only difference was that the evil perpetrators that acted in such volatile ways kept their doing so behind closed doors, and under the guise of a happy marriage. Though slavery had been abolished, modern slavery was still rife about the world, as there were thousands of people trafficked every day. Sadly, there were also still very vocal groups of people that didn't care for anyone of a different ethnicity or race to their own.

It wasn't often that Gweneviere contemplated the world around her, as she didn't want to think about what could've been. Would the world have been a better place if Gweneviere had listened to the Crone? Was Gweneviere to blame for the fact they didn't live in an even more accepting, forward-thinking world? Surely that was too much to ever put on one person's shoulders, no matter how powerful they were. Whenever she did feel the waves of 'what if's', they were soon squashed by the sheer amount of self-pity that Gweneviere felt. She didn't owe the world anything, in fact, she believed that she was the one short-changed by her outcome in life. She had to watch others be happy as her life fell apart, one loved one after another. Though she might've been three hundred and seventy-eight years old, deep down, she was still just a teenager with a broken heart that never healed. After accepting that she may never move on from Kambili, Gweneviere felt ready for death and had hoped that it would rear its ugly head soon.

Gweneviere was a frail skeleton of the woman, and witch, she used to be. Even her magic was dissipating in her final weeks; she struggled to light the fireplace most days. Yet still, she didn't have the willpower to end her miserable existence herself. She'd been the reason for too many lives lost, she couldn't bear to take her own, too. Instead, she laid in bed each night in the hopes that it might be her last day in this Godforsaken realm.

One otherwise ordinary day in New York, Gweneviere was walking home from her local grocery store. She walked with a cane in one hand and her brown paper bag full of groceries in the other. Her hunched back made it hard to lug the bag of supplies and, as she struggled along the sidewalk, the bag slipped from her weak grip. The bag hit the ground, making a mess everywhere. Eggs were splattered, milk spilt, and her fruit was bruised and dirtied by the tarmacked street. Gweneviere attempted to descend to the ground to salvage what produce she could, but as she did, she heard a familiar voice offering to help.

"Gweneviere?" a kind voice spoke. "Gweneviere, is that you?"

Kambili? Gweneviere's frail mind pondered, as she twisted and turned to get a look at the stranger. As Gweneviere just about managed to return to her somewhat upright position, her eyes began to refocus on the young woman's face until she recognised the kind voice.

"Nkechi," Gweneviere remembered, still butchering the pronunciation, as she always did.

Nkechi was an old acquaintance of Gweneviere's that she had tried to entice into joining her Manhattan coven. This was all just before the Marcidus attacked. Gweneviere hadn't seen Nkechi since, for many reasons, but boy was she glad to see her then. She was a sight for sore eyes indeed: her large curly locks bounced when she walked, and her beautiful hazel eyes made Gweneviere feel seen for the first time in a long time. Nkechi was a tall and slim girl, but had only in recent years become more confident in her looks. The patch of vitiligo that covered her face once made Nkechi feel inferior, but now she was a grown woman, with a clear mind and strong magic behind her, and she was proud of her unconventional beauty.

Just a few years ago, Nkechi would've been nervous at the sight of Gweneviere, but Nkechi noted that there was nothing to fear anymore as she smiled down at the frail woman.

"Gweneviere, is that really you? You look so..." Nkechi

began, before realising the next word might've been insulting.

"Old? It's okay, you can say it, my dear," Gweneviere joked.

Nkechi chuckled. "Yeah, sorry."

"Oh, it's fine, I think I look rather good for three hundred and seventy-eight."

"Yeah, I'll give you that!" Nkechi smiled back at that, having never been afforded the knowledge of her true age before. "Here, let me help you," Nkechi offered, as she bent down onto her knees in a split second to pick up the salvageable remnants of Gweneviere's shopping.

"Thank you, dear. Would you like to come back to my apartment for a cup of tea?"

In all honesty, Nkechi didn't have a lot of reasons to be nice to Gweneviere, after all, she had tried manipulating her in the past when it suited her, or the covens, needs. However, seeing her in such a fragile and lonesome state, Nkechi knew she'd spend the rest of the day feeling guilty if she didn't at the very least indulge the old woman for an hour.

"Yeah, sure," Nkechi agreed, bunching up the groceries in her arms so that Gweneviere didn't have to carry them any longer.

"Wonderful. So, how have you been?" Gweneviere asked, in the hopes that Nkechi's wasn't another life gone awry by Gweneviere's involvement.

"Well, I guess you could say it's been a weird and rough couple of years, but I got through it," Nkechi answered honestly.

"I'm sorry, I know you've not had an easy life either, but it's good to see you're on the other side of it now. Are you and

Kosum still friends?"

Nkechi and Kosum had always reminded her of herself and Poppy's friendship, at least before the betrayal. That was one thing, in particular, that had haunted Gweneviere for many years. Poppy had tried on many occasions to contact Gweneviere; she would use her magic to find Gweneviere's address and send her letters. She never showed up in person, as Gweneviere's final words to her always resonated in Poppy's mind and she didn't want to overstep. Nonetheless, she informed Gweneviere of any news in her life and always asked how Gweneviere was. She apologised again and again in each letter, in the hopes that one day Gweneviere would reply. That day never came. Gweneviere never replied. She was still too hurt by Poppy's actions. Poppy even sent a Christmas card every year, and although Gweneviere never returned the gesture, she did enjoy receiving them. Even as Poppy grew old – at the more standard witch rate – and had children and grandchildren, she never forgot to send one Christmas card. Gweneviere could see in the shaky handwriting that Poppy was becoming frailer over the years. One year, when the yule tide season came, Gweneviere sensed that Poppy might not have many Christmases left, and so she decided she would write back when she received her card. That same year, however, there was no mail from Poppy. At first, Gweneviere thought that Poppy had given up, or didn't care anymore, but when she remembered just how many years had passed and how many pointless years she had stayed angry with her, she realised that Poppy was gone. It was the second biggest regret of Gweneviere's life, after, of course, the day she left Kambili alone.

"Yeah, we're best friends." Nkechi smiled.

"That's great, take it from a stubborn old lady whose lost far too many friends in her time, don't lose her. Even if she did something unforgivable and you think you can never bear to look at her again, don't ignore her forever. Everyone makes mistakes, but when you've isolated yourself and the only person you want to talk to you can't because you're too busy being mad, it sucks, and it's not worth it. Take time, of course, to move on from things, but always make up, okay?"

"Yeah, of course. She's in a relationship with my cousin Nicole now anyways, so I can't get rid even if I tried," Nkechi joked.

"Oh, she's gay?" Gweneviere questioned, referring to Kosum.

"Oh, God, please don't ruin this and tell me you're one of those old timey homophobes now," Nkechi moaned, rolling her eyes.

"Me? God no. Quite the opposite, I was kissing girls before your great, great, great grandmother was born," Gweneviere cackled.

"What?! You're gay?" Nkechi exclaimed, surprised.

"Well, I believe the term is bisexual, but yes, I loved a girl once, and there's been no one else since," Gweneviere said, her voice growing quiet with grief.

"Oh, I'm sorry, that sounds awful. What happened?"

"I'll tell you everything over that cup of tea," Gweneviere said, as she fumbled in her pocket to find her door key, now that they were coming up to the apartment building.

Once inside, and with a steaming pot of tea between

them, Gweneviere told Nkechi her life story, leading up until the very moment they originally met. Nkechi was enthralled with the blow-by-blow telling of her life. Back when Nkechi had originally known Gweneviere, no one really knew much about her personal life, other than the fact that she lived with a countless number of cats – something that Nkechi was now learning, the hard way, was indeed a fact. She even had to pull a cat hair from her tea a few times. There had always been rumours about Gweneviere's past, but the rumours were nothing compared to what Nkechi was getting straight from the horse's mouth.

After listening to Gweneviere's entire life story, Nkechi felt sorry for her, and could appreciate what a horrible hand the cards of life had dealt her. However, Nkechi also knew that her disturbing past didn't vindicate the way she had treated people in more recent years, and she put that point across very clearly to Gweneviere.

"You're right, Nkechi, I have done awful things in my life, and now, at this ripe old age, I finally see that two wrongs don't make a right. But it's incredibly humbling to see that a young woman, such as yourself, has learnt that already," Gweneviere complimented the young woman, as well as finally pronouncing Nkechi's name right after many years of knowing her, which Nkechi appreciated.

"Hey, I'm not perfect either. I've done some *questionable* things," Nkechi said, light-heartedly.

"Yes, of course, as we all have, but you have the self-awareness to know what you did wrong. That is a powerful thing that some people can't be taught. I know I definitely played my part in what has happened in your past, and for that I'm sorry. Oh, how I wish I could just go back in time and redo everything. I would never have left Kambili that day. She'll never know how much I loved her."

"I'm sure she does know," Nkechi consoled, and as she did, she had an epiphany. "Didn't you mention that Kambili's parents had voodoo beliefs?"

"Yes, dear, why?"

"Well, her spirit may have been taken to Limbo with Papa Legba, especially if she has unfinished business, which, if you ask me, it most definitely sounds like you and her have unfinished business," Nkechi explained, though it went straight over Gweneviere's head – her mind certainly wasn't what it used to be.

"I'm not sure I'm following. What's Limbo?" Gweneviere asked, looking confused.

"It's a place lost souls go to aimlessly wander around in a terrified state forever."

Gweneviere's face was silently horrified.

"But... if she is there, then maybe I'll be able to contact her, and you could talk to her through me. Me and Papa Legba are pretty tight, if I do say so myself," Nkechi said, with a smug smile on her face that changed Gweneviere's worried expression to a hopeful one.

"You'd do that for me? After everything?"

"Gweneviere..."

"Call me Gwen."

"Gwen, you've done some bad things, but you understand that and you feel remorse. You deserve a second chance to be happy."

Nkechi cleared the coffee table in front of them and laid upon it on her back. Nkechi had become somewhat a pro at dipping into Papa's realms, and so she closed her eyes and let her mind wander through the spirit realm to Limbo.

It was a vast, foggy void with souls traipsing around in agony. Nkechi called out Kambili's name into the cold abyss. Kambili was nowhere to be seen, though it wasn't exactly easy finding one spirit among millions. Luckily, Papa Legba appeared through the fog beside Nkechi. He was a large man, or rather, deity. He had a white skull painted across his face and long, beaded dreadlocks flowing behind him. He wore a cloak that covered the rest of his body apart from the two large, bony feet that pointed out from beneath it. He looked down to Nkechi with a kinder face than he did most people who entered his realm.

"What are you doing here, my child?" he asked.

"I'm looking for a girl called Kambili. I believe she died three hundred and sixty years ago?"

"Hmm, oh yes, Kambili. 1666. I thought that poor girl would never make it out of Limbo, it's been so long," Papa thought aloud as he stroked his pointy chin. Papa knew of every soul that entered or passed through his realms.

"Yes, well, believe me when I tell you it's an even longer story of why it's taken until now," Nkechi jested.

"Say no more, my child. I shall fetch her."

With a raise of his arm, his cloak opened up to reveal a confused Kambili coming out from within it. She looked so scared and tired, though who wouldn't be after wandering an endless void for hundreds of years? Kambili looked up at Papa, and he gave her a reassuring look back.

"Here, my child, Nkechi will take good care of you."

"Hi." Nkechi smiled, with a small innocent wave to Kambili.

"Hello, why have you summoned me?" Kambili asked, though she was happy to be free from her zombie-like state.

"Gweneviere would like to speak to you," Nkechi explained.

"Gw-Gweneviere? My Gwen?" Kambili stuttered, shakily.

"Yes," Nkechi answered happily, already seeing their love for each other light up Kambili's gaunt face.

"I never thought I would see her again, I'll do whatever it takes to see her," Kambili exclaimed.

"I'll leave you to it, Nkechi," Papa said with a look of respect, as he once again disappeared back into the mist.

"Here, just hold my hands and I'll allow you to temporarily speak through my body, I can't hold it for long, though, as this plane will try and claim my soul too."

"Okay, I'll make it quick. Thank you, Nkechi, truly."

"It's okay, hopefully seeing her will release you from Limbo for good, and you can move onto paradise," Nkechi said, holding out her hands for Kambili to latch onto and begin the temporary possession.

The two of them joined hands and, back on the earthly plane, Nkechi's body sat up and swung around on the coffee table to face Gweneviere.

"Kambili?" Gweneviere slowly asked, as she held out hope.

"Gwen?" Kambili answered, confused for a moment until she realised how old Gweneviere was now, though it didn't change a single ounce of the love she felt for her.

Kambili, using Nkechi's body, swooped in for a long overdue hug, and as they pulled away, they were tempted to exchange lips, but it didn't feel appropriate doing so in someone else's body.

"Kambili, I'm so sorry. I should've listened to you and left when you said. They tricked me, they knew you would..." Gweneviere frantically apologised, before Kambili softly silenced her.

"Shh, it's okay, everything is okay. None of that matters. I haven't spent the last few hundred years thinking, 'well, I knew I was right'. Okay, maybe the first hundred," she couldn't help but tease. "I spent them thinking about you; how you were spending the rest of your life, how much I love you and how much I know you love me. So, tell me, what have you done with your long life? I can see you didn't get very good taste in home décor in the future." Kambili chuckled, looking around at the old, granny-style flat.

Gweneviere didn't laugh, her wrinkled face cast down in shame. "I've been horrible to everyone. I've let you down. I'm sorry."

"Hey," Kambili murmured, lifting Gweneviere's chin back in line with her own, or rather, Nkechi's. "Firstly, I'm sure some of those people deserved to see your horrible wrath," she jested. "But more importantly. You've been through more pain than most could ever imagine. And you've spent your whole life being sorry for things that simply aren't your fault. You've said you're sorry enough to span a hundred lifetimes. I'm not going to judge you on what you've done, it's clear you understand where you've gone wrong, and you don't need a lecture from me. Besides, I don't know what I would have done in your shoes, I would have probably gone a little crazy too, if you'd died in my arms. All that matters is that I love you, and I'll be waiting for you on the other side, okay?"

"What if I don't make it to the 'good place'?" Gweneviere asked, with a very real worry in her eyes.

"Then, Gweneviere Baxter, I will traipse through the depths of hell to find you. You won't lose me again, I promise."

"I love you so much," Gweneviere said, tearing up as she stared lovingly past Nkechi's physical body and into Kambili's soul.

"I love you too."

The two of them embraced once more before Kambili began to feel Nkechi's body turn cold; she could sense that time was up and prepared to say her goodbyes.

"Gwen, I don't know who Nkechi is to you, but thank her again for me. She's a gift from God," she said, placing a kiss on her forehead.

Gweneviere nodded.

"See you soon, Gwen." Kambili smiled as she laid Nkechi's body back down.

Gweneviere whispered, "See you soon, my love."

Within a split second, Kambili's soul left Nkechi's body and happily made its way to paradise having reassured Gweneviere that she'd never stopped loving her, and that she'd be waiting on the other side.

Nkechi snapped back into her body and shivered, her lips were just about to turn blue. Gweneviere mustered up the last bit of magic she had in her to warm Nkechi's body by wrapping her arms around her and generating a little heat.

"Thanks, that feels amazing," Nkechi said, as her shivering began to ease.

"No, thank you. I've waited three hundred and sixty years for a moment like that, you're truly a miracle." Gweneviere smiled up at her sweetly.

Nkechi had never met any of her grandparents, and Gweneviere was certainly the last person she ever expected to feel that kind of connection with, but in that moment, she did.

"It's okay, I'm just glad you got your second chance to be happy." Nkechi smiled, noticing the overall more joyous look on Gweneviere's face.

Gweneviere pulled herself up and hobbled over to a bookshelf, and from it she pulled out her mother's spell book. She blew the dust off it, having not used it in a good few years, before taking it over to Nkechi.

"Here, I want you to have this," she said, handing her the book.

"What is it?"

"It was my mother's spell book. She passed it on to me, and now I'm passing it on to you. It's magic, so once I change its ownership to you, only you can read and write its secrets."

"Oh, Gwen, are you sure?" Nkechi looked up from the book for reassurance.

"Of course, I can't think of anyone more deserving. Now here, give me your finger," Gweneviere requested.

"Okay," Nkechi replied, holding out her forefinger. "Ow!" she yelped, as Gweneviere pricked it and dropped her blood onto the pages.

Gweneviere whispered a spell under her breath, and suddenly the hundreds of spells materialised on the pages before Nkechi's eyes, and slowly became invisible to Gweneviere. There was something calming about that to Gweneviere, knowing that she'd never have to use magic again.

"Wow, that's magical." Nkechi chuckled at her own cheesiness.

"Now, promise me, when you look as old as I do, that you won't have any regrets."

"I promise, Gweneviere." Nkechi smiled.

"Hey, I said call me Gwen," Gweneviere light-heartedly instructed.

"I promise, *Gwen.*"

"Right, now, go on! Live your life! Don't waste another second on this old fart," Gweneviere said, having only ever looked as happy in that moment as she did back when she was with Kambili.

It was clear to them both that Gweneviere was ready to go.

Nkechi placed a kiss on Gweneviere's forehead before tucking the grimoire beneath her arm and leaving.

🔥

Not long after Nkechi left, Gweneviere took a match and struck it, for the first time in her life, throwing it at the fireplace. She laid back on the sofa beside it, and slowly drifted to sleep as she listened to its roaring crackles.

When Gweneviere finally awoke, she was in a world much kinder than ours. She was in a world with Kambili, and whatever name that world might've had, to Gwen, it was simple.

It was paradise.

CRANTHORPE
—— MILLNER ——
PUBLISHERS

Did you enjoy this book?

Why not leave a review, or email digitalmarketing@cranthorpemillner.com to sign up to our newsletter and receive advance copies of our upcoming titles.

www.cranthorpemillner.com